Reap What You Sew

Center Point
Large Print

Also by Elizabeth Lynn Casey and available from Center Point Large Print:

The Southern Sewing Circle Series
Sew Deadly
Death Threads
Pinned for Murder
Deadly Notions
Dangerous Alterations

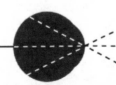

This Large Print Book carries the Seal of Approval of N.A.V.H.

Reap What You Sew

Elizabeth Lynn Casey

CENTER POINT LARGE PRINT
THORNDIKE, MAINE

This Center Point Large Print edition
is published in the year 2012 by arrangement with
The Berkley Publishing Group,
a member of Penguin Group (USA) Inc.

The text of this Large Print edition is unabridged.
In other aspects, this book may vary
from the original edition.
Printed in the United States of America
on permanent paper.
Set in 16-point Times New Roman type.

ISBN: 978-1-61173-523-9

Library of Congress Cataloging-in-Publication Data

Casey, Elizabeth Lynn.
Reap what you sew / Elizabeth Lynn Casey. — Large print ed.
p. cm. — (Center Point large print edition)
ISBN 978-1-61173-523-9 (library binding : alk. paper)
1. Sewing—Fiction. 2. South Carolina—Fiction. 3. Murder—Fiction.
4. Large type books. I. Title.
PS3603.A8633R43 2012
813'.6—dc23
2012016142

For my family, with all my love.

Acknowledgments

As always, when working on a new story, questions arise that need answers. And the people who provide those story-enriching answers are surely deserving of my thanks. So, to that end, I shall get to it . . . A huge thank-you goes out to my cousin, William Casey, for sharing his knowledge of the movie-making process with me. Another, equally huge thank-you goes to Darci Ettari for telling the kinds of stories that send me off into my happy place (and not holding it against me when I get that faraway look).

Chapter 1

Despite the plethora of scientific reference books to the contrary, Tori Sinclair had begun to wonder whether the speed of light had finally found its match. The cues had been subtle at first, many of them more indicative of a coincidence than a true shift in nature. But now, as she glanced at her watch, she couldn't ignore reality any longer. . . .

The women of Sweet Briar could, indeed, spread gossip around town at a pace that begged to be studied by modern physicists worldwide.

In fact, the proof had become so irrefutable, it could start a veritable avalanche of grant money for research labs near and far.

Case in point: The originating call had come into the library at ten fifteen. After securing all noteworthy details, Tori had called her predecessor, Dixie Dunn, with the news at ten twenty-five. Now, just three minutes later, she was looking across the main room of the Sweet Briar Public Library at two of her dearest friends—Margaret Louise Davis and her twin sister, Leona Elkin— who had, no doubt, arrived to verify the facts.

The only thing skewing her hypothesis, though,

was the blatant look of discomfort on Leona's flawlessly made-up face and the unexpected hesitation Margaret Louise showed as she approached Tori's position behind the information desk. It didn't fit.

"So, I take it you heard the news. Isn't it wonderful?" she prompted, before slipping off her stool and enveloping the sixty-something grandmother of seven in her arms. "I love the name, don't you? So distinguished-sounding."

Margaret Louise offered a less than enthusiastic hug in return, her voice distracted. "Names are good. Important, even." Spinning around on her Keds, the decidedly plump woman patted the counter area to her left and nodded at the elderly woman a few steps behind Leona. "Right here, Mamma. You can stand right here. Next to me."

Mamma?

"Mamma?" Tori repeated aloud, a smile stretching her mouth upward. "Is this your mother, Margaret Louise?"

Her eyes still focused on the petite woman at her side, Margaret Louise simply nodded as her slender and stylish sister pranced over to a nearby chair and sat down.

"She's visiting from Georgia for a few days," Leona said.

Margaret Louise drummed her fingers on the countertop. "Visitin' implies a short stay, Twin. And you know as well as I do, that ain't the case this

10

time." Waving off the argument that arose on Leona's face, Margaret Louise flashed a tentative smile in Tori's direction. "To answer your question, Victoria, yes, this is our mamma, Annabelle Elkin. Mamma, this is our dear friend Victoria Sinclair. She's as sweet and darlin' as she is pretty, ain't she, Leona?"

Leona squinted at Tori, her perfectly penned eyebrows barely moving. "She'd be a whole lot prettier if she would take the time to perfect a few of the techniques I've shared with her over the past two years."

Ahhh, yes. Leona's techniques. How could she forget?

She opened her mouth to speak, to remind her always-groomed friend that she didn't have the time or the inclination to spend three hours getting ready each morning, when a series of rapid movements out of the corner of her eye brought her up short. And then, just as quick, Margaret Louise's hand dipped into the tote bag on Annabelle's shoulder and removed four items. . . .

Tori's stapler.

Tori's paper clip container.

Tori's pencil holder.

And the apple Mr. Downing had given her on her way into work that very morning.

Without so much as a missed beat, Margaret Louise returned each item to its original spot and patted her mother on the back. Leona rolled her eyes.

"I think Victoria looks as beautiful as always." Margaret Louise gestured her now empty hand toward Tori and smiled at her mother. "Victoria is our librarian, and there's not a person in this town who doesn't adore her."

"That may be true for the live ones, but the dead ones? I'm betting they don't have quite the same warm and fuzzy where she's concerned," Leona mumbled.

Ignoring the pot-stirring barb, Tori reached across the information desk and placed a hand over Annabelle's. "Ms. Elkin, it is my pleasure to meet you. I couldn't ask for two better friends than your daughters. I'm very blessed to have them in my life."

And she was. A million times over.

In fact, of all the places she'd ever lived, she'd never felt more at home than she did right there in Sweet Briar. Sure, it had been tough going at first thanks to the unenviable task of replacing the woman who had served as head librarian for nearly forty years—a task that had been further complicated by doing it in a town that a) didn't take too kindly to outsiders and b) took even less kindly to *Yankee* outsiders. But, eventually, she'd made it through thanks to friends like Leona, Margaret Louise, and the rest of the Sweet Briar Ladies Society Sewing Circle—all of whom had taught her a thing or two about true friendship along the way.

Now, as she drank in every detail of Annabelle Elkin—the petite, slightly stooped stature, the thinning gray hair, the pronounced cheekbones—Tori couldn't help but wonder which of the qualities she'd grown to love in Leona and Margaret Louise had come from this woman.

Was Annabelle the reason Margaret Louise was so thoughtful? Had she been the wonderful grandmother to Jake growing up as Margaret Louise was to Jake and Melissa's ever-growing brood? Did she like to cook as much as her always-happy daughter?

Or was Annabelle more like Leona? Part bristly and cantankerous with an underlying dose of generosity? Did she have a thing for men in uniform the way Leona did?

They were all good questions. With answers she couldn't wait to learn.

Annabelle moved slowly down the counter, her gaze fixed on the pile of books Tori had been planning to shelve before Duwayne Morgan called.

Duwayne.

She clapped her hands softly and glanced back at her friends. "You haven't said what you think of the news yet."

"What news?" Margaret Louise asked, her focus never leaving her mother. "Have you and Milo finally set a date for gettin' hitched?"

Just the mere mention of her fiancé's name made her smile. There were times when she still found it hard to believe someone as wonderful as Milo Wentworth actually existed. He was warm, thoughtful, generous, kindhearted, and a million other pinch-worthy qualities all rolled into a package that was handsome to boot. And he loved and cherished her in a way she'd never known before.

Glancing down at the ring she'd finally allowed him to place on her finger, she couldn't help but feel giddy. Milo was truly one of a kind.

Her kind.

"Not an exact day, no. But we're looking at about this time next year."

"I believe they call that a shotgun wedding," Leona mused.

"Twelve months is a shotgun wedding?" she echoed in disbelief.

"It's less than eighteen months, isn't it?"

Tori held her hands up in surrender. "Can we get back to Nina and the baby, please?"

Margaret Louise and Leona sucked in their breath simultaneously. "Baby? Nina had the baby?"

Her mouth gaped open as she took in the utter shock on Margaret Louise's gently lined face. "You—you didn't hear?"

Leona crossed her ankles in delicate fashion, her mouth contorting in boredom. "Really, dear, you're awful at the cat and mouse game."

Cat and mouse game?

She pondered Leona's words for a moment only to shake them off in favor of being the one to *share* the news instead of always hearing everything last. "Yes. She had the baby."

Margaret Louise echoed Tori's original clap, her large brown eyes happy once again. "She did? When? It was a boy, wasn't it? I told you she was carrying that baby like a boy!"

She couldn't help but laugh. Whatever had Margaret Louise so subdued was long forgotten as the notion of a new baby in Sweet Briar took root for the grandmother of seven—soon to be eight.

One by one, Tori divulged the details her assistant's husband had so happily shared with her not more than twenty minutes earlier. "Duwayne and Nina welcomed their new son at nine thirty this morning. He's six pounds, four ounces and—"

"I knew she should've done more eatin'. Six pounds, four ounces? Woo-eee, that's tiny."

"Let Victoria finish, Margaret Louise."

She grinned at Leona. "It's okay. Your sister is excited."

"Is Nina okay?" Margaret Louise asked.

"Nina is fine. Duwayne said she made it through like a champ."

"And the baby?" Margaret Louise leaned forward against the counter. "What did they name him?"

"Lyndon James."

Leona nodded her consent ever so slightly. "Lyndon James. Lyndon James Morgan. That's a good name."

"Isn't it? I think it—"

A flash of movement at the far end of the counter made her turn just in time to see Annabelle shove a book in her tote. Before she could make sense of what she was seeing, Margaret Louise was at the woman's side, fetching the book—along with Tori's highlighter, cell phone, and hand sanitizer—back out of the bag, returning everything to its original location.

She opened her mouth to speak, but was saved by the sound of the front door opening.

Looking up, she waved at Beatrice Tharrington and her young charge, Luke, their unexpected arrival helping to dispel a tension she hadn't yet begun to understand.

"Victoria? Did you hear the news?" The youngest and shyest member of the sewing circle fairly ran to the information desk with the day's newspaper in her hand, her feet only slowing when she spotted Leona. "Oh. I'm sorry. I didn't know you had guests."

"It's a library, dear. That's what she's supposed to have." Leona shot an irritated glance in the general direction of her sister and mother, then turned to face the English nanny. "We already know about Nina and the baby."

Beatrice stopped, her cheeks taking on a pinkish hue. "Nina had her baby?"

Tori nodded. "A boy. Lyndon James."

"A tiny little thing," Margaret Louise supplied as she ushered her mother to a chair beside a less than pleased Leona. "Just six pounds, four ounces."

Beatrice's shoulders slumped. "I hadn't heard."

Tori rushed to ease any hurt feelings. "It just happened. In fact, I just now told Margaret Louise and Leona."

The nanny perked up. "Oh. Well that's splendid news. Ducky, really."

"Ducky?" Leona repeated. "Did you say *ducky?*"

Taking command of the conversation before it took a dangerous turn, Tori pointed at the paper in Beatrice's hand. "I take it the news you're talking about is something different?"

"News?" Flustered, Beatrice looked from Tori to Leona and back again. "What news?"

Luke wrapped his arms around Beatrice, the admiration and love he had for his nanny impossible to miss. "Tell them about the movie, Miss Bea. Tell them how they need people to be in it."

"Movie? What movie?" Leona asked, all traces of sarcasm and boredom suddenly missing from her ladylike southern drawl.

The six-year-old tugged on Beatrice's sweater. "Tell her, Miss Bea. Tell her."

"Oh. Yes. I guess I got sidetracked hearing about the baby." Slowly, Beatrice held the entertainment section of the South Carolina *Sun* up in the air. "They're coming. *Here.*"

"Who's coming?" Tori asked gently.

Beatrice placed the paper on the counter, stopping to smooth it with a practiced hand. "Warren Shoemaker."

"Who's Warren Shoe—"

"Hush," Leona commanded as she cocked her head of salon-softened gray hair a hairbreadth to the left, a clear indication she was processing the name and double-checking it against an internal data bank of men she'd either known over the past six and a half decades or hoped to know in the not too distant future. Sure enough, after barely a pause, Leona spoke, peering over the top of her glasses as she did. "Warren Shoemaker is only the most talked-about film director in all of England. He's talented, shrewd, extremely wealthy *and*"— she slipped a petal pink compact from her purse and flipped it open, inspecting her hair and face in its tiny mirror—"he's one of *Individual* magazine's top ten Most Handsome Men in Show Business for the eighth year in a row."

"He's gonna make a movie right here in Sweet Briar, isn't he, Miss Bea?" Without waiting for a response, Luke tugged on Beatrice's arm. "Miss Bea? May I go to the children's room? I'll be good."

Tori couldn't help but smile at the anticipation on the little boy's face—anticipation for a room she'd dreamt of for years yet executed in a matter of days. Knowing that it was just as loved by the library's youngest patrons made it all the more special.

Beatrice glanced at Tori. "Is that okay, Victoria?"

"Of course. There's a volunteer reader in there now if he hurries."

As Luke disappeared down the back hallway, Leona regained control of the conversation. "Warren is going to make a movie here in Sweet Briar? When?"

Tori looked down at the newspaper, skimming the opening lines of the full-page article she'd somehow managed to miss. She fought to bite back a squeal at the mention of the movie's name in the second paragraph. "Oh how wonderful! He's making a movie based on one of my favorite novels, *Memories of Autumn*."

"Isn't that the one where the male protagonist is dying of some sort of disease and he's all but given up on finding someone to share his life with . . . but then he does?" Margaret Louise asked from her spot beside her mother, her soft, pudgy hand fairly holding Annabelle's hand to the table.

Tori nodded before taking in the article once again. "It says here that our town square was selected as the location where Kevin—the protagonist—first sees Patricia. That scene, as well as a few other critical outdoor scenes, will film here in Sweet Briar with somewhere between ten and fifteen extras."

"I've always thought that would be tremendous fun," Beatrice said. "The kind of experience to write about in one's journal."

Leona waved away Beatrice's comment. "Have they cast the part of Patricia yet?"

Tori jumped her finger to the article's sidebar, her mouth giving voice to an answer she knew she'd find. "I would certainly think so, she *is* one of the two main . . . wait. Here we go. The part of Patricia will be played by Anita—"

"Because I think I could play that part very well. Men naturally fall for me so it wouldn't require the kind of overacting that is so prevalent in movies these days." Leona reached into her purse, extracted a tube of lipstick, and snapped her compact open once again. "When will Warren be arriving?"

Tori opened her mouth to speak, to tease her friend for making such a joke, but, in the end, she simply let it go. It was Leona, after all, Queen of Confidence.

"It seems funny Georgina didn't crow about this sooner," Margaret Louise mused. "Somethin' like this should've had her a-squawkin'."

Fellow sewing circle sister Georgina Hayes doubled as Sweet Briar's mayor, a job that had been all but left to her by a line of Hayes family members who had served in the same capacity during much of the town's lengthy history. While a master at her job, Georgina did have a habit of filling the group in on some behind-the-scenes gossip that was probably supposed to be behind-the-scenes for a reason.

"Maybe she was sworn to secrecy," Beatrice suggested.

"That wouldn't preclude her from telling us." With the preciseness of an artist, Leona touched up her lips and then lowered the crimson shade back into the tube. "We should always be the exception."

Tori shrugged and scanned still further down the page, reading to herself—and then aloud—a quote from Warren Shoemaker himself. "While searching for this particular setting in the book, we were taken by the people of Sweet Briar, South Carolina. In wanting to ensure that translation to the screen, we are only considering extras with a valid Sweet Briar address. To that end, we have not shared plans of this shoot in advance to preserve the integrity of our search."

When she reached the end of the quote she looked up, saw the dawn of understanding flash behind Margaret Louise's eyes. "Well, there's our answer. Georgina either didn't know because they didn't tell her . . . or, like the director, the town didn't want a host of outsiders scramblin' around tryin' to get notes from folks sayin' they live in so and so's shed or somethin'.'"

"Casting for extras starts tomorrow morning at seven. You're to bring a short bio and a picture." Beatrice clasped her hands in front of her and looked sheepishly from Tori to Margaret Louise and back again. "Do you think he'd cast me?"

Tori reached out, squeezed Beatrice's hands. "I think you've got as good a shot as anyone else."

Wrapping her fingers around the delicate handles of her clutch-style purse, Leona stood. "For an extra, I have to agree with Victoria. But in terms of Patricia? There's only one woman who can play that role the way it should be played and it's not this—this . . . Anita-Whoever-She-Is."

"Anita Belise." Margaret Louise pushed back her own chair then helped her mother to her feet, glancing into the woman's tote bag before surrendering it for the walk back to the counter. "What about you, Victoria? Will you try to get a part as an extra?"

"I don't know. I've never done anything like that before." She folded the paper article-side up and handed it to Beatrice, her gaze lingering on the headline sprawled across the top fold. "Besides, with Nina on maternity leave, it's not like I have anyone who can take my place here."

"You have Dixie," Beatrice reminded.

That was true, she did. But she didn't want to take advantage. The twosome had finally forged a tentative bond since Nina's bed rest, and the last thing Tori wanted was to retreat back to the days when she was top dog on Dixie's Most Hated List.

"If Dixie had her druthers, she'd be here runnin' the show. You know that, Victoria."

Margaret Louise was right. But still . . .

"I'll give it some thought," she finally promised. "Who knows, maybe you'll see me there, picture in hand, just like everyone else in Sweet Briar."

Leona took three steps toward the door and then stopped, turning back to look at Tori. "You might want to consider giving the director a lily-white version of your bio, dear. Perhaps something a bit more wholesome and ladylike."

"More wholesome and ladylike?" she echoed in confusion.

"I know that's a novel concept coming from a place like"—Leona shuddered dramatically—"*Chicago*, but if you simply focus on your job as a librarian and leave off your peculiar little habit of getting mixed up in murder investigations, then perhaps you'll have a chance at being cast, dear."

"Leona!" Beatrice whispered in a rare burst of outrage. "That's not nice."

"I'm not saying it to be mean," Leona countered. "Victoria knows that. I'm just guiding her the way I always do, isn't that right, dear?"

She nibbled her lower lip inward in an attempt to keep from laughing out loud. She was, after all, at work. In a *library*.

"Point noted, Leona. And I'll keep that in mind. Really. Sweet Briar and its residents have nothing to fear. The only"—she raised two fingers from each of her hands into the air to simulate quotes— "*death* facing us will be part of the movie."

Beatrice gasped. "So this character . . . the one who finally finds his soul mate . . . *dies?*"

"In the book, yes. But that doesn't mean the movie will go the same way. Movies often change a book's original story line. It's why so many book lovers resist seeing big-screen versions of their favorite tales." Tori stepped out from behind the counter and reached for Annabelle's hand. "It was so very nice to meet you, Annabelle."

A moment of clarity pushed the fog from Annabelle's eyes. "I remember that book, *Memories of Autumn*. It's a beautiful story."

Without thinking, Tori reached out, brushed a strand of thinning gray hair from the woman's wrinkled yet pretty face. "I agree."

Annabelle reached into her bag, a sudden bout of sadness tugging her lips downward. "I'm sorry. I didn't mean to take these." And then, just like that, the woman pulled out four more items pilfered from the information desk—a tiny snack bar Tori had tucked behind her computer, another book from the pile to be shelved, a Sweet Briar Public Library bookmark, and a penny.

She accepted the items as Annabelle handed them to her, resisting the urge to look at Margaret

24

Louise and Leona as she did. She didn't need to look at them. She could sense their discomfort as surely as she could any of the items she now held in her hand.

"Thank you for finding these for me," she said when the last of the items was safely back in her hands and the clarity the elderly woman had shown just moments earlier was all but gone. "I'd been worried about them. You're a good finder, Annabelle."

With barely a nod, the woman shuffled into step behind Leona as they made their way toward the door. Realizing Margaret Louise wasn't with them, Tori turned to find her friend lingering beside the information desk.

"Margaret Louise? Is everything okay?"

"Thank you, Victoria. The kindness you just showed my mamma was beautiful. I only wish my sister had been payin' attention." Margaret Louise swiped the back of her hand across her eyes and then stood up tall. "And don't mind her none, you hear? She didn't mean nothin' 'bout that dead body stuff."

She had to laugh. "It's not like it hasn't been true these past two years."

Margaret Louise's plump frame rose and fell with a shrug. "But she has a way of sayin' it like you did somethin' to make all those things happen. And you didn't."

"Don't worry, I didn't take any offense to what

25

Leona said. Truly. It was more funny than anything else." Hooking her hand inside Margaret Louise's elbow, she walked her to the front door and her waiting family as Beatrice left to join Luke in the children's room. "We're talking about a one- or two-week-long shoot, right? Really, what could possibly go wrong?"

Chapter 2

It took everything Tori had not to peel the aluminum covering off the plate and take a taste— or two—of the Mississippi Mud Cake she'd brought for that evening's sewing circle meeting. However, if it took Rose Winters much longer to open the door, she couldn't be held responsible for what she might do.

Chocolate was, after all, the main ingredient in the homemade treat, and chocolate was her biggest downfall. Always had been, always would be.

She tapped a few beats of a favorite tune with her foot as she waited for the oldest member of the group to heed her third knock. But no such luck. The door remained closed despite the line of familiar cars parked along the curb that served as confirmation of that week's meeting location.

Glancing at the still-covered treat in her hand, she contemplated the notion of giving up and heading home, of taking the unanswered door as a sign she might do well to indulge in a rare and much-needed night to herself, but she couldn't. For as appealing as a night of mindless TV sounded, it simply couldn't beat the pleasure she got from spending an evening with the crew.

Sure, she loved her job—being a librarian was all she'd ever wanted to do since she was old enough to read her first book. And Milo, well he'd single-handedly restored her faith in the opposite sex after her now-deceased cheating ex-fiancé had blown it to smithereens the night of their engagement party when she found him in the coat closet with one of her girlfriends. But her sewing circle sisters? They made her feel as if she truly *belonged*. And in doing so, Monday night circle meetings had become the wings that helped make the rest of her week soar.

She opened the storm door and knocked again, this time on the heavier, wooden door that Rose tended to keep bolted shut.

Rose appeared not a minute later, all visual bristles softening the moment she made eye contact with Tori. "I know you have impeccable manners, Victoria, but when I tell you to walk right in, I want you to walk right in."

Tori stepped into Rose's home, stopping just inside the foyer to plant a kiss on the elderly woman's cheek. "I'm sorry, Rose, I guess I didn't hear you. That's one thick door, you know?"

"That's why I wrote it on one of those yellow sticky things and stuck it to the storm door." Rose took the covered plate from Tori's hand and plunked it on the counter beside a half dozen other homemade treats. "You can read, can't you?"

"When there's something *to read,* of course," she said with as straight a face as she could manage before offering her elbow for the walk down the hall to Rose's sewing room.

Rose waved aside the assistance and, instead, brought her hands to her hips, narrowing her sights on Tori. "I just said I left a note."

She shrugged. "Maybe you did, but it's not there now."

Margaret Louise strode into the hallway, her ever-present smile widening still further at the sight of Tori standing beside Rose. "Victoria, you made it. I was beginnin' to think you'd forgotten us."

"Never." It was a simple response, yet no less true.

"She decided to stand on the porch for a while instead of following my instructions," Rose grumbled.

Tori nibbled back the urge to laugh, knowing the sound would only irritate Rose further. Rose, while sweet, didn't take kindly to being questioned. "If I'd seen a note, I'd have done as it said."

A flash of crimson rose in Margaret Louise's cheeks. "A note?"

Rose nodded.

"What color was it?"

"It was yellow," Rose snapped. "Stuck it on the door myself while you and Leona were yakkin' away in the kitchen."

Reaching into her pocket, Margaret Louise extracted a small yellow square of paper with writing on one side. "Is this the note you're talkin' 'bout?"

Rose's eyes narrowed still further as they latched onto Margaret Louise's left hand. "How is anyone supposed to know to come in if you've got my note in your pocket, Margaret Louise?"

Slowly, Margaret Louise reached into her other pocket and pulled out three more items—a single key on a light-up chain, a quarter, and a trial-size vitamin jar. "By any chance are these your things, too, Rose?"

Rose leaned closer. "That's my house key . . . and my vitamins."

"And the quarter?" Margaret Louise asked.

"How am I supposed to know if that's my quarter or not? I keep my loose change right over there on that hall table." Rose turned and looked toward the spot she'd indicated. "But since there's nothing there at the moment, I'd say it's probably mine."

Tori looked closely at the items in Margaret

Louise's hand, reality dawning just as surely as if she'd seen what had transpired with her own eyes. "Your mamma is here, isn't she?" she finally asked, not unkindly.

Margaret Louise merely nodded, the corners of her normally happy mouth turning downward.

And, just like that, Rose's bristly demeanor was gone, in its place the kind of deep-rooted compassion that had jettisoned her onto Tori's personal list of favorite people. Waving aside the items Margaret Louise held in her direction, Rose lowered her voice to a near whisper. "She's ninety-two, Margaret Louise. She walks without a cane, she lived with an elderly sister and no outside help until just three days ago, and she's in reasonably good health. So she got confused and took a few things this one time . . . I'm sure it's nothing for you to be worrying about."

Only it hadn't been this one time. Annabelle had lifted things on three separate occasions at the library just that morning. . . .

Dementia, perhaps?

Or maybe Alzheimer's?

Margaret Louise gently removed Rose's hand from her arm and turned it over, laying each of the recovered items into the elderly woman's palm. "Mamma has been doin' this for as long as I can remember. She did it at friends' homes when she dropped Leona and me off at birthday parties. She did it in our classrooms when she came to watch us in a program. She did it on my weddin' day, and at Jake's baptism party, and again when I lost Jake's daddy."

Tori swapped stares with Rose before they both turned to study Margaret Louise. "It's not her age?" Rose finally asked.

"Some of it might be. Things like the confusion and the forgettin', I s'pose. But the rest . . . no. She's a kleptomaniac hoarder."

Rose blinked once, twice. "A kleptomaniac hoard—what on earth?"

"It means she helps herself to things without asking. Usually it's things of little value." Margaret Louise pointed to Rose's hand. "Like an empty pill bottle or a light-up key chain. The difference with Mamma is that she prefers to take several things at one time in an almost hoarding fashion."

She took in everything Margaret Louise was saying, processed it against everything she'd seen that morning. Including the almost irritated way in which Leona regarded Annabelle. "Does she know she's doing it?"

"If she does, it's not in a malicious way. But tryin' to get my sister to see that is like tryin' to get an oink out of a pig that's already turnin' above the fire."

"Leona comes down on her?"

"No, Rose. She just ignores her—and the stealin'—as if it's not happenin'. Why I remember

31

goin' to a party when we were five or six. It was at Susie Hillmaker's house." Margaret Louise stared off into the distance as if she were revisiting an all too familiar time and place. "Susie had a grand house. When it was time to leave, Mamma came to get us. As we were walkin' out, she snatched up a few things—a hairbrush, a bobby pin, a penny, and a mint from some fancy glass jar on the hall table. Leona saw it, I know she did. She'd been walkin' right behind Mamma and right in front of me when it happened. But Leona kept right on walkin' . . . pretended she hadn't seen a thing. So when we got in the car, I had to take the things out of Mamma's purse and bring them back inside. After that, I never got invited to another party at Susie's house. Leona did, of course. But not me."

"Why not?" Rose asked in a shaky whisper.

"Because Susie's mamma thought I was a thief."

Tori sucked in her breath. "You never told them the truth?"

Margaret Louise shrugged. "I'd rather they think *I* was a thief than have them think something like that about my mamma."

It wasn't a surprise. Margaret Louise was the kindest, truest, most loyal friend Tori had ever had. And, judging by the misty haze clouding Rose's eyes, Tori wasn't the only one that felt that way.

She reached for Margaret Louise's hand, encasing it between her own. "Annabelle is lucky to have you."

"*I'm* the lucky one, Victoria. I learned how to be a mamma and a mee-maw by watchin' her."

Rose cleared her throat and then gestured toward the sewing room at the end of the hall. "I think it's time we start sewin', don't you?"

Margaret Louise and Tori fell into step behind the evening's hostess, each lost in thoughts the others could only guess. But that was okay. Friends and sewing—the cure for just about everything under the sun—were mere steps away and Tori wasn't the only one who felt that way.

She could see it in the way Margaret Louise's trademark smile returned to light her face. She could hear it in the way Rose's normally shuffled steps became almost weightless. And she could feel it in the way all remnants of tension in her own body seemed to magically disappear.

All conversation stopped as they rounded the corner into Rose's sewing room, the chatter that was as much a part of the weekly meeting as the sewing itself giving way to a round of smiles and a chorus of hellos.

"Victoria, we were afraid you weren't going to make it tonight," Debbie Calhoun said as she wiggled her way off the scrap of sofa she'd claimed for herself to give Tori a hug. Debbie was the group's triple threat—devoted wife to author husband, Colby, attentive mom to Suzanna and Jackson, and respected owner of Debbie's Bakery. "We're glad to see we were wrong."

"I wouldn't miss an evening with all of you unless there was a really good reason." Tori hoisted her sewing bag further onto her shoulder and looked around at all of her friends. "And there wasn't . . . so I'm here."

In the far left corner of the room, Georgina sat behind one of the group's portable sewing machines, her favorite straw hat balanced on the armrest of the love seat she shared with Leona. To Leona's left sat Melissa, Margaret Louise's daughter-in-law. Melissa was just finishing up the first trimester of her eighth pregnancy, a milestone that had her finally wanting to eat again.

Margaret Louise crossed the room and reclaimed her spot between Melissa and Annabelle while Rose shuffled over to the rocking chair that permanently resided underneath a gooseneck lamp.

Behind Tori sat Beatrice, who was busily searching through her sewing box, and Dixie— Tori's predecessor and on again, off again nemesis. At the moment, they were friendly enough, Nina's maternity leave providing the former librarian an opportunity to feel needed once again. What would happen once Nina was back, though, was anyone's guess.

"So what did I miss?" she asked, as she, too,

claimed a chair for the evening—a cushioned folding contraption nestled between Beatrice and Dixie.

Leona lowered her latest travel magazine to her lap and peered at Tori from atop her reading glasses. "Incessant chatter about Nina's baby, what else?" Lifting the magazine once again, the woman made a slight grimace. "Why on earth babies have to be such a topic of conversation all the time is beyond me."

Tori couldn't help but laugh at Leona being Leona—antimarriage, antichildren, anti-everything except wealthy and/or uniformed men. "They *are* cute, Leona. You can't deny that."

"*Paris* is cute, dear. She's fluffy, she's cuddly, and she is on her best behavior all the time." Leona's chin jutted upward with indignation. "Yet you don't hear me going on and on and on about her twenty-four/seven."

A snort of disgust came from Rose's direction, followed by a stamp of her foot on the wood floor. "You've only been here twenty minutes, Leona Elkin, and I've already seen three photos of that rabbit."

Leona sniffed. "Those were for *Patches's* benefit, not yours, you old goat."

Debbie, the consummate peacemaker of the group, raised her hands into the air, successfully thwarting an argument between the two most stubborn members of the circle. "Leona, I'm sure

35

Patches enjoyed seeing a picture of his mother. That was very thoughtful of you."

Leona lifted her chin still further only to bury it behind her magazine as Debbie continued. "I'm also sure that babies are cute, too. And since we've all just learned about Nina's new addition, I think it's quite normal for that to be a topic of discussion at the moment. Just as Paris's unexpected bout with motherhood was on the tip of everyone's tongue for weeks after our circle getaway."

It was true. Somehow, despite everything that had been going on at the time—not the least of which was the murder investigation into the death of Tori's ex-fiancé, and her unrelated yet long overdue acceptance of Milo's marriage proposal—the realization that Leona's beloved bunny rabbit, Paris, was a female and not a male had dominated its fair share of conversations both in and out of circle meetings. Some of that, of course, was simply the nature of the surprise. One minute, Leona was dressing Paris in neckties, and the next she was throwing a belated baby shower for the long-eared mother of seven.

And when Leona had elected to give one of the baby bunnies to Rose, every member of the circle had held their breath, wondering if the long-standing tension between the pair would finally subside once and for all.

It was a question that had been answered quickly and succinctly. No.

"Have you seen him yet?" Melissa flicked the end of her long, sandy blonde ponytail over her shoulder then plucked a cracker from a zip top baggie tucked between her thigh and the side of her chair. "Does he favor Nina or Duwayne?"

Just like that, the conversation was back where it belonged—in safe waters.

"I don't know. I haven't seen him yet. But Milo and I are planning to stop by the hospital tomorrow after work."

Dixie retrieved a baby blue gift bag from the floor and handed it to Tori, the woman's normally gruff demeanor disappearing behind a rare smile. "Then would you give this to them for me?"

"Of course, I'm sure Nina will be touched—"

"I have one, too, if you wouldn't mind," Debbie said, nudging a blue and white striped bag in Tori's direction with a gentle foot. "I went out on my lunch break as soon as I heard the news."

"Me, too," Beatrice said, indicating a carefully wrapped gift box on the end table beside her chair. "Luke and I were walking around the square after our visit to the library when we had to duck into Scarlet's Trunk so he could use the loo. While I was waiting, I saw the most lovely pram blanket for Nina's baby."

Within seconds, the tiny table beside Tori's folding chair was covered with an assortment of gifts for Nina and her new baby boy, including one from Leona, herself.

"See, Twin? Even with all your hullabaloo against babies, you can't resist their pull, either, can you?" Margaret Louise teased.

"It was a chance to shop. That's all," Leona mumbled before dropping her magazine onto her lap to cast a scrutinizing eye on the mayor. "So, what's all this about a movie being filmed here?"

Georgina stilled her hand mid–needle thread and shrugged. "What's there to tell? Warren Shoemaker is filming a few outdoor scenes on the Green over the next week or so. He'll be using about ten or fifteen extras from the town and, in exchange, he'll be donating a half dozen picnic tables and some bleacher seating for the festival grounds at the far end of the square. It's a win-win for the town."

A swell of conversation about movies and favorite actresses and actors ensued only to get cut off by an ever-growing impatience in Leona.

"Have you seen him?"

Georgina resumed her task at hand, stopping to moisten the tip of the thread between her lips. "Him, who?"

Leona rolled her eyes. "Warren Shoemaker, of course. Who else?"

With a practiced hand, Georgina knotted the end of her thread then pushed aside the portable sewing machine. "Of course. I saw him at city hall yesterday and—"

Leona's eyes narrowed behind her glasses.

"Why didn't you tell us? Why did we have to read it in the papers like the average . . . the average commoner?"

"It was city business, Leona."

"Like that's ever stopped you before," Leona countered.

"Well, it did this time." Georgina looped her left hand beneath the white eyelet pillow case, and set her right on top, guiding the needle through the fabric from below. "That bleacher seating will be a nice addition to our festivals and it wasn't worth losing out on that by breaking his trust. Warren was very clear about wanting to keep this call for extras under wraps until the last minute."

"I wouldn't have told a soul," Leona said between lips that were suddenly pouty. "In fact, I would have made a wonderful welcoming committee for Warren. It's good for people of culture and affluence to find a kindred spirit as quickly as possible when visiting a strange land."

"A *strange land?*" Rose echoed. "Good heavens, Leona, what on earth are you babbling about now?"

Turning her back to Rose, Leona continued, her words directed at Georgina yet intended for all to hear. "Do you know how I could reach him?"

Georgina stopped mid-stitch and met Leona's gaze straight on. "You can show up at the call for extras at seven o'clock tomorrow morning just like everyone else."

Leona's breath hitched in surprise. "But I'm not like everyone else. I—I have no intention of being a blur in the corner of some two-second-long camera shot."

Melissa laughed, the soft, melodic sound echoing around the room. "Oh no, Aunt Leona? Then what, exactly, do you *intend* to be?"

"Wait. I can answer this."

Leona turned and stared at Rose. "You can?"

"Of course. You intend to be"—Rose stretched her arms wide, the effort hampered by limbs riddled with arthritis—"a *star*."

Eight sets of eyes turned to stare at Leona, including one additional set belonging to that of her own mother.

"Is that true?" Dixie asked through a mouth that stopped gaping just long enough to pose the three-word question aloud.

Leona squared her shoulders. "Why wouldn't it be?"

Slowly, Georgina looked up from her pillow-case, pinning Leona with a steely eye. "The main parts have been cast . . . by professionals."

"Casting changes happen all the time." Leona lifted her magazine off her lap once again, her voice adopting a bored tone. "Did you know that John Travolta was supposed to be Forrest Gump? Or that Gwyneth Paltrow was supposed to play Rose in *Titanic*?"

"The main parts have been cast . . . by

professionals," Georgina repeated. "Though, from what I hear . . . no, wait. I shouldn't."

Leona dropped her magazine once and for all, her hands finding and grasping Georgina's arm in record time. "Yes, you should! Tell us!"

Lowering her voice to a whisper she could be certain was still audible around the room, Georgina leaned forward, eyes shining. "It seems there are a few folks connected with this movie who can't wait for it to be done and over with."

"Why? Are they having personality clashes or something?" Debbie mused.

Georgina snickered a laugh. "That's putting it mildly. In fact, from what I've been able to gather from a few of the folks behind the scenes, Mr. Shoemaker is spending as much time stamping out sparks as he is directing."

Eight hands stilled around the room, allowing eight bodies to lean in Georgina's direction. Waiting.

"Sparks? What kind of sparks?" Tori finally asked.

"Big ones," Georgina answered in a voice that no longer qualified for any kind of whisper. "You know, the kind of sparks that are just waiting to go . . . BOOM!"

Chapter 3

Despite it being her third autumn in Sweet Briar, the absence of colorful leaves and any sort of definable nip in the air still surprised Tori. So, too, did the annual appearance of Halloween decorations that suddenly graced nearly every storefront window that bordered the town square.

It simply didn't fit.

But as odd as orange pumpkins were on an eighty-degree morning, the festival-size crowd amassed along the perimeter of the square at seven in the morning was even more disconcerting.

The people of Sweet Briar were supposed to be working . . . or sending their kids off to school . . . or heading into Debbie's Bakery for their morning cup of coffee . . .

That would be normal.

That would fit.

This didn't.

"Woo-eee. You ever see anything like this, Victoria?" Margaret Louise mused as she leaned over the white fence surrounding the Green, her large brown eyes fairly dancing with excitement. "Why I believe every single person in Sweet Briar is here this mornin' and there ain't a fried dough stand or barbecue tent anywhere."

Tori nodded as she, too, took in the excited faces around them, everyone eager for a chance at two seconds of blink-and-you're-gone fame. "Debbie is probably beside herself with the lack of customers this morning."

"I doubt that considerin' she's right over there"—Margaret Louise pulled her hand from Annabelle's stooped shoulder and pointed to four familiar faces on the other side of the Green— "with Colby and the kids."

A warm feeling settled in her chest at the sight of the Calhoun family. It was inevitable, really. They had it all—success for her as a business owner and for him as an author, a tight bond as husband and wife, and two children who were happy, healthy, and kind.

"Oh, well then I guess Emma is running the show at the bakery this morning," Tori mused of the now college-aged girl who had become Debbie's right hand.

"Nah, Emma is over there"—Margaret Louise's index finger moved right, Tori's gaze following suit—"'bout ten people down from Debbie."

Sure enough, Margaret Louise was right. The strawberry blonde was using a nearby tree for support as she stretched her legs. "I don't think the bakery has been closed since I moved here. Except, of course, for Christmas."

Margaret Louise lifted her polyester-clad arms out to the side. "It's not like she'd have any customers today, Victoria."

Tori peered around at the crowd, the truth behind her friend's statement not hard to validate. In fact, the more she studied the crowd, the more she had to wonder who *wasn't* there.

"Hey sunshine, you're a tough woman to find." Milo Wentworth smiled his way into the line that bordered the eastern edge of the Green and bent down to kiss Tori. "Can you believe all of this? It's nuts."

The butterfly brigade that always took flight in her stomach at the sight of the handsome third grade teacher sprung into action. "Milo, hi!" Rising up on the balls of her feet, she met and raised her fiancé's kiss with one of her own. "I was wondering if you'd make it this morning." She glanced down at the silver link watch that graced her left wrist. "Don't you have to be at the school?"

Milo shook his head as he released Tori and offered a hug to Margaret Louise, who was beaming off to their right. "The kids have a two-hour delay today."

She stared at him. "Why?"

He raised his arms in a near-perfect replica of the same motion Margaret Louise had made just moments before his arrival. "Because the kids are all here with their parents."

"But it's a school day . . ." The protest died on her lips as she looked around once again, the excitement on everyone's face all the counterpoint she needed.

"I'm here! I'm here!" Leona fairly pranced into the line behind her sister, stopping briefly to kiss Annabelle. Then, craning her neck over the waist-high picket fence, she looked left, then right, her artfully enhanced brown eyes widening. "Have you seen him? Is he here?"

"I'm right here." Milo winked at Tori.

Leona paused then rolled her eyes. "Not you, dear. You're already spoken for." Slowly, and with more than a hint of dramatics, the sixty-something single smoothed her freshly manicured hands down the sides of her cinnamon-colored suit. "Though"—Leona's gaze traveled the full length of Tori's body before looking up at the sky in frustration—"why she dresses the way she does for you is beyond me."

She felt Milo's arms pulling her close, then releasing her just long enough to study her in a way that made her wish she had spent a little more time in front of the mirror that morning. But, at the time, the khaki-colored trousers and cream-colored blouse seemed a fine choice. She'd even braided a small section of her light brown hair and secured it with a clip. . . .

"I love the way Tori looks. It's one of the many reasons I asked her to marry me." He lifted her left hand to his mouth and gave it a gentle kiss. "But you look lovely as well, Leona."

She stifled the urge to laugh even as Margaret Louise gave in to it.

"Good heavens, Milo, don't encourage my sister. Please—"

A loud, panicked voice stopped Margaret Louise mid-sentence. "Hey! My cell phone is missing."

Tori turned, the look of confusion on the face of the teenage boy beside her suddenly mirrored by an elderly gentleman to Milo's left. "So is my camera!"

"And my knitting needles and yarn!"

Milo placed a calming hand on the elderly gentleman's companion. "Everyone check their bags one more time. Just in case, okay?"

The teenager reached into his pocket and felt around. "Nope. No cell phone."

The elderly man pointed at the spot on the bench where he'd apparently set his camera. "It's not here."

His female friend leaned down, opened her knitting bag wide, and gestured inside. "My needles and yarn were just here a minute ago."

"I'll go find Chief Dallas, let him know what's going on," Milo offered, his progress toward the sidewalk thwarted by a familiar hand.

"There's no need," Margaret Louise whispered. "Just give me a moment, will you?"

In a manner that was both tentative and sure,

Margaret Louise closed the unnoticed gap that had grown between herself and Annabelle, whispering something in the elderly woman's ear as she did.

"What's going on?" Milo's breath against Tori's ear did little to eradicate the intense sadness she suddenly felt—for both Margaret Louise and Annabelle.

Before she could answer, Margaret Louise returned, carrying the missing items. With a practiced hand, she handed each thing to its correct owner. "My mother meant no harm."

"Geez, lady, is your mom some sort of klepto or something?" the teenager asked before being shooed from his spot by the elderly man with the camera.

"No harm done." The man pointed to the woman at his elbow. "This is my wife, Mira, and I'm David—David McAllister. I'm the assistant director out at Three Winds."

She looked a question at Milo as the threesome spoke—her fiancé's warm voice quickly filling in the holes in her Sweet Briar knowledge. "Three Winds is a small group home for people with various challenges. They do good work out there." And then, "That's Leona and Margaret Louise's mom?"

Leona . . .

Tori leaned forward, tried to gage a reaction on Leona's face, yet there was none. Instead, Margaret Louise's twin was doing exactly what

47

she'd been doing since she arrived—hanging over the fence looking for any sign of Warren Shoemaker, completely oblivious to Annabelle's latest transgression or the fact that her sister was, once again, left to clean it up all on her own.

"Yes, that's their mom. Her name is Annabelle." Tori squeezed Milo's hand. "I'll be right back, okay?"

She sidestepped the ever-growing army of people in front of her and sidled up beside Leona. "Your sister could probably use a little help right now."

Without taking her focus off the Green, Leona shook her head. "Margaret Louise has it covered."

"Do you even know what it is she's covering right now?" she asked through teeth that were suddenly clenched. "Because from what I can see, you're a little too wrapped up in *this* nonsense."

Leona turned, dipped her chin, and stared at Tori through narrowed eyes. "It's the same thing that always has to be covered whenever Mamma is around, regardless of where we are or what we're doing."

Before she could reply, Leona continued. "What did she take this time? A haircomb? A button? Some poor child's neglected yo-yo?"

The slightest hint of a tremble in Leona's voice caught Tori by surprise and she found herself back-pedaling. "Look, I can't even begin to imagine how hard it is to deal with something like—"

"You're right. You *can't* imagine. So don't."
Leona waved her bejeweled hand in the direction
of the Green, a determined set to her jaw nipping
their current conversation in the bud. "So many
people hoping to be stars when only a handful will
even get a chance. It's fascinating, really."

She swallowed.

In the two years she'd known Leona Elkin,
she'd been treated to a host of interesting
revelations and Leona-declared rules. . . .

She'd learned that a woman should always wear
lipstick. Even at bedtime (a rule she didn't
follow).

She'd learned that Florida was an imposter in
the category of southern states.

She'd learned that sweet tea—never lemonade—will always have a place at a party.

She'd learned that even thirty-year-old men
could be charmed by a woman like Leona.

She'd learned to always have at least two chairs
on her front porch—to have less would be rude.

And she'd learned more than she ever cared to
know about cellulite-birthing foods (yet ate what
she wanted, anyway).

Indeed, some of what she'd learned from Leona
was silly, even trivial, but there had been important lessons along the way, too. Lessons that had
come about unexpectedly yet left a lasting
impression on Tori's heart.

Like the one that had her backing off and giving

Leona the space she seemed to need when times got tough. "So, did you bring a headshot?"

"Of course." Leona reached into her clutch and retrieved a picture that was a good twenty years old. "What do you think?"

She swallowed. "Um, uh . . . it's very nice. But don't you think they might like a more . . . um . . . *recent* picture?"

Leona glanced down at the photograph in her hand and sighed. "The female protagonist in the book was in her forties, right?"

Tori nodded.

"Well, I need the casting folks to see the kind of age range I can play."

"But you're not forty anymore, Leona." The second the words were out of her mouth she wished she could recall them. Instead, she rushed to soften a sentiment she hadn't meant to sound so harsh. "And while I have no doubt you could play the part, you have to realize that role has been cast. By Anita Belise, remember?"

"Roles can be recast, dear."

She made a face. "I'm sure that's true, Leona, but—"

Her words were cut short by a squeal from the other side of the Green . . . and another to their left . . . and their right.

Tori shielded the morning sun from her eyes, strained to see what the commotion was all about. But it was no use. She simply couldn't see a thing.

"Excuse me, miss? Are you here to play a background?"

She swung her head left, her gaze coming to rest on a man about her age, his impossibly tall stature making him difficult to miss in a crowd. Yet she had. Until he was at her side, studying her from all angles.

"A background?" she repeated.

"An extra."

"Oh." She couldn't help but laugh at herself. "Um, yeah, I guess."

"Did you bring a picture?" He pulled his left hand from the clipboard in his right and raked it through his already messy blond hair.

"I think so. . . ." Her words trailed off as she tugged her backpack purse down her arm and unzipped it, her focus thwarted only by the desire to read the teeny tiny name written on the lanyard around the man's neck.

Todd.

"*I* have one." With the ease and speed of a now-you-see-it/now-you-don't magic trick, Leona pulled her twenty-year-old snapshot from her clutch and plopped it on top of the man's clipboard. "I have amazing range. I can play a variety of ages. Including a forty-eight-year-old female who falls for a dying man."

The man lifted the photograph off his clipboard and held it out to Leona. "This is very nice, thank you."

Leona beamed. "You can keep it. I've got dozens more just like it."

"Yeah. Oooo-kay . . . thanks." A slow eye roll was followed by Leona's photograph finding a home at the bottom of the man's stack of papers. When he was done, he looked at Tori once again. Waiting.

"Oh. Right." She pulled a snapshot from her purse and held it outward, her silly pose on the picnic blanket, and the memories of Milo it evoked, bringing a smile to her lips. "Is something like this all right?"

He glanced down at the picture and then back up at her, giving an approving nod as he did. "Come with me."

"Me?"

"Uh-huh." With a quick hook of his finger, he beckoned Tori to follow as he turned and began winding his way through the crowd of people.

She, in turn, looked at Leona and shrugged. "Well, that was weird."

"It was." Leona's chin jutted into the air before she fell into step behind Tori. "Then again, I imagine he doesn't want to call attention to the fact I'm being considered."

She stopped short, wincing as Leona ran into her. "*You're* being considered?"

Leona sniffed. "Of course, dear. Why else would he have kept my picture and summoned me to follow?" Elbowing her way past Tori, Leona led the way, her pace closing in on Todd in short order despite the stylish heels she wore.

As they approached a heavily guarded opening in the fence, Todd raised his name tag to the security man posted behind a table at the entrance and turned around, pointing past Leona to Tori. "That one's with me."

And then, just like that, he disappeared into a sea of people with name tags just like his.

Leona slowed by the entrance just long enough to smile and bat her eyelashes at the guard. "Good morning, handsome."

The stocky gentleman, clad in black pants and a black T-shirt despite a day that already showed signs of unseasonably warm temperatures, held his hand out, effectively stymieing Leona's progress. "Not you, ma'am. *Her.*" He pointed over Leona's head at Tori. "The young one."

Uh-oh.

In an instant, the batting was over. "The young one?" Leona repeated, dipping her head to peer at the man's name tag. "Mr. Kelly, does that headset around your neck work?"

The man glanced down. "Of course it does."

Leona folded her arms ever so gracefully across her chest. "Then I suggest you use it to summon Warren."

Tori's mouth gaped open, her feet virtually glued to the ground.

"Warren?" Mr. Kelly echoed.

53

Leona merely nodded, filling in the last name in drawn-out syllables as one might do for a foreigner in a strange land. "Shoe-mak-er."

The guard released a nervous laugh. "I can't do that, ma'am."

Tori watched as Leona waved aside the man's refusal. "Tell him that Pooky is here."

"Pooky?" she mouthed along with the guard's question.

Leona drummed her coordinating cinnamon-tipped fingers on the edge of the table. "We met in Paris last year."

The slightest hint of crimson appeared in the guard's face as he lifted a small rope-mounted mic to his lips and spoke into it quietly, his gaze never leaving Leona's face.

Tori stepped forward, brought her lips to within mere inches of her friend's ear. "You weren't *in* Paris last year, Leona."

With a swat similar to that which would normally be imparted upon a pesky mosquito, Leona stepped closer to the table. Tori shadowed her. "What are you doing, Leona?"

"Watch and learn, dear. Watch and learn," Leona whispered before addressing the guard once again. "Warren will be extremely upset if he's not told I'm here, Mr. Kelly. *Extremely* upset."

Less than a minute later, the guard's skepticism was gone, in its place something much closer to worry.

"I'm sorry, ma'am. I'm just doing my job."

A triumphant smile spread across Leona's face. "I certainly understand, Mr. Kelly. We wouldn't want undesirables compromising the set, would we?"

Tori pushed her mouth closed and followed Leona through the opening first indicated by Todd, her mind whirling with questions Leona had no intention of answering anytime soon.

Except maybe one.

She ran to catch up with her friend. "Do you really know Warren Shoemaker?"

Leona slowed her step momentarily. "That's irrelevant, dear. What you should be asking is whether I truly intend to get the female lead. . . ."

She stopped and absorbed the woman's words. "You can't be serious."

"Oh but I am."

"Wh-what about Anita Belise?"

"What *about* her?"

She looked to her left and then her right, her voice dropping to a whisper amid the hustle and bustle around them. "It's her part, Leona."

"At this moment, that might be true." Leona stopped, then brushed a determined hand down the front of her skirt before resuming her diatribe, the nature of her words and the tone in which they were uttered unleashing an inexplicable shiver down Tori's spine. "But just you wait. That part will be mine . . . One way or *another*."

Chapter 4

The second they stepped through the opening, they were whisked apart—Tori toward a table heaped with forms, Leona toward a trailer on the far side of the Green.

"There you are, I thought I lost you," Todd said as he caught back up with Tori. "In order to work on the set, there are some forms you need to fill out. It's standard procedure and just requires some box-checking and a signature or two. Easy stuff, really."

Tori peered at the papers in front of her, the legal-style jargon making it hard to concentrate on much of anything besides the fact she'd actually been picked as an extra. Sure, she'd shown up that morning along with the rest of Sweet Briar's population. But how could she not? She was, after all, the epitome of a curious soul. It was why she'd gravitated toward books and libraries in the first place.

Todd grabbed a packet from the top of a stack and handed it to Tori. "When I turned around and you weren't at my feet, I was afraid the security detail let that older lady through instead of you."

She stopped reading and looked up. "Older lady?"

"Yeah." He lifted the papers on his clipboard and indicated Leona's picture with a careless flick of his index finger. "This one."

Setting the forms down momentarily, Tori pointed at the tiny microphone clipped to Todd's collar. "There isn't any sort of chance that someone could have just heard what you said, is there?"

He followed the path of her finger with his eyes, shaking his head as he did. "I'd have to press the button in order for anyone to hear me, and even then it only goes to people working on set, all of whom are wearing an earphone like me."

"Like Warren Shoemaker?"

Todd drew back. "Why would you ask that?"

"Because if it did, you'd be getting an earful right about now."

He let his various clipboard-confined papers fall back onto Leona's picture. "I don't understand. Do you know Warren?"

She shrugged then picked up her own packet of forms once again. "I don't. But apparently that"— she stopped, glanced left, then right—"*older lady* does."

A cloud passed over the man's face. "Excuse me?"

Reaching across the table, Tori plucked a pen from a plastic holder propped in the center.

"Something about a trip she didn't take and a name I didn't recognize."

He brought the clipboard to his chest and locked it into place with folded arms. "And what name might that be?"

She searched her memory bank even as a part of her brain was still wading through the forms' various clauses designed to make a person pull out their hair. "Um, I think it was something like Mook—no wait, Sook . . ." Her words trailed off as she worked to remember exactly what Leona had said.

Todd's eyebrows inched upward, first the left, then the right. "Pooky, perhaps?"

"Yes! That's it," she said. "Does that name mean something to you?"

"To me, that older lady, and hundreds of other women just like her." He lifted the mic to his mouth and pressed the button on its side. "Rick?"

Confused, she simply scrawled her name across the bottom of one of the forms and pushed it toward the bored-looking attendant behind the table. "I don't get it."

He released the button. "Do you read the gossip rags?"

She shook her head.

The response was met with a raised index finger and another press of the button. "Yeah, hey, Rick. You might want to look in on Warren. Seems you didn't brief Kelly the way you were supposed to on the whole Pooky connection. As a result, he let another one in not more than five minutes ago."

She let her eyes roam toward the trailer even as her ears remained steadfastly trained on Todd.

No sign of Leona . . .

"This one is older than the norm. Attractive enough, but older. I've got a picture if you want to see what she looks . . . what? Wait, wait, wait, I didn't catch that. Say it again."

Her gaze returned to Todd, to the disbelief evident in his eyes.

"They're w-*what?*" he stammered.

An image began to form in her mind—an image she quickly shook off.

"Are you certain?" Todd asked of the voice she'd have given just about anything to hear at that moment.

But even with the one-way conversation, the image still returned.

They were, after all, talking about *Leona.*

Todd brought the mic still closer to his lips and lowered his voice to little more than a whisper. "Do you think this one's the real thing? The real . . . *Pooky?*"

A few more seconds of inaudible conversation followed before Todd finally signed off, stunned. He let the mic fall back to his collar. "Wow. I don't know what to say. Except all hell's about to break loose."

She studied him closely. "Why?"

"Because Anita doesn't like competition. She's proven that again and again with each new Pooky that's walked through the door since shooting began—" He stopped suddenly, and waved his hand in the air. "You know what? I've already said way more than I should. You passed on breakfast this morning to be a part of the glamour and glitz, yes? So let's get to it, shall we?"

Not knowing what else to say, she simply nodded, her feet trailing behind his as they made their way across the Green to a large white tent that had been erected overnight. He talked as they moved, filling her in on everything she'd be doing over the next few hours.

"The scene you're being brought in for involves the moment when the two main characters see each other for the first time. Kevin—the main character—is deeply conflicted. He has recently learned he's dying and his life is plagued with regrets."

"I've read the book more than a few times," she said, the breathless quality in her voice warming her cheeks. "It's one of my favorites."

He nodded. "Then you know that the moment he sees this woman is magical. So it needs to be just perfect." When they reached the tent, he pushed aside a flap and motioned her inside. "We want the background to be quintessential small town—folks out walking their dogs, couples picnicking, children playing nearby. Yet, nothing so distracting that it detracts from the powerful emotion this scene must portray."

She fell into step behind him once again, dodging various microphone- and name-tag-wearing people every few steps. "So we're the silent background."

"Primarily, yes. Unless we see something in a particular extra that will make the scene stronger. But that, although next to rare, won't happen if there is even a hint of a personality issue with the key players. Especially in a scene involving Anita Bel—okay, here you go." Todd stopped in front of a tall redheaded woman with a spray of freckles across the bridge of her nose and a name tag slung around her neck. "Here's one of your extras, Margot."

The harried-looking twenty-something with large brown eyes and a serious case of bedhead merely nodded in Tori's direction, before pointing to a series of chairs, most of which were empty. To Todd, she said, "So far we've got four of our fifteen. Max and Chelsea need to pick up the pace if we're gonna have a prayer of getting this shoot going with the body count Warren wants."

Todd shrugged. "They'll find the rest. They always do." He shot a glance around the tent, his eyes taking in everything around them with an ease that surely came from experience. "Is Anita here yet?"

A snort escaped Margot's pencil-thin lips. "Oh

she's here all right and making everyone's life hell as usual." Dropping her voice so as not to be heard beyond their section, the girl's words morphed into a divalike mimic. "Do you think it might be possible to find a decent cup of coffee in this godforsaken town? Something that doesn't look or taste like mud?"

Todd released a matching snort. "So the pot I brewed wasn't sufficient?"

"Is it ever?" Margot replied, answering her own question before Todd could utter a word. "Which is why I was wandering the streets of Sweet Briar until about ten minutes ago."

Tori stood beside one of the empty chairs. "You could try Debbie's Bakery. They make better coffee than I found in Chicago."

Todd's questioning glance was met by a vigorous headshake from Margot. "The place was closed. As was everything else I tried in this one-horse open town."

"Oh. Sorry. That's right. Debbie and just about everyone else in town are here. Hoping for a chance to be an extra." Tori lowered herself onto a chair. "But if it was open, I suspect Ms. Belise would have been happy with that coffee."

A second, more sarcastic snort escaped Margot's nose. "You haven't met Anita the Great yet, have you? The coffee is never good enough, the lunch is never expensive enough, the crew isn't polite enough, the script isn't perfect

62

enough. And then, just when you think she's found every last thing to complain about, some poor slob's spouse sends in a treat for everyone after a long day on the set and she makes us throw it out because it's been within a ten-mile radius of a nut." Margot exhaled in frustration. "Trust me. *Ms. Belise* is never happy with anything or anyone. Except maybe War—"

A loud and decisive throat clear from Todd brought Margot's diatribe to an abrupt halt.

"So. Margot. I'll check in with Chelsea and Max and find out where they are in terms of extras, then I'll head back outside and see who else I can find." He waved his clipboard at Tori. "You good to go in here with Margot?"

Tori nodded. "I guess so, but"—she glanced down at her silver link watch—"do you know how long this will take? I'll need to be opening the library soon."

"Library?" Todd echoed.

"I'm the librarian."

"If you're going to do this, you'll need to find someone else to open and close for you today."

"Close, too?"

"Shots like this can go deep into the night, though we're hoping that's not the case today." Margot shooed Todd toward the door with her own clipboard. "We'll have a better chance, of course, if we actually find all the extras we need, isn't that right, Todd?"

He offered a dramatic salute in return. "Yes, ma'am."

And then he was gone, disappearing out the flaps of the large white tent, leaving Margot in charge of the meager slate of extras that had been corralled thus far. "Okay, so let me explain the shot you've been brought in to help with. The two stars are walking down the sidewalk. He, lost in thought over everything he's facing, and she simply enjoying the beautiful day. You four"—the woman pointed at each of the people seated in her section—"along with the other eleven or so my coworkers are supposed to be finding, will be our town. A few of you will be strolling the sidewalk, a few of you enjoying a picnic, one to two playing with a baby in a carriage . . . that sort of thing. Think you can handle that?"

Tori's head nodded along with those of the three other extras.

"Any questions?"

A teenager two chairs to the left of Tori slid to the end of his seat and balanced himself there with a toe. "Is this Anita chick really a witch?"

"That's being kind." Margot flipped back the top sheet on her clipboard and jotted something on the page below, her mouth still moving despite the deep concentration that created crease lines in her forehead. "But I didn't just say that, okay?"

"Your coworkers might get mad, huh?" asked a woman to Tori's right who looked vaguely familiar.

Margot stopped writing. "My coworkers? Huh! Not likely. Everyone hates Anita the Great. Well, everyone except the director. *He* thinks she walks on water."

"Maybe she's good at what she does," the woman offered.

Margot's eyes narrowed. "Oh, I don't doubt that at all. In fact, I suspect she's very good at what she does. Though, from what I've heard, she's got competition in that field should His Highness's preferred flavor—the mysterious Pooky—ever decide to show her face this side of the pond."

Tori's interest in the conversation sharpened to a fine point. "Pooky?"

Margot buried her face back among her papers, substituting her pen for a finger that skimmed its way from top to bottom. "Uh-huh. Aka the supposed eye candy that landed Warren Shoemaker on the front page of some French tabloid last year."

Eye candy?

Nibbling her lower lip inward, Tori did her best to sit still and let her fellow extras ask the questions that were begging to spew their way out of her mouth.

"I thought most of those stories were false," the teenager mused.

"Some, maybe. But not all. Not by a long shot." Margot's finger reached the end of the page then flipped it over the top of the clipboard. "That story made things mighty tense with Anita the Great for quite some time."

"They're involved?" the woman asked.

Margot shrugged. "Anita certainly likes to think so. And since none of us know exactly what the deal is between the two of them, no one has had the guts to actually make her pay for the way she treats everyone, movie after movie."

"That bad, huh?"

Glancing up from her paperwork, Margot pinned the woman with a stare. "You have no idea. No one does. Everyone thinks she's the epitome of the graceful, classy characters she plays. Yet nothing could be further from the truth."

Tori released her lip from between her teeth. "And if this . . . this Pooky suddenly showed up here?"

A maniacal laugh from Margot made more than a few heads turn in their direction, forcing the girl to lower her voice a few octaves. "Anita would rip her from limb to—"

"Margot! You won't believe what I just heard from Max!" A woman sporting a name tag similar to Margot's and Todd's fairly skidded to a stop at Margot's elbow.

"He actually did his job and found eleven more extras?" Margot commented dryly.

"Even better. Guess who's here."

A bored eye roll was followed by an exasperated sigh. "Who?"

66

Glenda, as her name tag read, reached out, grabbed Margot's upper arm in a grip tight enough to leave marks. "Pooky."

Margot's eyes widened.

Tori swallowed as her fellow extras leaned forward.

"You can't be serious. . . ."

Glenda's eyes shone with unbridled excitement. "That's what Todd told Max." Glenda pulled her hand from Margot's arm. "The pot is already up to five hundred bucks."

"Pot?" Margot asked.

"On who's going to survive until the end of the day—Anita or Pooky."

Reaching into her back pocket, Margot extracted a folded twenty-dollar bill and thrust it into Glenda's hand. "I'm in. Pooky is going down."

Tori rushed to cover her mouth with her hand but it was too late. Margot heard her laugh, anyway.

"Is there something wrong, Miss"—Margot flipped to the paperwork Todd had given her—*"Sinclair?"*

She dropped her hand to her lap. "Uh . . . no. Not really. I just, um, wouldn't have made that same bet."

Margot's eyes narrowed in on Tori's face. "Bet? What bet?"

"The one that has Pooky losing in a head-to-head with Ms. Belise."

Margot's mouth twisted into the kind of smirk most people reserved for idiots. "You don't know Anita Belise."

And you, my friend, don't know Pooky. Not by a long shot . . .

Chapter 5

There was something about a newborn baby that could make you forget everything—the day of the week, your job, your name, even your role as an extra in a movie. It was as if the pure innocence and wonder of a new life made all else pale.

At least that's all Tori could come up with to explain the total euphoria she felt as she left Westbrook Hospital hand in hand with Milo.

"Isn't Lyndon absolutely precious?" Tori asked as they crossed the main road and headed toward Milo's car. "I mean, he has to be one of the prettiest newborns I've ever seen."

"I have a sneaking suspicion you said that about Molly Sue when she was born, too." Milo released her hand just long enough to retrieve his key ring from his pocket and aim it at the car. "And I suspect you'll say it again when Melissa has number eight in the spring."

She smiled up at him as he opened her door and waited for her to sit down. "You're right. I'm absolutely hopeless when it comes to babies."

Leaning in, Milo planted a kiss on the top of her head. "That's okay. I thought Lyndon was pretty cute, too." He straightened up, shut the door, and walked around the front of the car to the driver's side, slipping in beside Tori in a matter of seconds. "Thanks for waiting to see Nina and the baby until I could go with you."

"My pleasure." Settling into the seat for the ride back to Sweet Briar, she released a quiet sigh into the shadow-filled car. "It's been my one moment of sanity all day."

"Ah yes, the life of a movie star," Milo teased as he pulled the car onto the road. "I should be jealous of you, you know. There I was standing next to you, waiting for my shot at daylong stardom, and the next—poof!—you were gone."

She froze. Milo was right. She'd disappeared from the line with Todd and Leona and never said a word to Milo about where she was going or what she was doing. Awash with a sudden onslaught of guilt, Tori sneaked a sidelong glance in her fiancé's direction. "Are you mad?"

The sound of his answering laugh chased away all worry. "Mad that you went over to talk to Leona and got snatched from the crowd for a movie? Are you kidding?" He pulled his right hand from the steering wheel and threaded it around Tori's left. "I was just playing. But I *am* curious."

Squeezing his hand, she leaned against the seat back once again. "Curious about what?"

"Everything. The process, what it was like on the other side of the fence, the celebrities you met . . . You know, the basics and that sort of thing."

She peered out the window as he reclaimed the use of his hand, the streetlamps and businesses that surrounded Westbrook Hospital giving way to the quiet countryside that would accompany them for the bulk of the twenty-five-minute drive east. "The other side of the fence was basically what you saw—tents for extras like me, trailers for people like Anita Belise, Zack Quandran, and the director, Warren Shoemaker."

"Did they feed you? Because Beatrice said movie sets put out a lavish spread for the cast and Margaret Louise was beside herself trying to figure out what they'd serve."

The mention of her friends made her sit up tall. "Were they upset they didn't get picked as extras?"

"Wait a minute. Who's asking the questions here?" When she didn't answer, his teasing tone was replaced with one of reassurance. "Hey. Don't go there, Tori. Beatrice and Margaret Louise were happy for you. We all were."

"But Beatrice is the one that called this whole movie thing to my attention in the first place."

His hand found hers again in the dark. "That might be true, but this is Beatrice we're talking about. She was just excited to be part of the whole experience. You should have heard her explaining everything to Luke." He squeezed her hand. "Really. It's okay. Now, if you don't mind, can we get back to my questions? We'll be back in Sweet Briar before we know it, and having answers might make it a bit easier to sleep."

She laughed. "Okay, let me see . . . Yes, they fed us. Bagels and croissants for breakfast, sandwiches and fruit salads for lunch, and more of the same for dinner." She stared down at her engagement ring as he disengaged his hand in favor of the steering wheel, the occasional streetlight making it sparkle. "There was a whole lot of sitting around for a shot that took all of about twenty minutes—tops. And during all that sitting-around time, I came to realize that my Monday night sewing circle meetings are not the only gossip game in town. A movie set—with bored extras sitting around—isn't too bad, either."

Their speed increased as they took to the wide open country roads that separated Westbrook from the next southern town. "Got an earful, huh?"

"I got a million earfuls about everything from local gossip to celebrity stuff."

"Local gossip?"

She nodded. "Did you know that Leeson's

Market is thinking about opening a second location in Tom's Creek?"

Milo slowed to avoid a possum in the middle of the road only to accelerate as they cleared the animal. "That's good, right? Means Leeson is doing well."

"True. Unfortunately Wendlyn's fruit stand isn't. According to one of the extras—Dusty, I believe—Carl Wendlyn is thinking about getting out of the business and heading down to Florida to do something else." She shifted in her seat, the long day of 90 percent sitting and 10 percent standing finally taking its toll. "But it wasn't just the locals who were gossiping. It was the set crew, too."

"Oh yeah?"

"Only their gossip centered around the industry. You know, other movie sets they've worked on, favorite directors, difficult actors, that sort of thing."

They slowed as they approached a four-way stop, Milo turning the steering wheel to take them south. "People on our side of the fence vacillated between wanting to catch a glimpse of Anita Belise and talking about how difficult she supposedly is during movie shoots. You hear anything like that inside?"

She couldn't help but laugh. "She was a favorite topic of conversation. And not in a good way. Seems she's rather diva-ish. Which, of course, only magnified the whole Leona—or should I say, Pooky—situation."

"Leona situation?" he repeated.

"You didn't know?" she teased. "Why our own Leona Elkin is now playing the starring role in her very own movie and moonlighting as Anita Belise's stand-in."

"Come again?"

Closing her eyes, she ran through the day's events in her thoughts, her lips providing the audio portion for Milo's benefit. "Apparently Warren Shoemaker and Anita Belise have a bit of a fling going on. It's been an on again, off again thing for about two years."

"Is it on or off at the moment?"

"On. Or rather, *was* until Leona marched her way on set masquerading herself as some dalliance Warren had in Paris last summer."

"Wait. What?"

"He calls her Pooky. Or, rather, the real woman he had his little encounter with."

Milo pulled onto an expanded shoulder and shifted the car into park. "Oh boy, *this* I've got to hear."

She waved her hand in the air. "I'm not sure I can explain it very well. I'm still having a hard time grasping the way this all went down in the first place."

"Try," he prompted.

"Okay. To make a long story short, Leona was

aggravated she didn't get picked as an extra. So she told this poor security guard at the gate that she was Pooky, the woman all the tabloid magazines have supposedly been whispering about for months."

Reaching up, Milo turned on the interior light, his eyes wide. "And?"

"Well, she's not . . . at least, I don't think she is. But she pulled it off. The guard fell for her line and let her in."

"And this director guy didn't throw her out when he realized she wasn't the right woman?"

She shrugged away her own disbelief. "Apparently not, because within an hour, the two of them were walking around the set like they were an item. A red-hot item."

"If I didn't know Leona, I'd have a hard time believing this. But I do, and so I'm not." He shook his head quickly, as if trying to come to grips with what he was hearing. "So how did this Belise woman take to her competition?"

"Not well. Not well at all. And she took her anger and frustration out on everyone around her—the security guard who let Leona through and will probably get his walking papers because of it; the assistant directors who didn't balk about Leona being cast as a stand-in for her during today's scene; the extras, like myself, who dared to smile at her when she walked by; Margot, Todd, Max, Glenda—all of the people who were just there, trying to do their job. By the end of the day, it was a miracle she hadn't been locked in her personal trailer with a lion trained to attack if she so much as opened the door."

"That bad, huh?"

"You have no idea." She reached across the center console and traced the edge of Milo's jawline with the tip of her finger. "I much prefer my boring life in this one-horse open town, don't you?"

He caught her finger with his and brought her whole hand up to his mouth. After a few gentle kisses, his eyebrows rose ever so slightly. "So where is Leona with all of this?"

"Smitten."

Laughing, he leaned forward, his breath warm against her cheek. "Does she realize a director doesn't wear a uniform?"

The million-dollar question. One she, herself, had posed to Leona midway through the day. She recited the answer as it had been given to her. "She does. But he does have *a title*. A very nice, *impressive* title."

"A title—"

She held up her hand to indicate she wasn't done. "And, we must not forget, his body."

"That good?" Milo inquired.

She had to concede Leona's point. She'd be lying if she didn't. "For a sixty-something guy, yeah, he does. Then again, he probably has a personal trainer and his own chef."

Milo retreated back to his seat, puffing out his chest in exaggerated fashion. "You still like me, though, right?"

"I *love* you," she said, swatting him playfully.

He shifted the car into gear and glanced over his left shoulder, pulling back onto the road that would take them to Sweet Briar. "So she's got this guy in her clutches?"

"Leona is trying, there's no doubt about that. But Anita isn't making it easy. She follows them around the set like a puppy after a bone. She seems to realize that leaving them alone together is detrimental to her standing as Warren's leading lady off set."

"Which means Leona is in full-blown scheme mode of her own, yes?"

That was what troubled her. Leona didn't seem to be scheming at all. Well, apart from the whole Pooky-impersonation part that still made no sense to Tori. Wouldn't Warren *know* she wasn't the infamous Pooky?

Tori glanced outside, thoughts whirling through her head as fast as the scenery passed her window. Another week or so of filming and all things connecting the big screen and Sweet Briar would be over. Warren would be gone. Anita would be gone. And Leona would be left behind. Maybe *that's* why she hadn't resorted to scheming. Because even though Leona might be smitten, she was also smart enough to know a lost cause when it was staring at her in the face, right?

Yeah, that had to be it. Leona was simply enjoying the game and the fact that her presence was driving another woman—particularly someone of Anita's fame and fortune—nuts.

"It's hard to believe that's the same place it was this morning." Milo's words cut through her reverie, forcing her back to the present. Sure enough, they'd arrived in Sweet Briar—a Sweet Briar that was far quieter than it had been just fourteen or so hours earlier. In fact, the only indication the whole day hadn't been a dream was the presence of a white tent and four trailers on the north side of the town square. "Seems as if nearly everyone has packed it in for the night."

She followed the path of Milo's finger to a triangle of three trailers set apart slightly from a fourth, the furthest trailer and two of the three in the triangle the only real sources of light against an otherwise darkened backdrop. Occasionally a flash of light could be seen bouncing along the sidewalk surrounding the Green, but, other than that, the movie set appeared essentially locked down for the night. Like her, everyone remotely connected with the day had to be close to exhaustion. And she had done little more than sit the day away.

"Could we do Debbie's another night? I'm getting very sleepy." She met Milo's eyes, grateful for the understanding she saw in them.

"I understand, sweetie."

He steered the car in the direction of the cottage, the peace and quiet of her new hometown settling around her like a warm blanket. A right, a left, and two more rights brought them to her front walk.

"Tori?"

The feel of Milo's hand on her shoulder snapped her from the sleepy fog that had rolled in somewhere between the town square and home. She pulled her head upright. "Huh?"

"You're going to have to forgo your bed for just a little longer."

She rubbed at her eyes and yawned. "Why?"

"Look there, on your front porch." Once again, Milo's index finger pointed the way for her sleepy eyes. "Pooky is waiting."

She'd run out of fingers and toes a long time ago when it came to counting how many times Milo had been virtually shoved out Tori's door by Leona Elkin. When Leona stopped by to chit-chat, he was welcome to stay, her eyelashes primed and ready for their trademark flirtatious batting. But when there was a crisis that might affect his perception of her, the signals she sent to encourage his departure were not to be missed.

Fortunately, Milo was a quick learner.

And a very patient man.

"I'm sorry about this, Milo," she whispered up

at him before peering into her living room at the sixty-something woman pacing a path between her favorite plaid armchair and the tiny sewing alcove in the far corner of the room. "I have no idea what's going on but I think it's best if I give her all my attention at the moment. As we all know, an ignored Leona is not a pleasant Leona."

Raking a hand through his already tousled hair, he leaned in, brushed a kiss across her forehead. "It's fine. Really. But try not to let her stay all night, okay? You need some sleep."

"I won't let her go on too long. I promise." She answered his kiss with one of her own before following him to the front door and watching him disappear into the night.

"I thought he'd never leave."

Tori spun around and flopped against the door. "Leona! That's not nice."

"Nice, schmice." Leona waved her bejeweled hand in the air then perched herself on the edge of Tori's armchair. "I need your help."

She felt her jaw slack open. Had she just heard correctly? Had Little-Miss-Know-it-All actually asked for help? From *her?*

"Goodness gracious, Victoria, must you stand there looking like . . . like . . . like a backwoods hillbilly who just realized indoor plumbing exists?"

The noise that started as a laugh ended up as more of a snort. "If I didn't know any better, I'd

79

think Margaret Louise was sitting in my living room instead of you."

Leona made a face. "I'm nothing like my sister, dear."

No kidding.

To Leona she simply shrugged. "Most of the time, I'd have to agree." Pushing off the door, she wandered into the living room, the cloud of fatigue that had zapped her energy during the final leg of the drive finally lifting. "So what's wrong?"

"That"—Leona clenched her teeth—"that horrible, awful leech of a thing."

She lifted the pile of unopened mail from the end table beside the couch then paused, Leona's words seeping into her mind. "What are you talking about?"

Swiveling her hips to the right, Leona crossed her stocking-clad legs at the ankles and nested her hands atop her lap. "Anita. Anita Belise."

Ohhhh . . .

She gave up on the mail, returning it to its spot on the table before claiming a front-row seat via the couch. "You had a run-in?"

Leona glanced at the ceiling and sighed. "To have a run-in implies we had to have been apart at some point. Which we were not."

"Huh?"

Leona's glance turned into a full-fledged eye roll. "I simply don't have time to address your grammar, Victoria. There are just too many other pressing matters at the moment. Like how to keep that woman from following Warren and me around like some sort of pathetic pooch."

"Perhaps you could ask her to leave?" she suggested.

Leona uncrossed her ankles and rocketed to her feet. "I tried that. I told her that Warren and I wanted a little time alone. I even went so far as to tell her why, but she preferred to act as if I were speaking Greek."

Tori took in everything Leona was saying, holding it up to the things Margot had shared that morning. "You do realize that Anita Belise and Warren Shoemaker are an item, don't you?"

"They might have been at one time—"

"You mean like yesterday?"

Ignoring her, Leona continued on. "Warren is desperate for some time alone with me."

She tucked her legs up underneath her and grabbed for the throw pillow on the opposite end of the couch. "He told you that?"

Leona stopped. "Not in so many words, no. But his eyes . . . his hands . . . they said it all."

His hands?

It was a question she opted not to verbalize as it invited an answer she really didn't want to hear. Instead, she chose one that had been gnawing away at her psyche all day long.

"Leona, how can you be Pooky if you weren't *in* Paris last year?"

With dainty strides designed to highlight her shapely legs, Leona made her way back to the armchair. "I can't. Because I'm not."

That part she'd pretty much figured out. "Then why didn't Warren have you tossed from his trailer the second you walked in his door?"

A knowing smile inched Leona's cheeks upward. "I simply made him forget all about Pooky."

"By . . ." she prompted.

"By this, of course." Leona waved her hands down the sides of her body. "He took one look and—voilà!—bye-bye, Pooky."

All righty then.

She tried another angle. "Does Anita think you're Pooky?"

Leona shrugged a perfectly waxed eyebrow. "I don't know what that woman thinks. All that I care about is how to make her go away."

"Bring a bag of nuts the next time you see Warren." Tossing the throw pillow onto the coffee table, Tori rose. "Would you like a cup of coffee? Hot chocolate? Cookies? Anything?"

"Why is it, when you have some sort of little issue, I'm always the first to offer sound advice, yet, when I need help, you get flippant?" Leona groused.

She rounded the corner into her tiny kitchen, calling over her shoulder as she did. "Who's being flippant? The nuts are your best shot."

"Victoria, please."

Poking her head back into the living room, she pinned Leona with a stare of her own. "She's allergic to them, Leona. Margot said they use nuts whenever the crew has had their fill of Anita. She even likened it to the garlic used to ward off vampires."

"Did you say *allergic?*"

"Yes, I did. Highly, actually." She stepped back into the kitchen and grabbed the teapot from the stove. "So, was that a yes on coffee, Leo—"

Her words were cut short by the clacking of Leona's shoes as they crossed the living room floor, the woman's answer coming with the slam of the front door.

With a flick of her hand, Tori filled the pot enough to accommodate the hot chocolate she'd be drinking alone. "I guess I'll take that as a no," she mumbled to no one in particular.

Chapter 6

It was doubtful she'd ever be able to look at the act of walking in quite the same way ever again.

Walk this way.

Stop.

Do it again.

No, no, no.
Too fast.
Too slow.

Again and again, the crew moved the extras around the southern end of the Green like chess pieces on a game board, directing everything from their facial expressions to the pace of their walk, to the aura they exuded. And when they finally got that stuff down, there was more to absorb.

Come from around the gazebo.
Lean over the fence.
Touch the tree.
Look happy.
No, that's too happy.

Being a part of the process, Tori couldn't help but wonder how movies ever got made. Especially when common everyday people were part of the mix.

"Okay, guys, you're doing good. Real good." Margot held up her hands and gestured the scene's extras into a huddle. "The guys have what they need, which means we'll be doing the actual shoot soon. Let's break for lunch in the tent and be back here in thirty. Sound good?"

A heavyset man shifted his weight from one leg to the other. "Mind if I eat the lunch my wife made me? Fruit and cheese doesn't really go all too far with me."

"Fine. Fine. But keep it in the tent, will you? The last thing I—or any of my coworkers—need is a dressing-down for unapproved food being too close to . . ." Margot's voice trailed off, her words drowned out by the sound of Tori's cell phone.

She felt her face warm. "Oh, wow, I'm sorry. I thought I had it on vibrate." Pulling the phone from her back pocket, Tori glanced at the caller ID screen.

Margaret Louise.

"If we're breaking for lunch, is it okay if I take this call?" she asked.

For a split second she thought Margot was going to protest, some song and dance about the need for total focus all but visible on the tip of the girl's tongue, but, in the end, all Tori got was a begrudging shrug. "Make it quick, will you? And if Kelly gives you any grief about not being with me, just show him your name tag. That guy's a little over-the-top where his job is concerned and I have enough to deal with without adding RoboCop to the list."

"He's still here after letting Pooky through?" one of the extras asked.

"He won't be for long if the short-lived careers of his predecessors are any indication," Margot mused. Motioning for the group to follow her to the food tent, she continued, her voice taking on an almost recitation quality as if the matter at hand was fairly routine. "Once he's outed as the chink in the armor, though, his fate is sealed. That's a given."

Tori stepped to the edge of the sidewalk to allow her fellow extras to get by, their excitement for lunch and a half-hour break bringing a much-needed bounce back to their steps. She glanced down at the phone again, Margaret Louise's name replaced by a missed call icon.

Without waiting to see if a voice mail had been left, she flipped the phone open and dialed the familiar number. It was answered on the first ring.

"There you are, Victoria, I was hopin' I'd get a chance to chat with you. How's it goin' over there?"

Wandering over to a nearby bench, she sat down, the warmth of the afternoon sun and the sound of her friend's always-cheerful voice making her smile. "It's going. This movie stuff is a whole lot of waiting with little bursts of nuttiness tossed in."

The woman's hearty laugh started in Tori's ear and traveled to her various tension-filled spots, relaxing her in seconds. "Were you hidin' behind the cupboard in my kitchen this mornin', Victoria?"

"Nooo, why?"

" 'Cause you took that phrase right outta my mouth, that's why."

"Phrase? What phrase?"

"That part about little bursts of nutti—"

Tori looked up as Todd and Glenda walked around the far side of the gazebo, the anger in

Glenda's voice pulling her away from her own conversation. "Can you believe that witch's nerve? It's not bad enough that she sees me as her personal gofer-girl—demanding coffee, insisting on the day's paper, sending me out for a better shade of eyeliner, making sure I've briefed everyone on exactly where she keeps her EpiPen in the event of a nut invasion, *and* expecting me to stand by ready to fan her in the event the South Carolina sun gets too strong for her—but now I'm supposed to be a *magician,* too? Capable of making a person disappear into thin air never to be seen or heard from ever again?" Glenda whacked her head against the clipboard in her hands. "I don't know about you, but I missed the vanishing bunny class when I went to film school."

"Victoria? Are you still there?"

She swatted at the air, Margaret Louise's words barely registering as she strained to hear the identity of the person responsible for Glenda's ire.

Todd stopped, swooped to the ground, and retrieved a napkin from the grass. Crumbling it in his left hand, he looked around for a trash can. "You think you're the only one who's had enough of Anita the Great? Hell, I was barely through the gate this morning and she was yanking me by the arm, threatening to have my job if I didn't find out who let Pooky in yesterday."

"Did you tell her?"

He tossed the napkin into a trash can beside a

tree some ten yards from where Tori sat, eavesdropping. "Of course I told her. It was Kelly or me. Though, cluing her in didn't make her disappear. Rather, she started running through a list of everything I've done wrong since we got here—not the least of which was leaving the extras in Margot's complete control." Todd looked to his left and then his right before reengaging Glenda. "My God, what did Margot do to Anita? She's virtually out for that girl's blood."

"What hasn't she done? What haven't *any* of us done to make that woman hate us?"

"I haven't done anything," Todd protested. "I do my job just like I'm supposed to."

"And so does everyone else." Glenda tucked her clipboard under her arm and headed toward the food tent, Todd at her heels. "The problem is this: Anita Belise hates anyone who isn't *her*."

"Or Warren. You definitely can't forget Warren."

"True. Though that's a sentiment that's beginning to look mighty one-sided, don't you think? I mean, did you see the way he looked at her this morning when she berated him in front of the whole crew for not returning her calls last night? I thought he was going to reach across the conference table and"—Glenda stopped mid-step and released a sneeze. "Ooh. Excuse me. Anyway, what was I saying? Oh, yeah. Trouble in paradise . . ."

If Glenda elaborated any further on the trouble, Tori couldn't make it out, the twosome's footsteps taking them out of her hearing range once and for all. But really, what did it matter? The only trouble in paradise Glenda could have been referring to where Anita and Warren were concerned bore the signature of one person and one person only.

Leona Elkin.

"Oh, Mamma, I think Victoria and I got disconnected."

The sound of her name in her ear brought her back to the present. "Margaret Louise, I'm so sorry. I—I was distracted for a moment."

"A moment?" Margaret Louise chided playfully. "Why, Victoria, a moment like that could see a rocket ship take off *and* land on the moon."

Her guilt at an all-time high, she searched for a way to make amends. Margaret Louise deserved better. "How's Annabelle doing?"

A hesitation made her sit up tall on the bench. "Margaret Louise? Is everything okay with your mom?"

"She was better yesterday."

"What happened?" she asked.

"I didn't get picked as an extra." Margaret Louise lowered her voice. "I don't know what it was, Victoria, but there was somethin' about being around all that hullabaloo yesterday that made Mamma come alive. Well, after that little incident with the people on line, anyway. Milo was such a dear helpin' to smooth everyone's feelings."

Tori lifted her face to the sun, its warmth and brightness lifting her spirits and chasing away the vestiges of fatigue that seemed born of the whole moviemaking experience. "I'll ask Margot if I can give your mother a little tour tomorrow. If she says yes, do you think Annabelle would like that?"

"Like it? Like it? Why, Victoria, I think that would be just the breath of fresh air she needs." A momentary muffling of Margaret Louise's voice lasted little more than a minute. "I just asked her if she'd like to come see you on the set and she's all tickled now."

"Well let me make sure we can do it before you say too much more," she cautioned. "Then again, I suspect Leona's current connection might serve us better than any I've made."

Something resembling a snort of disgust permeated the phone line, a sound that was both foreign and disconcerting coming from someone as sunny and positive as Margaret Louise. "If Leona don't like the bagger at Leeson's to know who her mamma is, she most certainly don't want some hotshot movie director knowin', either."

She glanced down at her watch as the security guard from the day before came into view, his footsteps heavy on the sidewalk. Sure enough, the thirty-minute lunch break Margot had given them was drawing to a quick close. "Would you like me to talk to Leona? See if something I say might make a difference?"

Again, Margaret Louise snorted. Only this time, it sounded more amused than angry. "It's no use, Victoria. I tried when we were kids, I tried when we were teenagers, I try all the time. Why, I just tried a dab ago when she showed up on my doorstep wantin' a crash course in bakin' brownies."

Tori nearly dropped the phone. "Leona wants to learn to *bake?*"

"I s'pose you can say that, though, it was more a case of me bakin' and my twin sittin' all prissy like at the table demandin' more, more, more."

It was Tori's turn to laugh. "I'm not sure I've ever seen Leona eat one brownie, let alone more. Has she forgotten her near-daily diatribe about the evils of junk food? And its propensity for breeding cellulite?"

"She didn't eat them, Victoria."

Pushing off the bench, Tori made her way in the general direction of the tent, Margaret Louise's one-eighty beginning to make her head hurt. "Wait. Didn't you just say she demanded more and more the whole time you were baking?"

"More and more *nuts,* not brownies."

She nodded at the security guard as they passed one another, the scrutiny in the man's eyes softening as she held up the temporary name tag justifying her presence. To her friend, she said, "You lost me."

"She wanted me to put more and more nuts in the brownies," Margaret Louise explained. "Why, by the time I was done, I darn near put an entire bag of walnuts in that bowl. I sure hope this Warren fella likes nuts as much as she thinks he does."

The meaning behind Margaret Louise's words filtered through her thoughts, rooting her feet to the sidewalk. "Leona is making Warren brownies?"

"She's *bringing* Warren brownies," Margaret Louise corrected. "*I* made—"

"With nuts?"

"Lots and lots of nuts. *Too many,* if you ask me. But try tellin' that pigheaded sister of mine that and, well, it'll be like talkin' to a wall. Leona wants to bring that man brownies with nuts tonight, Leona's gonna bring that man brownies with nuts tonight. It's that simple."

"Tonight, huh?" A knowing smile tugged the corners of her mouth upward as the reason behind Leona's request dawned hard and fast. "You know something, Margaret Louise? Your sister may be utterly helpless at sewing, and completely inept in the kitchen, but when it comes to plotting her way in front of a man and eliminating all competition from his eyes, she is second to none."

"You'll get no argument from me on that one, Victoria. No argument at all."

Chapter 7

There were times Tori couldn't help but wish life came with a remote control. If it did, she could fast-forward through the tedious parts—like board meetings and shelving—and pause the heart-stopping highlights—like being asked to marry the most amazing man she'd ever met—and rewind whenever do-overs were a really good idea.

In fact, if she had the means to make it happen, she'd shell out a million dollars at that very moment to rewind her way back to the previous day.

Then again, hindsight had always had that nasty little habit of being twenty-twenty.

"Mr. Kelly, are the handcuffs really necessary?" Tori asked, gesturing toward Annabelle's immobile hands locked in place behind the elderly woman's stooped back. "Ms. Elkin is ninety-two. She's not going to be making a break for it anytime soon."

"I was hired to do a job, Miss Sinclair. It's an important job that has me here into the night and back again before dawn. I take my responsibilities very seriously despite what some might have you believe to the contrary." Stan Kelly peeled off his black Windbreaker and draped it over the back of Annabelle's folding chair. "Handcuffs are used in response to criminal activity, and theft is most definitely criminal activity. The way I look at it, if a ninety-two-year-old can swipe things, a ninety-two-year-old can be handcuffed."

Seated beside her mother on the opposite side, Margaret Louise dropped her head onto the hastily erected card table with a thud, her normally booming voice dulled by exhaustion. "Mr. Kelly, my mother is not a thief. She—"

"Oh no?" Stan strode around the room, his face set in hard lines. "Then how is it that your mother was in possession of a wallet, a lighter, a wig, and a watch that didn't belong to her? Are you going to tell me that Zack Quandran simply gave those items to a woman he met for all of about twenty seconds?"

"Well, no, but—"

He bent down, slamming the top of the table with the palm of his hand. "Then how else do you explain those items being in your mother's possession if Mr. Quandran didn't give them to her?"

Silence blanketed the room as the guard looked from Margaret Louise to Annabelle and back again. "Well? I'm waiting. . . ."

Margaret Louise pulled her head up off the table and fixed a weary gaze on the man. "She took them."

"Finally!" Stan took two steps to the right then dropped into the empty chair beside Tori. Slowly, methodically, he reached into his pants pocket and extracted a package of gum. "*Now* we're getting somewhere."

"But it's not what you think," Margaret Louise quickly added. "My mother didn't take those things to be malicious or deceitful."

The guard unwrapped a stick of gum, folded it into his mouth, then tossed the rest of the packet onto the table in front of him. "She stole a man's personal possessions but wasn't trying to be malicious or deceitful?" He leaned back in his chair, a smirk of amusement lighting his dark eyes. "Oh, this oughta be good."

Margaret Louise blinked against the tears Tori saw building. But when she opened her mouth to speak, Tori cut her off at the pass. "Mr. Kelly, may I speak with you for a moment?" Pushing back in her chair, Tori rose to her feet. "In private?"

With a shrug, Stan clamored out of his chair and followed Tori into the foyer area of the security trailer. "Yes?"

A lump sprang into Tori's throat as she peered around the guard's shoulder in time to catch Margaret Louise placing a protective arm around her mother. While she couldn't make out the whispered words the younger woman said, she suspected it was some sort of loving reassurance. Margaret Louise knew no other way to be.

She pulled her focus back to Stan Kelly. "Mr. Kelly, do you have elderly parents?"

The man nodded. "But they're not thieves, if that's what you're asking."

"Neither is Ms. Elkin. She has an illness."

"Is that what they call stealing these days?" He worked his piece of gum around his mouth, parting his lips just enough to nibble the off-white material between his front teeth.

Fisting her hands at her sides, she stared at the man. "Have you heard the term *kleptomaniac,* Mr. Kelly?"

"Sure have." Stan crossed his arms and widened his stance. "It's someone who steals."

"No. A kleptomaniac has an illness. There's a difference." Again, she peered over the guard's shoulder, the lump quickly joined by a misting of her eyes at the heartache and worry on Margaret Louise's face. "Annabelle Elkin is a kleptomaniac hoarder, which means she helps herself to a number of things. She doesn't do anything with what she takes—she doesn't try to sell it, doesn't try to claim it as her own. In fact, she rarely remembers taking it seconds after the fact."

The guard stopped chewing and looked over at Margaret Louise, who had, once again, buried her head in her arms while Annabelle simply sat and stared. "Is that why she's got that vacant look in her eyes like she doesn't know what's going on?"

"I suppose it's a combination of that and being

old." Tori bobbed her head in an effort to reclaim Stan's attention. "She did the same thing at the library the other day. In the blink of an eye she took my stapler, my paper clip container, my pencil holder, and my apple and placed them in her bag before I even saw her hand move. Seconds later, her daughter was taking each item out of her bag and placing them back on the information desk. Annabelle seemed oblivious to the whole thing. It didn't bother her one bit that everything she'd just taken was being returned." Waving her hand in Annabelle's direction she continued, "She didn't care, Mr. Kelly, because she's not a thief."

He began chewing again. "I suppose Ms. Davis did give the items back to Mr. Quandran unprompted. . . ."

Finally a light at the end of the tunnel . . .

She nodded. "She did. And Ms. Elkin didn't resist at all, either."

Slipping his hand into the front pocket of his pants, Stan Kelly retrieved an oddly shaped key and carried it over to Annabelle. "Okay, I'll make an exception this one time." With gentle motions, he freed the elderly woman from the handcuffs and returned the key to his pants' pocket. "You just keep sitting right there."

When Annabelle didn't offer a response of any kind, he shrugged at Margaret Louise and returned to the hallway. Bending his leg at the knee, he braced his foot against the wall. "So what do you want me to"—he glanced toward the table and stopped. "She doesn't quit, does she?"

"Who? What?" She followed his gaze to the table, saw Annabelle's closed fist disappear into her voluminous bag.

Uh-oh.

Tori jogged into the room and laid a gentle hand on the elderly woman's shoulder. "Annabelle, may I have that back, please?"

Annabelle stared straight ahead, her eyes a veritable blank slate.

Margaret Louise's head shot up. "Mamma? Did you take something?"

"She took my damn gum," Stan groused.

With a practiced hand, Margaret Louise reached into her mother's tote bag and extracted the opened packet of gum that had been on the table just moments earlier. Handing it to the guard, Margaret Louise released a frustrated exhale. "I'm sorry. I wasn't paying attention."

The scowl on Stan Kelly's face stirred a sick feeling in Tori's stomach. Had all the progress she made disappeared that quickly? Were they back to square one?

She tried to think of something to say, something, anything that could bring Stan back to the place of compassion she'd glimpsed before Annabelle swiped his gum. But before she could find the right words, he simply waved his hand toward the door. "You're free to go."

To Margaret Louise, he said, "I expect you'll see to it that your mother doesn't come back here again."

Tori's friend nodded, her normal sunny smile nowhere to be seen. Stan, too, seemed to sense the woman's sadness, rushing to soften the harshness of his words just a little. "I came mighty close to losing my job this week and I can't have that. Not now. Not anymore. But if it makes a difference, banishing your mother from the set is nothing personal. We just can't have people's stuff walking off."

"I understand, Mr. Kelly. And I do thank you for not pressin' charges on my mamma." Margaret Louise hooked a hand underneath Annabelle's left arm and pulled upward, lifting the elderly woman to her feet. "I'll be sure to let my sister know how understandin' you've been."

Stan furrowed his brow. "Your sister? Who's your sister?"

"Leona. Leona Elkin."

He shook his head. "Can't say I know anyone by that name."

Tori linked her arm with Annabelle's right elbow and walked with the women toward the door of the trailer, Stan's footfalls bringing up the rear. "That's because she introduced herself to you by a different name," Tori explained. "One you apparently hadn't been made aware of prior to your first morning here in Sweet Briar."

"Oh? What name would that be?"

Before she could answer, they were interrupted by the squawk of the man's two-way radio. Stan reached down, unclipped the equipment from his belt loop, and held it to his mouth, pushing a button on the side as he did. "This is Kelly. What's your location, Todd?"

"Oh, hey, I thought you were gone."

Releasing a long exhale, Stan shook his head, his free hand making a rolling motion while his index finger pressed the radio button once again. "Is there a problem?"

"Um, well, I don't know, exactly. Anita didn't respond to her call to set so Warren asked me to check in on her. Anyway, that's what I'm trying to do, only she's not answering her door."

"Maybe she doesn't want to be bothered."

"It's time to tape her scene. It's not like her to ignore a call."

"Did you look in the window?"

"You really think I should?"

Stan rolled his eyes. "Forget it. I'm on my way."

"No, wait, I'll look."

"Good idea there, champ," Stan mumbled to no one in particular as Margaret Louise and Annabelle headed out into the bright morning sun. When the door closed behind them, he clipped the radio back onto his belt. "Well, Miss Sinclair, I guess I better head on out—"

The guard's words were interrupted by a yell

from the radio that echoed off the walls of the security trailer. "Kelly? Kelly, are you still there? You gotta come quick! I see her, I see Anita! She's just lying there . . . on the floor. I think she—I think she might be *dead!*"

Chapter 8

By the time she'd walked Margaret Louise and Annabelle to the gate and returned to the tent where Margot was to be waiting, any hope Todd's final radio call had been an exaggeration was gone. Directors, assistant directors, camera operators, makeup artists, and talent ran amuck, their normal tasks thwarted by a kind of chaos no editing equipment could ever quite duplicate.

Those who weren't running here, there, and everywhere were sitting, typing away furiously on their cell phones and BlackBerries, all confidentiality agreements long forgotten as they rushed to be the first to release the kind of news that would be splashed across every newsstand in the country within hours. Fellow actors of the deceased would be interviewed about her profound talent; her parents, if still alive, would be tracked down for the purpose of eliciting a quote designed to tug at the reader's heartstrings; and the town where she died would be jettisoned into the public eye until it grew bored and turned elsewhere.

It was a mess, an absolute mess.

Tori flopped onto a bench beside one of her fellow extras, a woman named Callie who lived on the outskirts of town. "Do we know what happened?"

Callie paused her fingers atop the mini keyboard that sat in her lap and looked up, her eyes glowing with excitement. "Anita Belise is dead! They found her in her trailer not more than twenty minutes ago."

Already in the know on those details, Tori simply nodded. "I mean, do they know what happened? How she died?"

"Not yet, but every time another member of the crew comes up to Margot, I start reading lips." Callie looked left, then right before leaning in to make sure her words were heard by no one else but Tori. "A friend told me once that you can make *millions* if you're the one who breaks a story for *The Inquiry*. The more details you can provide, the bigger the payout."

She studied the woman closely. "You also signed a confidentiality agreement. You break that, and you could end up paying back more than you make."

"Not if I'm an"—Callie held the index and middle fingers of both hands into the air and moved them up and down—"*unnamed source. If I'm one of those, no one around here would be the wiser, you know?*"

I would be.

Shaking her head free of the desire to pontificate about the many differences between right and wrong, Tori turned the subject back to the facts at hand. Callie's decision to seek money from tragedy would be on Callie, not Tori. "What have you learned so far?"

Again, Callie looked both ways. Again, she leaned as close as she could to Tori's ear. "Seems she died sometime around eleven or so last night. Though how they know that is beyond me."

Tori glanced at her watch, noted the passage of nearly twelve and a half hours. "She must have been in full rigor mortis when they found her. That happens at about twelve hours."

Callie pulled back, the left corner of her lip curling upward. "You mean like what happens to the raccoons on the side of the road when animal protection takes too long to show up?"

"I guess. It's when the body is at its stiffest before beginning the process of softening up again."

"Ewww. How do you know that?"

More experience than I ever thought I'd have?

"Cop shows," she lied, hoping the woman would accept her answer and move on.

Callie took the bait. "Yeah, see, that's why I

don't watch those things. They give me the willies."

Tori nodded only to stop in conjunction with Callie's elbow in her side.

"Here comes another one," Callie whispered. Picking her cell phone off her lap, the woman positioned her thumbs over the miniature keyboard as Glenda sidled up beside Margot, bubbling with the latest scuttlebutt—scuttlebutt Tori didn't need lipreading to discern.

"Rick got ahold of Todd. They know how Anita the Great died."

Tori mirrored Callie's not too subtle lean forward. Margot's eyes widened. "How?"

Aware of the golden egg she possessed, Glenda pursed her lips. "I'm not sure I should say. Rick doesn't want to get Todd in trouble."

"The hell he doesn't," Margot argued. "Rick's been after Todd's job since the day Fifth-Cousin-Once-Removed Warren got him this gig in the first place. And you know that as well as I do."

Tori and Callie exchanged looks. So Rick—the often talked about but rarely seen crew member—was related to Warren Shoemaker . . . Now his presence on set made sense. Nepotism always superseded incompetence.

Glenda held up her hands. "Okay. Okay. You win. Sheesh."

Tori and Callie waited along with Margot as Glenda took in a dramatic inhale, releasing it with maddening slowness. "She was finally done in by her biggest nightmare."

Margot's eyes widened once again, this time accompanied by a gaped mouth from which she seemed unable to recover.

Glenda nodded. "Yup, you heard me right."

Callie's thumbs stopped moving. "What was her biggest nightmare?" she whispered.

Tori's shrug was cut short by Glenda's next words.

"Why on earth she didn't reach into that damn drawer for her EpiPen is beyond me. Then again, she probably didn't know what to do when one of us wasn't around to fetch it for her like a trained pooch."

Tori felt her mouth drop as wide as Margot's.

Callie poked her in the arm. "What? What'd I miss?"

Margot recovered long enough to ask the question pinging through Tori's mind. "Why didn't she call for help?"

Glenda made a face. "I wasn't there to open her phone for her and dial the number, I guess."

"C'mon. If you're dying you're going to call for help no matter who you are. It's only three numbers—9-1-1. It's not that hard."

"Well, she didn't. Or no one came. We are in Sweet Nothing, South Carolina, you know."

Callie's thumbs paused above her keyboard. "That's Sweet *Briar,* South Carolina."

105

Go, Callie . . .

A thundercloud of anger clapped behind Glenda's eyes. Gesturing toward the extras, she looked at Margot. "What are they still doing here?"

"I haven't been told to dismiss them."

"Well, then, dismiss them," Glenda hissed. "It's not like taping is going to resume the moment the witch's body is removed from her trailer. She was, after all, *the star*."

Margot offered her grudging agreement along with the semblance of an appreciative smile. "Okay, ladies and gentleman, I guess we're going to let you go. If something changes, we have your numbers on file. But for now, it doesn't make much sense to keep you."

"Damn," Callie mumbled. "I still don't know how she died."

"Nuts. She died from eating nuts." Tori rose to her feet and made her way over to Margot, who still looked as stunned as she had the moment Glenda shared the news. "Margot? Are you okay?"

Margot stepped back, removing herself from Glenda's immediate vicinity just long enough to shake Tori's hand. "I'm just . . . shocked. I can't believe this happened. I mean, this woman *berated us* on a daily basis about her allergy. So I don't get how she died from ingesting nuts."

"She probably didn't know."

Tori and Margot both turned toward Glenda.

"How could she not know?" Margot asked. "I mean, that woman quizzed everyone who walked by with so much as a carrot."

Glenda grabbed a pretzel stick from a nearby snack table. Popping it into her mouth, she sucked off the salt and then popped it back out again. "Maybe someone lied."

"Lied?" Margot echoed. "Why would they do that?"

"Why wouldn't they?" Glenda mused. "We are, after all, talking about Anita the Great, remember? The most hated person on this and virtually any other set."

Margot's mouth hung open momentarily before recovering long enough to form a sentence that sent chills down Tori's spine. "But if someone lied, that would mean Anita was *murdered*."

Glenda popped the now salt-free pretzel back into her mouth and chewed with careful precision. When she was done, she merely nodded, the light in her eyes a dead giveaway to the excitement she harbored at the possible truth behind Margot's words. "It would, wouldn't it?"

"But who would—"

Glenda continued on, undeterred from her conspiracy theory, rescuing another pretzel stick from the near-empty bowl. "Apparently Anita never saw *Snow White* as a kid. 'Cause if she had, she might have thought twice about that half-eaten brownie they found next to her body."

• • •

It was no use. She simply couldn't focus on the order she needed to place. Or the shelving that needed to be done. Or even the letter from Felicia Donovan, the young adult author Nina had been trying to track down for months despite being on bed rest prior to Lyndon's birth. The fact that the writer had agreed to headline the library's First Annual Holiday Book Extravaganza that December wasn't even enough to distract Tori from the worry that had gripped hold of her heart and refused to let go.

Anita Belise had died eating a brownie—a brownie laced with the very nuts that sent the actress into anaphylactic shock, from which she had been unable to recover.

The news had sent Callie's thumbs a-tapping and Tori's heart racing. Only their reactions were for very different reasons.

By learning the reason behind Anita Belise's death, Callie stood a very real possibility of making the kind of money she would never see any other way. The woman's fifteen-second chance at fame may have been gone because of the tragedy, but the tragedy, itself, had the potential to open new and different doors. Lemons into lemonade and that sort of thing.

Yet for Tori, the reason behind the actress's death brought something completely different. It brought fear. For Leona.

She supposed her antennae should have been up when she learned of Leona's sudden interest in brownies. She even supposed her radar should have been pinging off the roof when she first realized Margaret Louise had made the nut-filled brownies upon Leona's request. But, deep down inside, she'd already made all of those correlations. She'd just assumed Leona would use the brownies as a way to keep Anita away and, thus, Warren all to herself. In fact, Tori had found the idea to be rather clever.

Unfortunately, it had all gone down very differently. And now the target of Leona's baking-by-proxy idea was dead because of those very same brownies.

"I don't know what that woman thinks. All that I care about is how to make her go away."

The memory of Leona's words sent a fresh chill down her spine. Question after question crowded her thoughts, making every task she tried to complete at the library futile.

Reaching onto the shelf beneath the computer, Tori pulled out her cell phone and checked the screen. No missed calls. She sighed. Why wasn't Leona returning her calls? Had the police shown up at the antique shop and carted her friend away? Was Margaret Louise hiding her twin in her basement—a nose-twitching Paris nestled nearby in her brand-new bejeweled bunny carrier?

"If Leona were here, she'd tell you not to scrunch your face like that, Victoria. It invites wrinkles."

Tori straightened up tall on the stool and did her best to smile at Dixie. Although trying at times, her predecessor-turned-nemesis-turned-begrudging-friend had been an absolute godsend the past few months. In fact, without Dixie's willingness to fill the void left by Nina's bed rest and subsequent maternity leave, Tori would be forced to run the library single-handedly. A tough task in its own right, it would be darn near impossible with everything else that was going on. Not the least of which was the very real possibility that Tori would soon be finding herself watching Leona from the front row of a courthouse, doing her best to support her friend during a fairly cut-and-dry murder trial.

"But, since Leona isn't here, I'll take a different route," Dixie announced as she came around the information desk and pulled a second stool up to the computer. "Is everything okay? You look as if someone took your world and gave it a good shaking."

She pushed the keyboard tray away and turned to face Dixie. "I couldn't describe my mood any better if I tried."

Dixie gestured her hand around the virtually empty main room. "I know it's quiet today, but that's okay every once in a while."

"No, it's not that. It's—"

Dixie tsked her tongue. "I know, Victoria, you don't have to say it. You're upset you got cut, aren't you?" Sliding off the stool, Dixie made her way over to the opposite side of the circular countertop and began sorting through the pile of returns, grouping them effortlessly by genre. "I'm sure it's disappointing, but those movie folks did you a favor. Librarians shouldn't be involved in movies. It's almost a betrayal of what we stand for if you think about it. We should be advocating *reading,* not sitting on one's backside staring at a screen letting someone else do the imagining for us."

She almost asked why Dixie had been at the Green along with everyone else that first day, but she let it go. Why risk upsetting the applecart? Any momentary satisfaction that would come from such a retort would be short-lived. Instead, she simply laid out the simple fact. "I wasn't cut."

Dixie set a mystery novel down on its pile and turned to face Tori. "You weren't cut?"

She shook her head.

"Then why are you here? Shouldn't you be over there?" Dixie pointed her finger in the direction of the Green. "With all those people who should be in here reading, instead of standing there waiting for a chance to see someone famous?" The words were barely out of the woman's mouth before the accusing glare took over. "You're not worried I

111

can't handle things here by myself, are you, Victoria?"

It was a silly question but one she answered anyway. Dixie was the type of woman who needed pats of reassurance all the time, especially where her dedication and competence toward the library was concerned. "Of course not, Dixie. You've been amazing these past few months."

The glare gave way to the slightest hint of a sparkle. "I have, haven't I?" Dixie went back to the stack of returns, sifting through the next four titles in quick order before turning toward Tori once again. "Then if you weren't cut and you're not worried about things here, why aren't you working on the movie?"

She stepped down off the stool and joined Dixie in the corner, working through the second stack of returns with matched efficiency. "Because the movie is temporarily, if not permanently, on hold."

"On hold?" Dixie parroted. "But why? Have they decided Sweet Briar is not good enough for them?"

She had to laugh. Like their dear friend, Rose Winters, Dixie was fiercely loyal to the town she'd called home since infancy. Those who talked irreverently about Sweet Briar quickly found themselves on the receiving end of both women's ire. "No, no, nothing like that. It's just that something unexpected happened that necessitated a halt in production."

Dixie's eyebrow rose. "Oh? Then why is there still such a large crowd standing around the Green?"

"Because instead of watching a movie being made, now they're watching news unfold." Tori dealt the remaining books into their correct piles—national history, local history, mystery, romance, reference, young adult, and children's.

Upon placement of the last book, Dixie swooped up two of the piles and made her way toward the appropriate shelving. "News? What kind of news?"

She grabbed the stack of local history titles and joined Dixie out on the floor. "Anita Belise is dead."

Dixie gasped, nearly dropping her books at her feet. "Did you say *dead?*"

She nodded. "They found her in her trailer just a few hours ago."

"But she was so young," Dixie protested, her feet rooted to the floor in the center of the mystery aisle. "What could possibly have happened?"

Tori closed her eyes briefly, inhaling deeply as she did. "Um, from what I've been able to gather, it sounds as if she had an allergic reaction to something she ate."

"People with allergies must be so diligent," Dixie mused as she slowly resumed the task at hand. "Why, if I had an allergy to something, you can be sure I'd be asking questions about every-thing that even resembled food."

That's assuming people would tell you the truth . . .

She grabbed for the corner of a shelf as a wave of guilt crashed over her from head to toe. What was she thinking? Leona Elkin was her *friend*. . . .

In a flash Dixie was at her side. "Victoria? Are you okay? Do you need to sit down?"

Shaking her head, she willed herself to breathe. "I'm—I'm okay. I just have a lot on my mind and I'd really like to talk to Leona. Have you seen her today by any chance?"

"Actually, I did. She came prancing in here around eleven, I believe. Said she wanted to leave a surprise for you." Dixie meandered down the aisle, shelving books left and right. "She was in a weird mood."

Tori set her own remaining stack on the edge of a shelf. "Weird? Weird how?"

"All giddy like a high school girl," Dixie explained in a voice that was suddenly bored. "You know the type, Victoria. They spend hours droning on and on about some boy that happened to look twice at them in the cafeteria that day."

Before she could respond, Dixie continued. "The way Leona got with Investigator McGuire, and Curtis, and that magazine owner who was in town to give Margaret Louise the award for her Sweet Potato Pie last year. That's why I figured there must be someone new on her radar. Somebody who's all but made hell freeze."

She shot a look at Dixie. "Made hell freeze?"

Dixie nodded. "When else would Leona Elkin be spotted with a plate of something homemade in her hand?"

"Homemade?" She swallowed.

"She breezed in here with a plate of brownies, claiming she helped make them. Said she had a few left over and that you'd appreciate them for her cleverness."

Tori took a step forward, her legs more than a little resistant. "Where are these culinary master-pieces?"

"In your office." Dixie pointed toward the stack of books Tori had left unshelved. "I'll take care of those. You go sit down, enjoy one of Leona's brownies."

Sit down . . .

Sit down . . .

"Oh, and Victoria?" Dixie's voice broke through her reverie, the woman's unexpected words rooting her feet to the ground just as surely as any glue ever could. "She told me to be sure and tell you they did the trick."

Chapter 9

For the first time since the fire and subsequent renovation of the office she shared with Nina, Tori didn't stop in the doorway and smile. In fact, she didn't stop at all, her feet propelled forward by one thing and one thing only.

Brownies.

And while her friends might argue such a reaction was, in fact, normal for her, she knew it wasn't. Because as strong as her sweet tooth was, her love for the Sweet Briar Public Library was even stronger.

For as long as she could remember, libraries had always fascinated Tori. Even as a very little girl, she'd preferred a trip to the library over one to the park. As she grew into her teens, she'd been known to talk a date or two into going to the library rather than one of the more acceptable venues like bowling alleys or movie theaters. Graduation from college had brought her first real job at a library and she'd savored every moment, her only real distraction being her goal of running her own library one day.

Now that she was where she'd always hoped to be, her days were consumed with the everyday tasks that accompanied her position as head librarian, while her evenings were often spent thinking of new ideas and programs to make the Sweet Briar Public Library even better.

So far, the children's room she'd opened across the hall from her office was her most prized accomplishment to date, but she loved each and every change on its own merits. Nina's teen book club was off to a nice start with more and more kids signing up for each meeting. The coffee nook Dixie had lobbied for over the summer was a nice addition, too, earning rave reviews from the elderly patrons as well as the moms who brought their toddlers to story time each week. And the office renovations that had been necessitated by the fire two months earlier had ended up being a blessing in disguise, providing her and Nina—when she returned from maternity leave—with more functional space.

Yet none of that mattered at the moment in light of what had happened to Anita Belise. Or, rather, what Leona may have *done* to Anita Belise.

Tori crossed her office with several long strides and sank into her desk chair, her gaze riveted on the foil-wrapped plate positioned dead center on her desk. A note, in Leona's pristine handwriting, was taped to the top.

Suddenly, the one-track mind that had gotten her to that exact spot didn't seem like such a good idea anymore. Because if she opened the note and it said something about the murder, Tori would be an accomplice after the fact if she didn't share what she knew with the authorities. If she didn't open it at all, any worry she had about Leona's involvement in Anita's demise would remain just that. Worry.

Worry couldn't put you on a stand.

Worry couldn't lock a friend in jail.

And worry didn't necessarily entail a guilty conscience if it went unshared.

Or did it?

"Ugh," Tori moaned. She reached outward, pulled the plate and its accompanying note in her direction, the sound of her heart beating double time in her ears. Slowly, carefully, she opened the envelope and extracted a folded notecard from inside.

Victoria,

While I must take credit for the vast majority of your successes since coming to Sweet Briar, I feel it necessary to applaud you for one of your very own.

Ms. Belise's nut allergy, as you so smartly suggested, proved to be the perfect way to get rid of her once and for all.

Let's go to dinner soon and celebrate, shall we?

All the best,
Leona

The beating in her ears stopped as her mouth gaped open. Leona had done it, she'd actually done it. . . .

Tori's mouth went dry as she read the note a second and third time, the words and their meaning remaining unchanged no matter how many times she sent up a mental prayer for the contrary.

"Hey there, sweetheart, you look as if you've seen a ghost."

She read the note a fourth time. Still, no change.

"Tori? You okay?"

Looking up, she saw Milo standing in the doorway, worry etched in his eyes. She opened her mouth to speak, to tell him how glad she was to see him, yet nothing came out.

In an instant, her fiancé was at her side, crouching beside her chair as he looked up at her. "What's wrong? Did something happen to Nina's baby?"

Nina's baby . . .

"Hey." He stood, pulled her from her chair, and wrapped her in his arms. "Talk to me, Tori. What's going on?"

She tried to find words that wouldn't make her sound like an idiot. But she failed. "Margaret Louise . . . put in walnuts . . . and now she's dead."

Milo jumped back, horror evident where worry had been only seconds earlier. "Leona is dead? When? How?"

119

The babbling continued. "I didn't tell her to . . . I just said it . . . and now"—she pointed at the brownies—"she's gonna be sitting in an electric chair and she doesn't even *cook!*"

She felt his hands on her shoulders as he turned them both around until he was able to lean against her desk. "Tori, slow down. I'm not following a thing you're saying. Can you take it from the top? Slowly?"

Take it from the top . . .

She blinked once, twice, Milo's face suddenly coming into focus.

Get a grip, Tori. . . .

"What's this about Leona?" he prompted.

She inhaled slowly, willed herself to find a coherent explanation before the man in front of her went running for the hills, her engagement ring in his pocket. "I'm sorry. I just don't know what to do with all of this." Slowly, she pointed at the foil-wrapped plate, its contents all but certain.

"This?" He swiveled his body to the left just long enough to retrieve the plate and peel back its covering. A smile crept across his face. "Um, Tori . . . these are brownies."

She swallowed.

"I know."

"Since when have you had a problem knowing what to do with a brownie?" he teased, retrieving the top bar from the mound on the plate and waving it under her nose.

Pushing it away, she shook her head. "Please, Milo, that's not funny."

He dropped the brownie back onto the plate and set it down on her desk once again. "Okay, I'm lost. What's going on?"

She took a deep breath and brought him back to the beginning. "Remember when Leona was waiting for me the other night when we got back from seeing Nina and the baby?"

"Yeah . . ."

"Do you remember how I told you Leona was getting frustrated at the way Anita was following her and Warren around like a puppy? Refusing to give them so much as a second alone?"

"Yeah . . ."

"Well, after you left I made a silly suggestion to Leona."

He crossed his arms in front of his chest in amusement. "What kind of suggestion?"

"I suggested she go the garlic route."

"Huh?"

She tried again. "Just as garlic repels vampires, I suggested Leona try nuts to repel Anita."

Milo's head tilted to the left. "Nuts?"

"Nuts," she repeated. "Anita's allergic to them. So much so, she demands all nut products be kept some two hundred yards away from her at all times."

Understanding dawned in Milo's eyes. "Ahhh. I see. Did it work?"

"Too well." She closed her eyes only to open them and find Milo staring at her with blatant curiosity.

"How so?"

She swallowed.

She silently counted to ten.

She swallowed again.

"Anita is dead."

Milo's mouth dropped open.

"Dead," she repeated in whispered confirmation.

"What are you saying?"

Tori took a deep breath and then filled in the rest of the gaps. "Leona decided to take my suggestion and whip up a batch of brownies . . . with nuts."

Milo teed his hands. "Wait a minute. This is a joke, right?"

She stared at him. "A joke?"

"Leona Elkin doesn't cook," Milo pointed out by way of explanation. "You know that, I know that, heck, all of Sweet Briar knows that."

"Margaret Louise made them for her."

His hands returned to his side. "Okay, that makes more sense now."

She turned toward the large plateglass window that overlooked the hundred-year-old moss trees surrounding the library, desperate for the sense of peace the view normally afforded. But it was no use. Instead, she began to pace. "Anyway, Margaret Louise made the batch of brownies to Leona's specifications."

Milo pointed at the plate. "Lots of nuts, right?"

"Right." She stopped long enough to study the plate and then began pacing again. "Then, to the best of what I can figure out, Leona took them to the set. But rather than use them as a way to keep Anita at bay per my idea, she apparently gave her one to *eat,* instead. Next thing I knew, I was with Margaret Louise and Annabelle in the security trailer and the call came in about Anita."

"You sure she's dead?" he finally asked, the disbelief she'd felt all morning now evident in his voice.

She nodded. "I'm sure."

"And Leona? Where is she?"

Stopping mid-pace, Tori dropped into the cozy armchair in the corner and rested her head in her hands. "I have no idea. No one has seen her all morning. Except for Dixie."

"Dixie saw her?" Milo echoed.

She poked her head up. "She did. Here."

"And?"

Tori stood and made her way back to the desk, her gaze, once again, fixed on the plate of brownies in the center of her desk. "She brought me a thank-you gift."

She could sense Milo following her line of vision, heard the slow intake of air as he realized what she was saying. "These are those?"

"I think so," she whispered. "Look." Slowly,

deliberately, she held the notecard in Milo's direction. "She left a note."

She gave him a second to read Leona's words, then another few seconds to read it again. When he finally looked up, she shrugged. "Pretty damning stuff against Leona, huh?"

For a moment Milo said nothing as he studied Tori closely, his usual happy-go-lucky demeanor missing in action. And as she continued to meet his eye, she realized the worry was back, only the worry he now sported sent a shiver down her spine.

"Wh-what?"

He reached out, took her hand in his, and squeezed it tight. "If what you're telling me is true, Leona isn't the only one implicated in this note."

She looked from Milo to the note and back again. "What are you talking about?"

Slowly, he released her hand, pointing to the second paragraph of Leona's note.

Ms. Belise's nut allergy, as you so smartly suggested, proved to be the perfect way to get rid of her once and for all.

She heard the gasp as it escaped her mouth, felt the way her mouth grew dry and her hands moistened as the reality of Milo's words hit her with a one-two punch.

"Oh, Milo, what am I going to do?"

Chapter 10

Somehow she made it to closing, the comings and goings of the patrons providing some semblance of a distraction from the never-ending questions and second-guessing that ran on a continuous loop in her thoughts. Sure, she'd tried to let Milo's pledge of help quiet the voices, but it was hard.

Milo was right. If Leona went down for Anita Belise's death, Tori would be right there beside her as the brains behind the operation.

"I guess I'll be seeing you tomorrow since the movie stuff is on hold," Dixie mumbled, gathering her purse and her keys with quiet efficiency. "Then again, if you feel like taking a day off, I could certainly cover things. It has been a rather busy week for you."

Three months ago, Tori would have taken Dixie's suggestion as yet another indication her predecessor hadn't let bygones be bygones. But now, after working so closely together during Nina's predelivery bed rest and the aftermath of the library fire, she knew differently. Dixie no longer seemed to blame Tori for her earlier-than-intended retirement. In fact, the woman actually found opportunities to praise her replacement for the work she did, even going so far—on one momentous occasion—as to say the board had made a good decision in hiring Tori.

No, any disappointment she heard in Dixie's voice came from a simple need to work in a place that meant as much to her as it did Tori.

She studied the elderly woman closely, the stooped shoulders of three months ago gone, now replaced by a quiet confidence that was impossible to ignore. "You know something, Dixie? I think I might just take you up on that, if it's okay."

Dixie's face brightened. "Really? You mean I can run things around here tomorrow?"

"If you're willing, I'd be grateful," she said. The time off would enable her to clear her head and come up with a plan. As Milo had pointed out before he left, they needed any and all information they could find on Anita Belise's murder. Tracking down Leona would be the first step in that endeavor.

"I'll be here at eight." Dixie marched toward the front door only to stop a few feet shy of her destination. "You've made an old lady feel good about herself again these past few months, Victoria. And for that, I thank you."

She felt the lump that formed in her throat and worked to swallow it back. "You're very welcome, Dixie. But, truly, it's been my pleasure."

And with that, Dixie was gone, her shuffled footsteps disappearing out into the night. Tori rose and made her way over to the same door and threw the dead bolt. At the sound of the familiar click, she felt her shoulders slump in relief.

Wearing a smile when all she wanted to do was scream was hard work. Keeping the fear and the questions at bay, even harder. But now that the library was closed and Dixie had left, she didn't have to pretend any longer.

Funny thing was, now that she could focus on the trouble in front of her, she couldn't help but wish for the distractions to return. They were easier. Much, much easier.

A faint tapping from somewhere down the hall caught her attention.

Tap. Tap. Tap.

Tap. Tap. Tap.

She pulled her hand from the engaged lock and walked toward the sound, each subsequent tap growing louder and louder as she headed down the hallway and toward her office.

Reaching into the darkened room, she turned on the overhead light.

Tap, tap, tap, tap, tap . . .

She glanced toward the window in time to see a shadow duck behind the line of bushes that ran along the building's exterior. And in that instant she knew who'd been tapping.

Turning on her heels, Tori headed back into the

hallway, only this time, instead of making a left toward the main room, she turned right toward the back door. With a careful push, she peeked around the corner. "Leona?" she half whispered, half yelled. "Is that you?"

Silence.

"Dixie left. It's just me."

A rustling in the bushes was followed by a string of mutterings about snagged panty hose and then, finally, Leona pushing her way past Tori, Paris clutched protectively in her arms. "If I had to spend one more second crouched in that position I was going to start bargaining away all sorts of things—including all future interest in men."

"Like that would ever happen," Tori joked. The words were no sooner past her lips before she remembered how many times she'd called Leona's phone over the past seven or eight hours. "Where have you been? I've been trying to reach you all day!"

Leona led the way into Tori's office and flopped onto the armchair. "Now you sound like Warren."

Tori paused in the doorway. "Warren's been trying to reach you, too?"

Leona sighed. "And this surprises you, dear? Haven't I told you before that all I have to do is snap my fingers and men follow me around like lovesick puppy dogs?" Lifting Paris into the air, Leona pulled the bunny close for a quick nose nuzzle. "One might think a man of Warren

Shoemaker's stature would be different, but he's not. Then again, I'm one of a kind, dear, aren't I?"

You can say that again . . .

"You didn't call him back?"

Setting Paris back on her lap, Leona shook her head. "Of course not. When you're too quick to respond, they lose interest."

She stared at the woman. "When did you last talk to him?"

Leona waved her manicured hand in the air. "Last night. After I brought over the repellent."

"Repellent?"

"The brownies, dear." Leona shifted in her seat, straightening her back just enough to afford a view of Tori's desk. "Oh good, I see you got my thank-you gift."

"I, uh—"

"Everyone who tried them loved them, and I still had more than enough by the time I got to Warren's trailer to keep him happy. And you know what? They worked like magic. Once I told Warren what was in them, he was much more insistent that Anita stay away from us." Leona threw her head back in amusement. "She argued of course, even went so far as to say the brownies and I should be removed from the set entirely, but, of course, Warren disagreed."

She opened her mouth to speak but slammed it shut when Leona continued.

"I wore my fitted red suit . . . the one that makes me look devilishly exciting. Warren was an absolute goner the moment he saw me in it. By the end of the evening, I'm willing to bet Anita Belise was wiped from his radar once and for all."

"You can say that again," she whispered as she sank into her desk chair for the second time that day.

"I've wondered many times, over the past two years, whether anything I've said to you about men has made it into that pretty little head of yours. But now, after your idea with the nuts, I have to say my coaching has been relatively successful, Victoria. To come up with such a fabulous way to get rid of a pesky gnat like Anita was positively enlightened."

"Enlightened?" she echoed in disbelief as she pinned Leona with a stare to end all stares.

Leona rolled her eyes. "Would you prefer to have me say it was *genius?* Would that be more to your liking, dear?"

"I only mentioned nuts as a way to keep Anita away and give you some time alone with Warren. I certainly didn't intend for you to use them to *kill* her, Leona."

The woman's head dipped forward so she could peer at Tori across the top edge of her glasses. "Good heavens, dear, what on earth are you babbling about?"

She studied Leona's bewildered expression, a

question forming on her lips in the wake of an impossible to comprehend realization.

"Leona? Where, exactly, were you today?"

With the preciseness of a pageant contestant, Leona scooted forward in her chair, swiveling her knees to the left. "Why I brought you your thank-you gift, dear, and then I drove into Tom's Creek to that wonderful little day spa that's just opened. It's not what you'd find in one of the European cities, of course, but it'll do in a pinch." Lifting her hand from Paris's back, she waggled her fingers in the air. "The manicurist I had did a wonderful job with the French tips, don't you agree?"

With barely a pause, the woman continued. "She tended to chat on and on about some such drivel or another, but seemed to get the hint fairly quickly when I reached for a magazine." Leona brought her hand back down to Paris and stroked the rabbit's back ever so gently. "Clients shouldn't have to pay that kind of money to listen to someone else's problems for an hour. Though between me and you, dear, the lives of people in the backwoods can be extremely entertaining."

Tori leaned forward against her desk, grateful for the support the piece of furniture afforded. "So you were never on the set today?"

"I believe we've gone over this lesson, dear. One must not appear too easy, remember?"

"Easy?" she repeated.

"I saw Warren last night and, by the time I left, I had him virtually eating out of the palm of my hand. To return so soon would dampen some of the mystique."

She swallowed. "So you haven't spoken to Warren since last night?"

Leona offered a mischievous grin. "That's right, dear. Remember, it's about building mystique."

Leona didn't know . . .

"Wait. Why were you sneaking around in the bushes just now if you don't know?"

Leona gasped. "I wasn't sneaking. I was ensuring Paris some privacy while she used the restroom."

"Privacy?"

"Of course. She deserves nothing less." Leona's hand stopped mid–bunny stroke. "What is it you think I know, dear, besides the fact you look as if you could use a nap and a new under-eye concealer?"

She waved Leona off as she worked to process the woman's story. "If that's all you were doing, why were you tapping on my window with a pebble just now?"

Leona's face took on a crimson shade. "I made a little bit of a mistake this morning, one I didn't notice until I was walking up to the library just before Dixie left."

"What kind of mistake?"

Crimson turned to scarlet as Leona's gaze

moved to the floor. Tori's followed suit. "Do you see my shoes, dear?"

"Your shoes?" Confused, she took in her friend's burgundy pumps, their height and style more suited to a twenty-year-old than a sixty-something. Then again, they were on Leona . . . "What about your shoes?"

Leona rolled her eyes. "You don't see the color difference between the two?"

Tori leaned still further across the desk. "Uh, no . . ."

With a dramatic sigh, Leona reached down, removed her shoes from her freshly pedicured feet, and set them atop Tori's desk. "One is slightly browner."

She squinted. "It is?"

"It is," Leona confirmed.

"But they're the same shoe."

"The same style, yes, but they're slightly different shades. The true burgundy was purchased for this suit"—Leona ran her free hand down the side of her tailored skirt and jacket—"the browner ones for a pantsuit I got a few weeks ago."

"So a slight discrepancy in the color of your shoes made you tap on my window rather than knock at the door?"

"Precisely. I didn't want to risk someone seeing me like . . . like this."

If it were anyone else, she'd call the story

preposterous. But, since it was Leona—the same Leona who made Tori swear on her grave never to tell another soul about her footy pajamas—the story held water.

And proved, beyond a shadow of a doubt, that Leona truly had no clue about the fate that had befallen her chief competitor, Anita Belise.

Which meant it was up to Tori to fill in the blanks.

She pointed at the brownies. "Did you offer one to Anita?"

Leona pulled her shoes from the top of Tori's desk and repositioned them on her dainty feet. "While that might have been my backup plan, I never had to go that route. I simply showed up at Warren's trailer after shooting was over for the night and presented them to him as a special treat. True to form, less than five seconds after my arrival, that insufferable woman waltzed right through the door as if she owned the place. I swear, it's as if she has a security camera like Mr. Kelly's hooked into her trailer so she can watch Warren's comings and goings."

Plucking a pen from her top drawer, Tori worked her thumb and index finger down its shaft, flipping it over and repeating the motion when she reached the bottom. "So what happened when she walked in on the two of you?"

Leona's sudden smile reached all the way to her eyes. "She took one look at the plate of brownies sitting in front of Warren and nearly tripped over her own two feet in her haste to leave, never showing her face again the rest of the night." Paris twitched her nose in Leona's direction as if she, too, were enthralled with the results. "Warren said if he'd had any idea just how quickly the prospect of nuts could clear Anita from a room, he'd have tried it himself a long time ago. Though, to be quite frank, I'm not sure if that's true. I rather think he likes having multiple women pursuing him."

Tori set the pen on the desk and released an audible sigh. "Well, if you're right, he'll have to find a replacement for one of you."

Leona's left eyebrow slid upward. "A replacement? For me?"

"No, for Ms. Belise. After all, she's the one who is no longer in pursuit."

In an instant, Paris was hovering above Leona as the woman showered the bunny with air-kisses. "Our dear Victoria is being rather cryptic today, isn't she, Paris?" Slowly, she brought the rabbit back down to her lap. "Shall we indulge her by asking her to get to the point or shall we just wait her out?"

"Anita is dead, Leona."

Leona's head snapped up. "Did you say *dead?*"

"Yes, I did."

The woman's mouth gaped ever so slightly. "H-how? When?"

She considered the notion of calling Leona on

the less than attractive pose but opted, instead, to save retribution for another day, when its effects would have a more humorous reaction.

Now was not that time.

Recalling Glenda's words about the state of the victim's body when it was found, she answered Leona's second question first. "Maybe around eleven last night, give or take an hour or so."

Leona set Paris on the end table beside her chair, her hands visibly shaking. "What happened?"

"What happened?" she echoed as Leona's head bobbed in response. "Are you sure you want me to answer that?"

"I asked, didn't I?"

Tori sucked in a deep breath, allowed it to release slowly while she searched for the most delicate way to break the news. But before she could form the words, Leona beat her to the punch.

"The brownies killed her, didn't they?"

All Tori could do was nod, the enormity of Leona's situation suddenly making it impossible to speak.

The same, though, could not be said for Leona. "It's about time my sister was knocked off that domestic pedestal she's been prancing on for decades."

She stared at Leona. "Your *sister?*"

"Why are you looking at me like that?" Leona's perfectly waxed left eyebrow arched upward. "It's not *my* cooking that just killed a person."

Chapter 11

She hadn't intended to stop at Margaret Louise's on her way home. She really hadn't. It had been an excruciatingly long day heaped with more stress than she ever could have imagined and the one place Tori had been envisioning when she'd finally locked up the library for the night had been her bathtub.

Yet, less than ten minutes later, there she was, standing on her friend's front porch, straining for the sound of voices or laughter on the other side of the door before lifting her hand to knock. If there was chatter, the tub would win out.

"I sure hope you don't press your ear to the door like that with Leona. There's no tellin' what you might hear if you did."

Startled, Tori spun around, nearly knocking herself over in the process, her gaze darting around the shadowed porch in search of the person that matched the voice. "Margaret Louise? Is that you?"

"Indeed it is."

Lifting her hand to her brow line in an effort to block out the too-bright exterior light, Tori squinted toward the darkest corner of the porch, her gaze slowly making out the faintest lines of a familiar shape. "I had absolutely no idea you were sitting there."

"I kinda figured that." Margaret Louise shifted her weight ever so slightly, the aging porch chair beneath her body voicing its immediate displeasure.

She stepped toward the voice, the woman's subdued tone catching her by surprise. "Are you okay?"

"I'm tryin' to be."

It was a simple answer yet no less shocking from a woman who exuded positive vibes morning, noon, and night. Tori hurried to Margaret Louise's side. "Trying to be?"

Margaret Louise nodded.

"Are the kids okay?"

Again, Margaret Louise nodded. "They're fine. Sweet and ornery just like always."

She sank into the nearest chair and studied her friend. "*Ornery* isn't a word I'd use to describe your grandbabies."

"You ain't seen 'em clamoring for more cookies when the tray is empty."

She laughed. "True."

"You ain't seen 'em when they're called in for supper in the middle of a game."

"But they come, right?"

Another nod. Another creak of the chair. But still, no smile.

Leaning forward, she rested her hand on Margaret Louise's knee, a troubled thought filling her mind. "Is Melissa okay?"

"Doctor said baby number eight is developin' just fine."

Relief flooded her body. "Thank God. You had me worried there for a minute."

Margaret Louise's hand fluttered in the air. "No need to worry. Kids are fine, grandbabies are fine, everyone's fine."

"I'm having a hard time believing that."

And, just like that, the façade was gone, Margaret Louise's shoulders slumping in a way Tori had never seen. "I did something awful today, Victoria."

"You? Oh come on. I find *that* even harder to—Wait." Her stomach roiled as reality dawned, ushered in by the memory of Leona's words not more than thirty minutes earlier. "Oh dear God, please don't tell me you're putting any stock in what your sis—"

Margaret Louise stared down into her lap, the corners of her mouth inching their way south. "I checked her into Three Winds this afternoon."

She shook her head in an effort to follow the conversational one-eighty they'd just taken. "Her?"

"Mamma."

Confused, she waited for the woman to fill in the gaps, bringing her up to speed once and for all.

Margaret Louise didn't disappoint, though the despair in her voice made the explanation painful to hear.

"When we were sittin' there, in that nice man's trailer, I realized her behavior is hurtin' other people. People who don't understand. I try to explain it, try to fix it, but no matter what I say, no matter how quickly I try to put things back, they still look at her like she's crazy." Margaret Louise dropped her head against the wooden slats of her chairback and closed her eyes. "It hurts to see people lookin' at my mamma that way. She's a good person—a sweet and lovin' person. She can't help this problem she has."

A sigh shuddered through the woman's body followed by words that were strangled with unshed tears. "In Three Winds, no one will look at her that way anymore."

For a moment she said nothing, Margaret Louise's pained explanation making it difficult to know what to say and how to say it. But, in the end, she went with her gut, hoped what she had to say would make a difference to this woman who had been nothing short of wonderful to her. "I think you did the right thing, Margaret Louise. I truly do. If that man we met the other day was any indication, Annabelle will be in good hands there."

Margaret Louise looked up, a spark of hope flashing in her eyes. "You saw it, too?"

"It?"

"With David McAllister—that nice man at the casting call the other morning. The one whose camera Mamma . . . took." The hope intensified as Margaret Louise searched for some sort of validation from Tori.

A validation she couldn't help but give. Reaching across the gap between them, Tori pushed a strand of hair from her friend's tired face. "You mean the kindness? The understanding? The patience? Yes, I saw it. It was impossible to miss."

Margaret Louise's shoulders slumped still further in her chair, though this time, Tori was willing to bet it was from relief rather than despair. And she was right.

"You have no idea how much I needed to hear that, Victoria." Margaret Louise pushed off her chair and stood, her trademark smile returning. "But I don't want Mamma to ever feel as if I dumped her off without a look back. I want to visit her every day, maybe get her back to sewin' again. That always used to make her happy."

Grateful for the return of the real Margaret Louise, Tori stood, too. "Does Three Winds have an activity room?"

Margaret Louise beamed. "Oh, Victoria, this place is beautiful. It has a sunporch, an activity room, a lunchroom that looks like one of those bistro places my sister is always goin' on 'bout, and even a hair salon so Mamma can get her hair done each Saturday just like she likes."

The idea that had prompted her question magnified tenfold. "Do you think Mr. McAllister would let us have a sewing circle meeting there from time to time?"

"A circle meetin' . . ." Margaret Louise's words trailed off in favor of a hand clap. "Oh, Victoria, what a wonderful idea! We could add Mamma to the rotation. I could bring her to the meetings no matter where they are and then, when it's her turn to host, we'll bring the circle to Three Winds. That way she feels included!"

Buoyed by Margaret Louise's reaction, Tori continued, a second thought forming on the heels of the first. "And those rag quilts you mentioned making in the past? We could make that our latest group project and let Annabelle give them to her fellow residents. I bet she'd like that."

"I know she would." Margaret Louise took three steps forward and pulled Tori in for a bear hug. "Why, I'll talk to Mr. McAllister in the mornin' and see if we might be able to have a meetin' there on Monday. It was supposed to be here, but I don't think anybody would mind if we moved it to Three Winds, do you?"

Ever so gently, Tori extricated herself from her friend's surprisingly powerful arms and stepped back, each member of the sewing circle flashing before her eyes as she considered the question. "I can't imagine it would pose a problem for anyone except maybe Melissa if she needs to bring Molly Sue along."

Margaret Louise waved away any concern. "Jake should be home. He knows circle night is the only time Melissa ever takes without those young-uns. But even if she needed to bring Molly for some reason, that child is good as gold. Plop her in a travel pen with some dolls and books and she won't make so much as a peep. God sure gave them an easy time with that one."

"And Jake Junior, and Julia, and Tommy, and Kate, and Lulu, and Sally, too. Which makes me think it's more about good parenting on Jake and Melissa's part than some luck of the draw."

"Why that's nice to hear, Victoria." The proud grandmother of seven beamed. "So you think everyone will be okay with . . ."

Tori studied the woman closely as silence claimed the air around them. "Margaret Louise? Are you okay?"

"Leona."

"Leona?"

"My sister."

And just like that, the reason she'd come to this home, this place for a boost, was back in the forefront of her mind. Right alongside yet another, newer, realization.

"Have you seen her today?" It was a rhetorical

question in many ways, especially since she was 99.9 percent sure of the answer.

"I was with Mamma all day, remember?"

She nodded.

"Which means I didn't see Leona." Margaret Louise gestured for Tori to follow her to the door. "My twin finds it far easier to forget 'bout Mamma if she simply turns a blind eye. That way she don't have to be embarrassed. So if there's anyone who is goin' to have an issue with a meetin' at Three Winds, it'll be Leona."

"I hope you're wrong."

"I know I'm not."

Tori fell back a step as Margaret Louise yanked open the door and led the way into the lovingly messy house that was inhabited by one yet loved by many—its interior making all who entered feel at home whether they were one year old or eighty. Step by step she made her way down the hallway, peeking into each and every room as they passed.

The kitchen, with its wide counters and side-by-side double stovetops, was truly the heart of the home—providing the workspace Margaret Louise employed to fulfill her insatiable need to experiment with recipes while serving up plenty of room for the hungry masses that always seemed to be on hand to taste test the fruits of her labor. The country-style table on the far side of the room accommodated one high chair and seating for ten more, perfect for the kind of family gatherings so many people associated only with holidays yet were a regular occurrence for the matriarch and her close-knit family. The lingering smell of freshly baked chocolate chip cookies and the colorful magnetic letters arranged to say, "We love you Mee-Maw," only completed a picture that needed no further clarity.

The parlor was next, its raised floral wallpaper and decorative crown molding the only indication of the room's formal status, a child-sized wooden kitchen set, miniature baby buggy, and toy chest overflowing with stuffed animals and building blocks setting the record straight for all who crossed its threshold.

By the time they reached the family room, Tori was more than ready to curl up on one of the well-worn sofas with an afghan and her sewing box, the only snafu being the warmer than normal autumn temperatures and the fact she didn't *have* her sewing box.

Margaret Louise flopped onto a chocolate brown armchair and lifted her swollen ankles onto the matching ottoman. "I've been flappin' my jaw like a hummingbird flaps his wings ever since you got here and now it's your turn. What's got your beehive in an uproar?"

Hooking her leg beneath her body, she sank onto the matching sofa opposite Margaret Louise, her mind casting about for something she could say that would stop just short of the truth.

"I'm missing Nina at work," Tori said. She grabbed hold of a nearby throw pillow and hugged it to her chest. "It feels like forever since she was there."

Margaret Louise's eyes narrowed. "Least she's had the baby now."

"True." Tori studied the pillow closely, finding a loose thread near the bottom left corner and wrapping it around her index finger again and again. "And boy, is Lyndon adorable."

"Now, Victoria, don't you pee on my leg and tell me it's rainin' 'cause I ain't havin' none of that, you hear?"

She stopped mid–finger wrap and stared at her friend. "Excuse me?"

"Quit your lyin'."

She looked from Margaret Louise to her purple-tipped finger and back again, her finger unraveling itself from the makeshift noose she'd created. "I don't know what you're talkin'—I mean, *talking* about."

"You didn't take ten laps around the barnyard just to tell me you miss Nina."

Her mouth hung open just long enough to allow her ears to process yet another foreign expression. "Ten laps around the barnyard? What barnyard?"

"My house is not on the way home from work."

"I knew you'd understand my feelings." She knew it was lame, but she tried it nonetheless.

"I might understand them if I knew what they were."

"I miss Nina."

"And . . ."

"Um, I'm tired?"

Margaret Louise pointed toward the window. "Your bed is 'bout half a mile that way."

"I, uh, was hopin' to see Lulu?"

"Lulu goes to bed at eight o'clock . . . in her own house." Margaret Louise wiggled her toes atop the ottoman. "You could look me in the eye if you'd quit beatin' 'round the bush and tell me what's on your mind, Victoria."

She knew the woman was right yet, still, she was afraid. Margaret Louise had too much on her plate already with looking after Annabelle. The last thing she needed was any angst her sister's dilemma was certain to cause. Especially when the police finally came knocking at the door of the deadly brownie's ultimate creator.

"I don't know how to say it." She swallowed once, twice.

"Seems to me it'd be a lot easier to just spit it out rather than keep hemmin' and hawin' the way you're doin' now."

It was true. Besides, it was only a matter of time before the gossip the woman had managed to miss while looking after her mother caught up once and for all.

"Did you happen to notice the way Mr. Kelly ran

from his trailer shortly after you and your mother left this morning?"

"Can't say I did. I reckon a train could have rumbled past my head after we left and I wouldn't have noticed. Seein' Mamma in handcuffs like that shook me to my boots. All I was thinkin' was how best to help her before we crossed paths with someone less understandin' in the end."

She felt her shoulders slump. "Oh."

"Why do you ask?"

Why indeed.

"Was there something wrong?" Margaret Louise inquired with all the persistence of a dog in search of a bone.

It was no use. It was time to come clean. Delaying the inevitable was making it worse. "Anita Belise is dead."

"Anita Bel— wait. You mean the big fancy actress?"

She nodded.

"Isn't she the one my sister was fumin' 'bout just last night? The one that kept gettin' in the way of Leona's latest conquest?"

Again, she nodded, the remaining details still to be told making it difficult to speak.

"That's awful, Victoria."

"There's more," she whispered.

"Good heavens, Victoria. What more can there be?"

Closing her eyes, she counted to ten, willed

herself to find the courage to say what needed to be said. When she reached the last number, she felt her lashes part. "She . . . She died eating a brownie."

"A brownie?" Margaret Louise echoed. "What kind of brownie?"

She swallowed against the lump that threatened to cut off her speech, the answer to her friend's question threatening to choke her where she sat. Finally she found the words if not the volume.

"Yours."

Chapter 12

By the time Tori unlocked her front door, all thoughts of a bath were gone, in their place one very distinct image that involved a comforter being pulled over her head and absolutely no contact with the outside world for the next fifty years. Or, at least, until the whole Leona/Margaret Louise fiasco was resolved. But even as her feet led her toward the proper setting, she knew it was an exercise in futility.

Sure, she could climb into bed, even pull the covers over her head and pretend the world didn't exist. But that's all it could be—pretend.

Anita Belise was dead.

And she was dead because of a brownie—a brownie made by Margaret Louise and used by Leona as a way to get rid of Anita Belise.

Granted Leona hadn't intended for the actress to die, but she had, and that, alone, was enough to make either, or both, of the women a suspect should the starlet's death be classified a murder. And judging by the widespread knowledge of Anita's allergy among those who worked with her on set, the likelihood it was an accident seemed next to nil.

Dropping her car keys onto the catchall table just inside the family room of her tiny cottage, Tori released a sigh to end all sighs. The intuitive side of her knew there wasn't anything she could do about the situation at that exact moment. Time would tell what direction the circumstances surrounding Anita's death would take. Unfortunately, it was the rest of her that couldn't let it go. Especially when two of her favorite people stood to lose everything should those circumstances end up pointing a finger in their direction.

She wandered aimlessly around the room, stopping periodically to adjust a throw pillow, move a knickknack half a centimeter to the left or right, stoop to pick up a piece of lint from the floor. By the time she reached the sewing alcove off the far side of the room, she was desperate to do something real, something capable of chasing the worry from her thoughts if only for a little while.

She stopped beside the refinished desk she and Beatrice had picked up at a garage sale little more than three weeks earlier and ran her finger along the delicately carved horse and buggy design that graced the top of her antique sewing box. Ever since she'd first laid eyes on the box in Leona's antique shop two years earlier, she'd thought of her grandmother, a woman who had taught her so much about sewing, and books, and life in general. Not a day went by she didn't miss their time together or wish they could have just one more sewing lesson, one more hug. But just as each glimpse of the box made her think of her grandmother, so, too, did it conjure up thoughts of the woman who gave it to her as a gift.

There was no doubt about it, Leona Elkin was a force to be reckoned with. She was equal parts ornery and prickly, yet, for those who took the time to notice, she also had a pinch of sensitivity and generosity. The fact the sewing box was even present in Tori's home was proof of that.

Shaking her head, Tori forced herself to focus on something else—something besides a path that would surely lead her right back where she'd been when she walked into the room. She removed the tray of thread from the box and set it on the table, reaching into the bottom section of the box with a practiced hand.

Rag quilts for the residents of Three Winds was sure to be a fun project and she found herself looking forward to Monday night's meeting just so they could get started. Sure, the weekly meeting of the Sweet Briar Ladies Society Sewing Circle was already a highlight thanks to the priceless friendships she'd formed with its members, but when they came together to complete a project for someone less fortunate, it was even better.

Buoyed by the new image in her mind, Tori carried the box over to the sofa then returned to the desk for some fabric. Rag quilts needed squares, lots and lots of squares. And while she knew her fellow sewing sisters were more than capable of cutting fabric squares on their own, the task would save them time on Monday night and keep her busy until it was time to climb into bed for real.

When she reached the sofa once again, she plopped onto its comfy cushions and retrieved her scissors and tape measure from the box. Slowly but surely she began cutting squares—seven-inch by seven-inch sections that would eventually come together to create a homemade blanket for Annabelle's new neighbors. The project itself would be fairly simple, but the result had the potential to be significant.

Tori was halfway through cutting her fourth square of fabric when her cell phone chirped to life, the familiar jingle bringing a knowing smile to her lips. No matter how tired or frustrated she was on any given day, one thing could always bring her clarity.

Milo.

Leaning forward, she plucked her phone from the table that housed her keys and snapped it open, her smile growing still wider.

"Hi Milo."

"Hi yourself." The rumble of his voice sparked a tingle of awareness down her spine. And, just like always, that tingle launched a butterfly brigade in her stomach. "What's going on?"

She forced herself to focus on her fiancé's voice, the way it warmed her heart and soul with hope for their future together. But just as surely as it did, she knew, too, that it was only a matter of time before that same warmth had her pouring out her fears to the one person who always made her feel safe.

"I'm cutting some fabric for a project the circle is going to start on Monday."

"Oh? Tell me about it."

Closing her eyes, she leaned her head against the back of the sofa, Milo's genuine interest in her hobby still surprising at times. Before he'd come into her life, she'd just assumed all men were like her ex-fiancé Jeff—a little self-absorbed, a little clueless.

But Milo had shown her otherwise. Or, at the

very least, proved that molds could be broken.

"Remember Annabelle? Margaret Louise and Leona's mom?" Without waiting for an answer, she continued, her mouth just as eager as the rest of her to avoid talking about the elephant in the room. "Margaret Louise got a place for her at Three Winds and—"

A long, low whistle filled her ear. "Wow. I imagine that had to be hard for someone like Margaret Louise."

"It was. And it still is, I suspect. But deep down inside she knows it's for the best. Annabelle is going to get herself in trouble one of these days and Margaret Louise feels this is the best way to protect her from a world that isn't always so quick to understand a mental illness."

"I guess I can understand that."

Shifting the fabric squares and scissors onto the coffee table, she snuggled into a corner of the sofa and pulled a throw pillow to her chest. "But even though she knows it's for the best, she's still worried. She doesn't want Annabelle to feel lonely or, even worse, discarded."

"So where does the circle come into play with all of this?"

She gazed at the squares she'd managed to cut so far, the enthusiasm for her idea intensifying. "Well, first of all, we're going to see if the director at Three Winds will allow us to hold an occasional circle meeting at his facility. That way Annabelle can feel as if she's hosting a meeting from time to time."

"She's going to be a member?"

Tori offered a futile nod. "I think she'll be an honorary member . . . when she's up to coming."

She could hear Milo's smile through the phone. "Nice."

Buoyed by his reaction, she got to the specifics of the project. "We thought it would be nice if she was part of a group project that would benefit some of her fellow residents. So, we're going to make rag quilts—if the rest of the circle is in agreement—that Annabelle can give out to her neighbors at Three Winds."

"I like that. A lot." Milo's voice deepened. "You came up with this idea, didn't you?"

Her face warmed at the accuracy of his assessment. "I suggested it, but Margaret Louise agreed right away."

"That's because the two of you are cut from the same cloth."

"The two of us?"

"The two of you," Milo confirmed. "You're both nurturing and caring, you both put others before yourselves, and you're always trying to come up with ways to make people feel welcome."

"You certainly nailed Margaret Louise." She plucked a piece of lint off the pillow with her free hand. "I swear, that woman—"

"I nailed you *both*." Milo made a stretching

sound in her ear and then sighed. "Oh, sorry about that. I didn't get my run in after work and my body is protesting a bit."

She felt her cheeks inch upward at the image that formed in her head. "If you'd feed it a little chocolate it might stop protesting."

He laughed. "Seems to me, when you eat chocolate, all your body does is demand more."

Realizing an argument would be useless, she skirted his statement, bringing their conversation back to him. "Why didn't you get to run?"

"I couldn't get my mind off you and that note, for starters."

She closed her eyes. Somehow, between work, bringing Leona up to speed on Anita's death, and Margaret Louise's worries about Annabelle, Tori had almost forgotten about the note that could, in the eyes of the police, incriminate *her* in the crime.

"I'm sorry."

"No, don't be. What happened to that actress is not your fault. It just bothers me that Leona worded that note in such a way as to implicate you in what happened."

She swung her legs to the side and sat up, her mind suddenly churning too many things to stay still. "She didn't know."

"Who didn't know?" Milo asked.

Rising to her feet, Tori meandered her away around the room, no destination to be had. "Leona."

"You lost me."

She tried again. "Leona didn't know about Anita's death until this evening . . . when I told her."

"Why didn't she pick up her phone one of the million times you tried to call?"

"She was at a day spa in Tom's Creek."

"A day spa?" he echoed.

"She was playing hard to get."

"Hard to get for who?"

Tori rounded the corner into the kitchen and stopped in front of the cookie jar, her stomach fairly pleading a junk food sanity check. She reached for the cap and twisted. "Warren."

"Warren?" A pause of disbelief was followed by raw confusion. "But I thought the whole reason she wanted to get rid of Anita was to have Warren to herself."

"It was. And it worked. But then she had to make sure he didn't take her for granted."

"Didn't take her for . . ." Milo's voice trailed off only to return to its original disbelief. "Wow. Women like Leona never cease to amaze me, you know?"

She understood what he was saying, she really did, but, still, she rushed to defend her friend. "Leona's been hurt. Her way of dealing with that is to never give the upper hand to another man ever again."

"And by holding every man to the yardstick

created by the guy who hurt her, she's only hurting herself."

Milo was right. She knew it. He knew it. And everyone who'd ever found a new and better love the second time around knew it. But putting your heart back together only to put it on the line once again wasn't always easy. Some, like Leona, never could. Others, like Tori, might give it a chance yet take the whole process in slow motion, second-guessing reality at every major turn in the road.

She gazed down at the ring finger of her non–cookie holding hand, the diamond solitaire presented months before she'd found the courage to accept it and the question that it accompanied shimmering in the light.

"Not everyone has someone like you on the other end of a second chance," she whispered, as much to herself as to the man on the opposite end of the line.

"Not everyone has someone like you on the other end of a second chance, either," Milo said, referencing his late wife, Celia. "But had I not leapt, had you not leapt, we'd both be casting about in a life that would be far less special."

"I love you, Milo." It was all she could think to say. Yet it fit. Perfectly.

"I love you, too. Which is why that note Leona left on your desk has me so worked up. It makes you sound as if you were in on what happened to that actress."

She nibbled a bite of chocolate chip cookie, Milo's concern suddenly seeming less worrisome. "Yeah, but Leona wrote that note before she even knew Anita was dead. Therefore there was nothing to imply."

"That's assuming the police believe Leona in the first place."

"She wasn't anywhere near Anita's trailer," Tori protested, the cookie-induced calm disappearing all too quickly.

"That's what she *says*."

"Milo," she gasped. "Are you saying you don't believe her?"

"No. But I'm not sure the police will. She baked the brownies."

"Margaret Louise did," she corrected.

"And whose idea was it to make them in the first place?"

She opened her mouth to protest only to shut it just as quickly, the picture Milo was trying to create suddenly crystal clear.

Chapter 13

Tori turned east onto Main, instinctively lifting her face to the early morning sun. If the forecasters were right, the day promised to be a beauty with nary a cloud in the sky. But, try as she might, she couldn't seem to shake the lingering fog that had rolled in during her conversation with Milo and lingered throughout the night, wreaking havoc on her sleep as well as her psyche.

It was only a matter of time before questions about the brownies began.

Where did they come from?

Who baked them?

Why were they given to a woman so highly allergic to one of their key ingredients?

And, last but not least, did the person who gave them to Anita know that she was allergic to nuts?

They were questions the police would ask.

With answers she could already answer . . .

They came from Leona.

They'd been baked by Margaret Louise.

The intent behind them had been to keep the victim at bay.

And, unless you were deaf, it was impossible

not to know. Everyone on set knew Anita was allergic to nuts.

Tori stopped in her tracks, a slight breeze plucking a few stray tendrils from her updo.

"Everyone on set knew," she mumbled. *"Everyone."*

Todd . . .

Margot . . .

Glenda . . .

And countless others like them who found Anita Belise to be more than a little insufferable.

The key was finding the right needle in a very large haystack.

Glancing to her right, she drank in the sight of her beloved library, its calming and steadfast presence calling to her sleep-deprived body like a warm hug. Glancing left, she took in the tents and trailers that dotted the far side of the town square, the hustle and bustle that had brought the former movie set to life virtually nil now that tragedy had come knocking.

She knew which way she wanted to turn. She also knew which way she *had* to turn.

Step by step, she followed the same path she'd made twenty-four hours earlier, a path that no longer led to a new experience for her mental memory book, but, rather, critical answers to questions that were no more than a few hours away. Tops.

She'd been on the receiving end of those kinds

of questions one too many times. And it wasn't a place she wanted to be ever again.

A familiar, burly figure emerged from a nearby trailer as she approached, his gait reminiscent of a mother lion Tori had seen at the Chicago Zoo years earlier—the animal making no bones about its job as protector and how it felt about the notion of people coming too close.

"Good morning, Mr. Kelly."

The security guard stopped just inside the fence line, his stance easing ever so slightly, his answering response coming via a quick nod.

"In all the chaos yesterday, I'm afraid I may have left something in the tent." She tilted her head a hairbreadth to the left and offered up a wide smile. "Would it be okay if I took a moment to look around?"

"What is it?"

"What is what?"

"The item you left behind," the guard prompted through narrowed eyes.

She searched her thoughts for something that sounded believable, the need for yet another white lie making her feel all the more guilty. "I . . . uh . . . left a . . . small notebook I'd been jotting work notes in during down times. It's . . . it's got information I need to enter into a computer at work this morning."

The second the words were out, she drew back, surprised at just how easily she'd concocted an answer that sounded fairly believable. Perhaps some of that was because she had, in fact, used that exact notebook while sitting in the tent before Margaret Louise and Annabelle had arrived for their set tour. Perhaps some of it was because she had, in fact, been looking for that very notebook not fifteen minutes earlier before heading out the door. The difference, though, was that she'd found it. And it was safe and sound in the purse that hung from her shoulder at that very moment.

Semantics . . .

Shaking any sense of a moral misstep from her conscience, she added a few blinks to her smile. "It won't take me long. . . ."

For a moment she thought he was about to decline her request, her attempts at female persuasion not as finely tuned as those of someone like, say, Leona. But, in the end, he waved her through. "It's a good thing you waited until now to come back and look. Had you come back yesterday afternoon, or even into the evening, I would have had to tell you no."

"Oh?" It was a lame inquiry but one she hoped would do the trick.

It didn't disappoint.

"This place was a circus yesterday—studio personnel, publicity people, police officers, you name it. You'd think the Queen of England had been murdered."

"Murdered?" she echoed. "They think Ms. Belise was murdered?"

A slight crimson rose in the guard's face, followed by a tightening of his jaw. "I didn't say that."

"No, but you likened the commotion to that of a murder."

He ran a hand down his face, stilling the motion at his chin. "Look, nothing is official. And if you quote me as saying otherwise, I'll deny everything."

"I understand. . . ." She let the words disappear into the air in an effort to prompt further discussion. The effort, however, was met with the sweep of the man's hand in the direction of the tent.

"Look around the tent all you want, but that's it. If I see you wandering around the grounds or catch you anywhere near the victim's trailer on one of my cameras I'll throw you out, you understand?"

"Absolutely." She reached out, touched his arm briefly. "Thank you so much. If I find this notebook, it will save me a ton of time once I get to work."

Once again, Stan Kelly acknowledged her words with a nod of his head, leaving her to follow the makeshift path that led to and from the main tent and the only chance at digging up answers she could craft on such short notice. Yet, as she got within steps of her final destination, she wasn't exactly sure where to start.

Inhaling sharply, Tori pushed back the flap of the main tent and peered inside, the once bustling interior now inhabited by only a handful of studio personnel. She recognized a few of the faces from her time spent in this very spot, but none well enough to approach, even with casual conversation.

"Tori?"

She looked to her right, a smile creeping across her face at the sight of Margot. "Oh, hey, how are you?"

Margot ran a hand through her already unkempt hair and shrugged. "Worried."

Tori stepped further into the tent, letting the flaps close in her wake. "Worried? Why?"

Dropping onto the nearest folding chair, Margot exhaled a strand of red hair from her cheek. "First, I'm worried about my job. I'm hired gig by gig and I was counting on this one lasting awhile. Second, I'm not exactly used to keeping my feelings for someone like Anita under wraps. But, if I don't, then the cops might start looking at me once they figure out what the rest of us already know."

It was hard not to sound too eager, to pounce on the girl's every word, but if she'd learned one thing about situations like this over the past two years, it was to take things slow. To do anything else might jeopardize her end goal.

The lost notebook was only going to buy her so much time. She needed to use it in ways other than trying to pry a turtle out of its shell. "Oh?" Tori wandered over to the nearby snack table, her interest in finding a pretzel at the bottom of one of the near-empty bowls far less intense than that of knowing whether her nonchalance was paying off.

Fortunately, Margot's mouth was on some sort of autopilot, spouting out so many gems Tori couldn't help but wish she could pluck her supposedly missing notebook from its spot inside her purse and take notes.

"I mean, c'mon, what are we, in Mayberry here? Is Barney Fife the chief of police?"

Not sure whether to defend her new home or to agree on some level, Tori opted, instead, to stay mum. Margot wasn't the type that necessarily believed in two-way conversation, anyway.

"It's not like Anita's allergy was some hush-hush secret. Shoot, they practically had to trip over a billboard advertising that fact when they went in to retrieve the body."

"Billboard?" She knew she was taking a chance asking something that might derail the woman from her ramblings, but she couldn't resist. The answer could potentially be important.

"You know, a big sign. Though, calling it a billboard might be a slight exaggeration—but only slight. I mean, this woman wore a medical ID bracelet, drilled every new hire about what to do if she came within five feet of a nut, and had more than one sign inside her trailer letting everyone know, in no uncertain terms, that nuts of any kind weren't allowed. Ever."

She opened her mouth to speak yet shut it just as quickly when Margot continued. "So why they're not dragging each and every one of us into one of those windowless rooms with the swinging lamps overhead and the gun-toting partner behind the one-way mirror is beyond me. I mean, hello, a woman was just murdered, people! Granted she was aggravating and obnoxious and more than a little full of herself but still . . . someone killed her."

"You're that sure she didn't just make a mistake? Maybe think the brownie was nut-free?"

Margot stared at her as if she'd grown three heads. Three insanely inept heads. "The only way that could have happened is if the person giving her the brownie was a mute. Because Anita the Great didn't touch a piece of food without asking for a rundown of each and every ingredient."

"So someone lied to her?"

"For starters." The curious statement had no sooner left her lips when Margot sat up tall and pointed at Tori. "Wait a minute. How did you get in here? The set is closed to extras and other nonessential personnel."

It took every ounce of willpower she could

muster not to ignore the girl's question in favor of their previous discussion. But she knew she couldn't. Not if she wanted to get a jump on the police investigation that was sure to be under way in a matter of hours.

Summoning her best theatrical abilities, she sank onto the edge of a chair and made a face. "Would you believe I was getting ready for work this morning and realized that little notebook I'd been jotting in during breaks was missing? And I need some of that information for an order I'll be placing this afternoon. Nearly tore my cottage apart looking for it until I realized the last place I could picture it was"—she shifted forward in her seat, glancing behind and around the circle of folding chairs—"somewhere around here."

Margot leapt to her feet, grabbing her clipboard off a nearby table as she did. "Well, you didn't leave it here. I'd have noticed it by now if you had."

"Maybe I dropped it and it got kicked under the table." Tori rose to her feet, as well, the presence of the floor-skirting tablecloth providing a momentary reprieve from her pending dismissal. "It's worth a shot."

"Suit yourself." Margot flipped back the first page on her clipboard and consulted the next. "It's weird, you know? All this quiet. It's like holding a bone and having no dogs to give it to."

Anxious to keep their dialogue going, Tori offered a few understanding noises as she dropped onto her knee and made a show of lifting the tablecloth and scanning the notebook-free floor.

"Don't get me wrong, it's kind of nice not to be dealing with a bunch of amateurs for a little while, but even that's better than this holding pattern we're in now, waiting to see what happens with the movie." Margot glanced up from the clipboard, a faraway look in her eye. "Whoever did this was rather shortsighted."

"Shortsighted?"

"Sure, we're all rid of the diva and her nonstop drama—some of us more glad than others about that, I'll admit—but, without her, there's no guarantee the powers-that-be will recast." Margot turned on her heels and headed toward the far exit of the tent, her ankle boots making soft clacking sounds against the temporary floor laid down by the studio. When she reached the end, she turned around, cut her hand through the air. "And without a leading lady, this all goes away."

Chapter 14

By the time Tori walked through the door of Debbie's Bakery, all she could see in her mind was a plate of chocolate—what kind didn't matter—and a jumbo-sized cup of hot chocolate.

She'd been down this road enough times to know it was her body's way of craving a boost—something, anything to get through the rest of the day. But as enticing as the image was, she knew deep down inside it wasn't going to matter.

All day long she'd done her best to focus on the library. She'd shelved, she'd tracked orders, she'd had a conference call with the board regarding the fast-approaching First Annual Holiday Book Extravaganza she'd been working on for months, and she'd read five stories to a handful of fascinated toddlers—all while dodging her fair share of glares from Dixie over coming into work when she said she wasn't. And even with all of that, she hadn't been able to get her mind off Anita Belise.

Or, rather, the *murder* of Anita Belise.

Because try as she might to think of a million ways the woman's death could have been an accident, she knew in her gut it wasn't. Educated adults with serious food allergies didn't take eating lightly. Especially educated adults like Anita Belise, who told everyone under the sun about her allergy. The notion that she'd take a bite of a nut-laden brownie without a care in the world simply didn't stack up.

Someone lying to the actress about the brownie's true ingredients, however, did. . . .

Which is what had her worried.

If Chief Dallas was as predictable as Tori knew

him to be, it wouldn't be long before he paid the first of many official visits to his top trio of suspects—Leona, Margaret Louise, and her.

She knew this because they were the easy suspects. And Chief Dallas tended to latch onto the easy for far too long.

"Earth to Victoria, earth to Victoria, come in, Victoria. Do you copy?"

Shaking her head, she forced her focus onto the young girl behind the counter staring at her with a mixture of amusement and curiosity. Step by step, she closed the gap between them. "Sorry, Emma, I guess I was someplace else just then."

Emma giggled and pushed a strand of strawberry blonde hair from her lightly freckled face. "I saw you walk in and then . . . boom . . . you just stopped. Like your feet were stuck to the floor or somethin'." Bobbing her head to the left, the girl lowered her voice so as not to be overheard by anyone else. "I was hopin' Mrs. Calhoun wouldn't come out and see you, maybe think I hadn't mopped well enough."

A smile tugged her lips upward. "Trust me, Emma, Debbie is well aware of what a gem she has in you. She's also well aware of how lost in thought I get at times."

The sparkle in Emma's sapphire blue eyes dulled ever so slightly. "Are you okay?"

She made herself nod. "Fine. Just a little distracted, I guess."

"Jumbo-sized hot chocolate?" Emma asked, her hand reaching for the largest to-go cup they stocked without even waiting for Tori's answer. "The caramel brownie is really good. It's a new recipe."

At the mention of the treat, Tori felt her stomach churn. She held up her hand. "The caramel part sounds good but the brownie part, not so much. How about a cookie or a pie of some kind?"

Emma stared at her momentarily before turning her attention to the glass case that separated them from one another. "Um, okay . . . there's a caramel pie and—"

"That sounds great." Reaching into her purse, Tori extracted a crisp ten-dollar bill and held it in the young woman's direction. "How's school going?"

After the treat was plated and the to-go cup filled to the top, Emma took the money and shrugged. "It's going, I guess. It's not as much fun as working here, though."

"Taking classes at the community college is giving you options. That's all. When you're done, if you want to stay here, I'm sure Debbie would be thrilled." Tori grabbed hold of the pie plate and her drink and took a step backward, gesturing toward the far side of the seating area with her chin. "I'll be over there."

Slowly, she made her way through the maze of lattice-back chairs to her favorite table in the back right corner of the bakery. The table was a high top like all the others, but this particular one was where she'd sat with Milo on their very first date. That alone made it a special place to sit. The fact that it afforded a perfect view of the front door and the large plateglass window overlooking the heart of Sweet Briar didn't hurt, either.

She slid onto her stool-high chair and looked around, familiar faces dotting several nearby tables.

Two years earlier, she'd been the proverbial fish out of water, the new Yankee librarian in a town of southerners who'd known each other all their lives. But now, she was one of them, her presence earning smiles and waves just like any lifelong Sweet Briar resident.

Some of that, she knew, was because of her work at the library. Patrons who saw her behind the counter day in and day out had grown to accept her as one of their own. And it was a good feeling.

Some of it, too, was the simple fact that kids had a way of forcing adults to see things differently—especially kids who came in contact with Tori on a semiregular basis either through story time, the teen book club, or via visits to the children's room she'd created in an old storage room of the Sweet Briar Public Library.

But most of it had to do with her sewing circle sisters. Through them, she'd become a true member of the community—a member who had the endorsement of some of Sweet Briar's most respected residents. People like Georgina Hayes, the town's beloved mayor, and Rose Winters, the elderly retired schoolteacher who had, at one time or another, taught virtually every member of the town.

Even more than the acceptance they'd helped her gain, the women of the sewing circle had given her a home. A place where she always felt loved and cherished.

"Emma tells me there's something troubling you."

Tori looked up from her pie plate and smiled at the thirty-something bakery owner who doubled as one of her dearest Sweet Briar friends. "Oh, Debbie, I didn't see you standing there."

"Further proof that I have a genius working for me." Debbie pulled a cloth from her belt and wiped off her flour-dusted hands before claiming the vacant chair across from Tori. "So what's going on?"

"Just craving a treat, that's all."

Debbie pointed at Tori's cup. "When you order a jumbo-sized, it's more than just a craving."

She couldn't help but laugh. Debbie and Emma had her habits down pat. "Am I really that transparent?"

"Yes." Reaching upward, Debbie released her long sandy blonde hair from its holder and let it cascade down her back for all of about three seconds before gathering it together once again, this time securing it a bit higher on her head. "So what is it? Wedding plans? The library? The end to your run as a movie extra?"

Leave it to Debbie to hit the nail on the head—even going so far as to strike nails Tori knew were there, yet had managed to forget for the moment. She wrapped her hands around the cup, savoring the warmth against her skin. "Yes. Yes. And in ways you can't even imagine."

A flash of intrigue skittered across Debbie's pale blue eyes. "Oh?"

She nodded.

"I want details." Debbie leaned back in her chair and gave Emma a high sign followed by a quick sweeping motion. Seconds later, the college-aged girl was out from behind the counter, dustpan and broom in hand. Debbie looked back at Tori. "Well? What are you waiting for? I need details."

"Of which part?"

"All of it."

Desperate for a little fun, Tori took a bite of caramel pie. "I—I don't know where to start."

Debbie rolled her eyes. "You're such a tease."

Tori took a second bite. "Hmmm, okay . . . the wedding. I've done absolutely nothing so far. I haven't looked for a dress. I haven't put a hold on the church, I haven't found a reception hall, I haven't—"

"You need to, you know." Debbie set an elbow on the table, propping her chin on her hand as she did. "Twelve months will slide by really fast if you're not careful."

Twelve months.

Twelve months until she became Mrs. Milo Wentworth . . .

She shook her head against the flood of panic that threatened to consume her where she sat. "I'll get to it. Soon. I just have to get a few other things off my plate first."

"Like the Holiday Book Extravaganza?"

The enthusiasm in Debbie's voice was contagious and she found herself pushing all images of fatal brownies and Leona in prison stripes from her thoughts. "I had a conference call with the board this afternoon. Looks like we might have Felicia Donavan inked as our guest of honor."

Debbie clapped and squealed. "Felicia Donovan? Are you serious?"

She nodded, a smile playing across her own lips at the mere notion of having an author of Donovan's stature in Sweet Briar. For an event *Tori* was putting together. "Seems she feels as if Sweet Briar is the perfect place to launch her first-ever holiday book."

"Wow. If you pull this off along with everything else you've got planned, this event is going to be a smashing success."

"From your mouth, Debbie Calhoun, from your

176

mouth." If she was honest with herself, though, she was every bit as hopeful for the first-ever Holiday Book Extravaganza as Debbie. Only Tori's hope was mixed with a generous helping of realism where similar events were concerned. Publicity was the key to all of it. "As soon as we ink her, I'm going to need to put your marketing committee to work."

Debbie sat up tall. "If you ink her, there won't be a person in the state of South Carolina who won't know about this event. You have my word."

"I'm counting on that." She paused her fork above the half-eaten pie and studied her friend, a miscellaneous thought pulling her back to her original funk. "Hey, can I ask you something?"

"Sure. Shoot."

"Did you cater any of the food for the movie set this past week?"

Debbie nodded. "I did. We did box lunches for the crew on the first day and some snack platters for a production meeting later that same evening. It was fun, but a little nerve-racking, too."

"Nerve-racking?" she echoed.

"I mean, I'm over the top about cleanliness in the kitchen anyway, but having the fear of God put in you regarding nut contamination has a way of making you neurotic."

She stared at her friend? "What do you mean?"

"The star. Anita Belise. She was deathly allergic to nuts. So much so, the kitchen had to be triple-scoured before making anything that would end up on the set." Debbie released a long sigh. "And then she goes and eats something with nuts anyway."

Before Tori could utter a word, Debbie continued, her voice a mixture of disbelief and sadness. "I know this sounds awful, Victoria, and I don't mean anything bad, but, I have to tell you, I'm just so grateful that the brownie that did her in didn't come from here."

The brownie that did her in . . .

She dropped her fork next to her plate. "You know about that?"

Debbie shrugged. "Everyone knows about that. At least they do if they read the paper."

Tori scrunched her brows. "Paper?"

"Uh-huh." Slipping off her stool, Debbie marched over to the front door, plucking a *Sweet Briar Times* from a rack just inside the entrance to the bakery. When she returned to the table, she set the copy beside Tori's plate. "For the first time I can ever recall, the day's paper came out late. But, based on the lead story, I can see why." Debbie spun the paper around so the top story and its accompanying headline were impossible to miss.

Actress Dead After Fatal Bite

Halfway down the article, a pull-out box contained a quote from Chief Dallas.

"We will find out who killed Ms. Belise one way or the other."

She scanned the article, drinking in every detail she could find, including the one about the victim's lifelong allergy that had made her vigilant about food. So vigilant, in fact, that the nature of the actress's death pointed to one thing and one thing only.

Murder.

"This isn't good," she whispered. "This isn't good at all."

"What are you talking about?"

Glancing up from the paper, she forced herself to focus. She knew this was coming, she really did. But now that it was here, in black and white with a nice vow from Robert Dallas to boot, she felt sick.

"W-we need an emergency circle meeting. Tonight."

"We do?" Debbie asked. "But why?"

Tori pushed her plate across the table and stood. "Because we need to put our heads together and figure a way out of this."

"Figure a way out of what?"

She could feel Debbie's eyes boring into hers yet she couldn't meet them. Her focus, her attention kept flitting to the quote from Chief Dallas. "This, this *mess*."

"Victoria, I'm sorry, but I don't know what you're talking about."

Sweeping her hand across the article, Tori put words to the worry in her heart. "We need to figure out a way to keep Leona and Margaret Louise out of jail."

"Out of *jail?*" Debbie gripped the sides of the table and leaned forward, her voice a shrill whisper. "What on earth are you talking about, Victoria?"

Shaking her head, Tori continued, Debbie's question disappearing beneath a sentiment she hadn't yet finished. "And me, too."

Chapter 15

If she'd been thinking even semiclearly, Tori never would have uttered the notion of calling an emergency sewing circle meeting aloud. Especially in the presence of Debbie Calhoun, a woman who'd surely been a worry-sniffing dog in some sort of previous existence.

However, any clarity she once possessed had been swallowed by the fog that had settled in Tori's brain the moment Anita Belise was found dead with a half-eaten homemade brownie beside her body. The fact that the brownie had been baked by Margaret Louise at the urging of Leona and upon Tori's own offhand-yet-meant-to-be-humorous suggestion only made things worse.

Fortunately, though, Debbie's *current* existence boasted a plethora of abilities including one Tori, herself, had yet to master.

It wasn't that Tori was sloppy per se, but her house wasn't party-clean twenty-four/seven, either. Nor did she own a bakery that could meet the snacking needs of eight women with little more than an hour's notice.

Still, she couldn't help but feel a little guilty as she rounded the corner onto Debbie's street, a pitcher of sweet tea in her hands. *She* was the one who'd called the meeting. Therefore *she* was the one who should be hosting.

Stopping at the mouth of the sidewalk that led to the Calhoun home, she inhaled deeply, silently praying for the peace and tranquility that surrounded her friend's home to be transferred to her via osmosis. Yet, for the first time, the southern beauty with its pale yellow two-story exterior and wraparound porch failed to do what it had done on other visits. In fact, even the large moss trees that shaded the expansive yard on either side of the home did little to boost her spirits, igniting not so much as a single memory or vision of the future.

"If you're going to stand there mourning your best friend, you could consider stepping two feet to your right so the rest of us could get by, you know." Rose Winters shot a gentle elbow into Tori's non-pitcher-holding side and shuffled past, her trademark cotton sweater buttoned up to the top despite the pleasant autumn temperatures. "Or, better yet, you could come inside with me and tell everyone what's got your britches in such a twist that you couldn't wait until Monday to get us all together."

And, just like that, the oldest member of the Sweet Briar Ladies Society Sewing Circle managed to accomplish what Debbie's picture-perfect home couldn't. Sure, the smile was one of amusement rather than true contentment, but still, it was a smile. . . .

Tori took a step forward and planted a kiss on the elderly woman's gently wrinkled face. "Sorry, Rose. I didn't know you were behind me. Guess I was lost in thought."

"Milo do something stupid?" Without waiting for a response, Rose placed her hand in the crook of Tori's arm and slowly made her way up the expansive porch steps.

She laughed. "No. Milo's great."

"Dixie set the library on fire again?"

Tori stopped mid-step and looked over her shoulder. "Shhhh! Do you know how long it's taken to get Dixie to a place where she doesn't talk on and on about the fire?" Resuming their slow and deliberate gait, she shook her head. "The only thing that quieted her down was seeing my

182

renovated office and watching me move back in two weeks ago."

"You didn't answer my question."

She rolled her eyes skyward. "She didn't set the *only* fire we had, Rose. You know that. It was sabotage, remember?"

At the top step, Rose pulled her hand from Tori's arm. "Then I'll go with my first assessment. Did you lose your best friend?"

The Rose-induced smile slipped from her face. "I have many best friends, Rose."

"Then which one of us is the reason behind that frown you're wearing?"

Reaching around Rose's frail body, Tori fisted Debbie's front door with two quick knocks and then pulled it open, the movement causing the last of the ice cubes to clank against the sides of the glass pitcher. "I—"

The sound of footsteps behind them made them both turn in time to see Leona waltzing her way up the porch steps, a stack of travel magazines in one hand and a choker-wearing Paris in the other.

"Good heavens, Leona, are you trying to make Paris look like a streetwalker?"

Leona's gasp echoed around them, Paris's ears perking upward in the process. "A streetwalker?"

Rose stopped in the middle of the doorway. "All that neck thing is missing is a few spikes."

Leona glanced down at the garden-variety bunny nestled in her left arm, her perfectly plump lips pursed. "The only people who would think that are people with no fashion sense." Pulling her focus from her beloved Paris, Leona fixed it, instead, on Rose. "You know, people like you, Rose. People who think cotton is for something other than granny panties."

"Ahhh yes, this from the woman who prefers dental floss for such things." Rose's left nostril flared ever so slightly as she turned back to Tori. "Really, Victoria, you should see the kinds of things Leona uses as undergarments."

Tori lifted her free hand into the air and resisted the urge to shudder. "Ladies, this discussion has taken the path commonly known as Too Much Information. Truly."

"You're here! You're here!" Debbie breezed into the foyer, removing the pitcher of tea from Tori's hands while simultaneously bestowing Rose with a hug and acknowledging Leona with a welcoming nod. "Everyone else is already here and settled in the family room."

"I want a chair as far from that woman as possible," Rose mumbled as she extricated herself from Debbie's arms and started down the hall. "In fact, if you don't mind, perhaps you could put her in another room entirely."

Debbie's hand flew to her mouth in an attempt to cover the smile that was sure to agitate the elderly woman. Then, without breaking the eye contact she sought with Tori, she addressed the woman scowling in the doorway. "Leona? What did you say this time?"

Leona's mouth gaped. "What did *I* say? Why does everyone always think it's me?"

"Because it usually is?" Debbie laughed.

"Humph." Leona looked down at Paris and shook her head. "This is why I don't let you outside, little one. Intelligence and beauty invite jealousy."

Debbie opened her mouth to speak only to shut it as Tori wrapped her arm around Leona's shoulders. "Rose took the first shot this time."

"And she took it at Paris." The corners of Leona's mouth drooped. "She was just sitting there, in my arms, minding her own business and twitching her sweet little nose when that old bat lashed out! Said Paris"—Leona reached across her body and covered the bunny's ears with the stack of magazines—"looked like a—a streetwalker!"

Tori watched as Debbie's gaze flitted downward, her lips twitching in response. "I think Paris's choker is lovely, Leona."

Leona's face brightened. "Of course you do. You have taste, darling." Pulling the magazines away from Paris, Leona started down the hall, her voice and demeanor void of any remaining hurt feelings.

Tori watched her go, the woman's poise taking her by surprise. "She just doesn't get it, does she?" she mumbled beneath her breath.

"Doesn't get what?" Debbie asked.

"How much trouble she's in." Lifting her hands to her sides, she let them fall back down just as quickly. "How much trouble her sister and I are in as well."

All hint of lingering amusement was chased from Debbie's stance by concern. "I haven't been able to think of anything else since you left the bakery. It got so bad Colby stopped all discussion at the dinner table this evening until I explained my preoccupation."

"What did you say?" she asked quickly. As much as she adored Debbie's husband, the man did write a local column for the Sunday paper. The last thing they needed was for Chief Dallas to be given a road map to the masterminds behind Anita's deadly brownie.

Debbie shrugged. "What could I say? You didn't tell me anything other than Leona's aversion to stripes and your concern for Margaret Louise should she be kept from her grandbabies."

Realizing the burden she placed on her friend, she reached out, gently squeezed the woman's forearm. "I'm sorry. I really am. But I'm ready to talk now."

Looping her arm inside Tori's, Debbie led the way down the hall and into the living room, a hush falling over the assembled circle members as they stopped in the entryway.

Beatrice jumped to her feet, her soft British

accent breaking through the sudden bout of silence. "Victoria? Are you okay?"

Before she could respond, Margaret Louise patted the vacant spot on the sofa to the left of where she sat with her mother, Annabelle. "Come. Sit."

Tori crossed the room, claiming the suggested spot with a mixture of appreciation and fore-boding. Sure, she was glad to be there, surrounded by friends who would do anything for each other. But as comforting as that thought was, the notion of stirring up yet another hornets' nest was also disconcerting.

"Hello, Victoria."

Startled, she turned to Annabelle and smiled, the oddly familiar voice and greeting so reminiscent of Margaret Louise. "Annabelle, hello. I'm so glad you were able to make it tonight."

"I'm grateful for the invite."

She met Margaret Louise's eyes, the delight in her friend's face impossible to miss. The whisper in her ear only served to underscore the reason she already suspected.

"Mamma is having a good day today."

"I can see that," she whispered back. "And I'm glad."

"So why the emergency circle meeting?" Georgina Hayes asked from her spot on the deacon's bench to the right of the hearth. Pulling her straw hat from the top of her head, the mayor of Sweet Briar addressed Tori with unbridled curiosity. "Is there a problem at the library?"

Before she could formulate a response, Dixie chimed in. "Everything at the library is wonderful. Isn't that right, Victoria?"

She nodded.

"Is something wrong with Milo?" Melissa placed a hand on her ever-increasing baby bump and lifted her feet onto the dark brown leather ottoman Debbie had no doubt positioned within striking distance of the mother-to-be. "I saw him at Leeson's Market after school today and he seemed okay to me."

"Milo is fine."

"Then what's wrong?" Beatrice asked once again. "You look a little peaked."

Rose's eyes widened just before a cough riddled her body momentarily. When she'd composed herself, the elderly woman sat forward in her rocking chair and surveyed Tori from head to toe and back again. "Please tell me you're not sick, Victoria."

Slowly, Tori looked around the room, the concern on Rose's face matched on seven others.

She rushed to offer some semblance of reassurance, though how much reassurance reality would offer was anyone's guess.

"I'm not sick. I'm just worried. About Leona and"—she leaned forward, peered at the woman seated beside her—"Margaret Louise."

"And you, too," Debbie interjected via a whisper.

She nodded. "And me, too, I guess."

Leona lowered her travel magazine to her lap. "I can understand being worried about my sister— she doesn't eat healthy at all. And I can understand being worried about yourself—your inability to retain my makeup tips is rather alarming. But being worried about me? I don't understand that. I have the perfect life. Just ask Paris."

At the sound of her name, Paris's ears perked forward from the travel pillow Leona had lovingly placed beside the armchair she, herself, graced. "See?" Leona continued, pointing at the rabbit. "Even Paris knows life is good."

Margaret Louise cleared her throat. "She's worried 'bout us 'cause of our hand—our *perceived* hand—in Anita Belise's death."

Georgina gasped. "Lord Almighty, Margaret Louise, what on earth are you talking about?"

Suddenly, the thought of calling an emergency circle meeting with the town's mayor, of all people, didn't seem like such a good idea. Tori swallowed, tried to think of a way to backpedal them out of the situation, but it was no use. Too much had been said already.

Instead, she worked to soften reality a wee bit. "I'm just a little concerned that Chief Dallas will latch onto the fact that Margaret Louise baked the ill-fated brownie most likely responsible for Anita's death."

"You did?" Georgina and Beatrice asked in unison.

Margaret Louise nodded. "My sister can be mighty hard to turn down when she starts beggin' and pleadin'."

Leona peered atop her glasses. "I did no such thing."

"Oh no?" Margaret Louise challenged. "Then what do you call this?" Pushing off the couch, the plump sixty-something made her way over to a table in the corner of the room and leaned across it with a dramatic flair. "You're such an amazing cook, Margaret Louise. I've always envied you that talent. If I had that ability, I'd be able to make Warren his favorite dessert of all—brownies with lots and lots of nuts."

Leona's face turned crimson at the imitation. "I don't sound like that."

"Yes you do," chorused seven voices.

"Hmph." Snatching her magazine off her lap, she raised it to her face only to let it drop back down. "It worked, though. You made the brownies just like I wanted you to. Just like *Victoria* suggested."

She felt the weight of seven sets of eyes. "I didn't suggest brownies. I made an offhand comment about a bag of nuts and having some time alone with Warren."

"That would have been much too obvious, dear," Leona mused. "The brownies were much more subtle."

"I wouldn't call murder *subtle,* Leona." Georgina rested her head on the seat back and shook her head. "Will there ever be a murder in this town that doesn't come back to someone in this room?"

"Not as long as Victoria is here."

Tori's mouth gaped along with the others in the room.

"Leona!" Debbie hissed. "You take that back."

Bending her fingers to her palm, Leona studied the results of her latest manicure. "Why? It's true, isn't it? Until Victoria moved to town, there hadn't been any murders here at all. Then, poof, she shows up bringing all that Chicago karma with her and look what's happened."

Tori laughed.

"How can you be laughing, Victoria?" Debbie asked as she rose to her feet and began pacing around the room. "Leona is saying awful things about you right now."

"When does our resident hussy not say awful things?" Rose quipped from her rocking chair.

Leona's eyes narrowed. *"Hussy?"*

Rose glared back. "If the shoe fits . . ."

"Here we go," Melissa mumbled, flipping her long blonde hair over her shoulder. "I am so glad the kids aren't here to see this."

Tori jumped to her feet, her fingers splayed in the air. "Ladies, please. I didn't call this meeting so—"

Movement at the end of the couch cut her off mid-sentence. Turning, Tori saw Annabelle's hands disappear into the infamous tote bag, a vacant stare on the woman's heavily lined face.

Uh-oh.

A quick glance at Margaret Louise told her everything she needed to know. Annabelle's antics had gone unnoticed—a good thing in light of the stress Margaret Louise was under.

"So, why, exactly, did you call this meeting?" Beatrice's voice, quiet yet firm, broke through the verbal sparring taking place around the room. "What can we do to help?"

Pulling her focus from Annabelle, Tori fixed it, instead, on Beatrice, her words addressing everyone in the room. "For starters, we can stop the senseless arguing. That doesn't help anyone. After that, we can try and put our heads together and create a list of people who had it out for Anita Belise."

"From what I gathered during my time with Warren, there's not enough paper in the world for a list like that." Leona scooted forward on her chair, uncrossing and then crossing her delicate ankles once again. "She wasn't liked, dear."

Rose braced her foot against the floor and

began rocking her chair. "Neither are you, Leona. But that doesn't mean we're going to kill you."

Leona drew back as laughter bubbled up around her. "Well, I've—"

"*I've* been reading Agatha Christie lately and there's always a number of possibilities," Beatrice chimed in, her eyes gleaming. "Several of those even have motive. But only one was pushed past the brink enough to do it."

Tori mulled the nanny's words as heads nodded in every corner of the room. "You're exactly right, Beatrice. It doesn't matter how long or short the list of Anita-haters may be. Only one person hated her enough to kill her. We find that person, and everyone else is in the clear."

Chapter 16

Tori turned the key to the right and pushed, the telltale aroma that was home guiding her feet across the threshold. No matter how much headway she had or hadn't made with her friends in the quest to identify Anita's murderer, one thing was certain . . .

They'd had fun.

Lots and lots of fun.

Never in her wildest imagination could she have

dreamed of the various murder scenarios a group of women, armed with sewing boxes and threaded needles, could concoct.

First, there'd been Dixie. Aside from the fact her plot was something out of the game Clue, the notion of Colonel Mustard with a deadly brownie had earned its fair share of laughs.

Then Rose had stepped into the limelight, and her tale of a jealous stand-in hell-bent on taking over the film's lead role had held actual merit . . . until Leona had happily pointed out that *she'd* been used in that capacity the day before the murder. And that she didn't need a brownie to get the role.

Beatrice, although sweet, had obviously been reading too many murder mysteries as of late, and so much of what she'd proposed hadn't made its way onto the piece of paper Debbie had thrust into Tori's hand.

Margaret Louise had been curiously quiet, the earlier bout of preoccupation that had enabled Annabelle's slick ways to go unnoticed short-lived. As a result, rather than be the partner-in-crime Tori had relied on many times in the past, Leona's twin had sunk into the role of concerned daughter.

Leona had been useless as always, her contribution to the topic at hand nothing more than superficial. Though, by the time the evening was over, there wasn't a sewing circle member who couldn't recite which male suspect looked the best in his clothes.

Debbie and Melissa had been the most helpful, their suggestions of wounded egos and retribution carrying the most weight. After all, in just the time Tori had been an extra, she could name a few production folks who weren't Anita Belise's biggest fans.

Deep in thought, Tori shut and locked the door behind her, then tossed the keys onto the hall table as she made her way toward the kitchen. The rational side of her brain told her she wasn't hungry, that the cookies and pie Debbie had lavished on the sewing circle had been more than enough. But it was the other side—the side that tended to crave sugar whenever she was stressed—that had her feet on autopilot all the way over to the cookie jar next to the sink.

Yet three Oatmeal Scotchies later, she was still stressed. The list she'd made at the meeting contained just four names.

Glenda.

Todd.

Margot.

And Warren.

She knew the last name was a stretch, the possible motive dubious at best, but still, it had its place. Especially if Warren truly had a thing for Leona and felt Anita was a detriment.

Tori sank onto her chair at the tiny kitchen table,

her thoughts spinning in a million different directions.

Warren was wealthy, successful, and more than a little handsome. The press he was getting on the movie was substantial. So why would he even consider doing away with the woman who brought in droves of moviegoers all by herself?

"He wouldn't," she said aloud, the sound of her voice in the otherwise empty kitchen bringing her up short. "Great, now I'm talking to myself."

Shaking her head, she looked down at the list she'd compiled, her gaze focusing on the first name.

Glenda.

She spun around in her chair and reached into a nearby drawer, plucking a pen from its depths. If she'd learned anything over the past two years, it was the need to consider all possibilities, all avenues.

"Glenda . . ." she said aloud. "Glenda."

Closing her eyes, she called up an image to go with the name.

No more than about twenty-five, Glenda Goodnight, as her name tag read, had mousy brown hair and large hazel-colored doe eyes. The young woman's propensity for salt-free snacks did little to help a waistline that could best be described as chunky.

Beyond the physical stuff, though, Tori didn't know much except that Glenda appeared to be one step above Margot on the movie set totem pole. At least in terms of dealing with extras.

Then again, now that she thought about it, she'd overheard Glenda refer to herself as Anita's personal gofer-girl—a role the woman neither relished nor appreciated.

Tori felt her excitement building. Glenda had motive. She'd resented the way Anita bossed her around, always snapping at her for one thing or the other. Perhaps, the girl had hit her limit and snapped.

She glanced back down at the paper, her hand poised and ready to draw a circle around Glenda's name until she looked at the one below.

Todd.

Unlike Glenda, Todd was closer to Tori's own age. Super tall with sandy blond hair, Todd was one of those guys you tended to overlook. It wasn't that he wasn't attractive, because he was, in his own way, but there was something about him that made him fade into the background unless he was talking.

His job on set was easier to identify than Glenda's since he'd been the one canvassing the crowd that first day, culling extras from the line and bringing them to Margot. Like Glenda, he, too, had shown little affection for the movie's female lead, citing the woman's constant threat to his job security during the same conversation Tori had overheard while talking to Margaret Louise on the phone during a break.

In fact, if she remembered the fruits of her eavesdropping correctly, Anita had threatened Todd's job on a regular basis. Something that surely grew tiring if not downright infuriating for Todd.

But did it become infuriating enough to kill her? Maybe.

She circled Glenda's name and then Todd's, her eyes drifting one line lower to the third name on the list.

Margot.

In an instant, the image of the tall, leggy redhead with the large brown eyes and slightly sloppy demeanor flashed before her eyes. Like Todd's job, Margot's was also easy to determine since Tori had spent virtually all of her time as an extra under Margot's supervision. Margot had been the one to make sure they understood their tasks, knew where they could be and couldn't be, and shuttled them to the set as they were needed. Patient for the most part, Margot hadn't minced words about Anita any more than the other two, yet, for only being in her early to mid-twenties, she'd seemed keenly aware of the fact that Anita's participation in the movie was crucial for all of them.

Then again, that awareness only seemed to come into play after Anita was dead.

Deflection, perhaps?

She scribbled her thoughts on the paper even as her mind registered the last name on the list.

Warren.

That one still made no sense. However, perhaps it was something *about* Warren that played into Anita's murder. . . .

Could another woman have been after Warren? Someone other than Leona? Or—

"Since none of us know exactly what the deal is between the two of them, no one has had the guts to actually make her pay for the way she treats everyone, movie after movie."

Tori dropped her pen onto the table as Margot's words filtered through her thoughts. The *who* and the *why* behind Anita Belise's murder might still be up for grabs, but the *when* behind the crime was starting to sport the faintest outline of a shape. A shape that had Tori wishing she'd bypassed the cookies altogether.

By the time Tori climbed into bed, her head was pounding. Every single person on her list— except for maybe Warren—had motive to kill Anita Belise. They resented her, despised her, and daydreamed of the day they'd be rid of her.

Yet, until that week, there'd been no real opportunity.

Leona's presence had changed that. And for one daring person, it had been all that was needed.

Who that person was, though, was anyone's guess.

Including hers.

The ring indicating Milo's goodnight call broke through her reverie, bringing with it a mixture of relief and anticipation. Hearing his voice before she closed her eyes each night was better than any sleep aid she could find in a pharmacy. Glancing at the clock beside her bed, she rolled over and grabbed her cell phone.

"Hi there."

"Hi, yourself." Milo's voice, warm and strong, filtered through her ears, blanketing her chest with a feeling of contentment. It was a feeling she knew wouldn't last, especially in light of everything she wanted to share with him, but, for the moment, she'd take it.

"How was school today?" Slipping under the covers, Tori settled back against her pillow. "The kids getting excited for Halloween?"

"I think bouncing off the walls is a more apt description." Milo laughed. "But, other than that, school was good. How about your day?"

For a moment, she actually considered telling him about work, but opted, instead, to get to the heart of her answer. "We had an emergency sewing circle meeting this evening. At Debbie's house."

"Oh? Who called it?"

"I did."

Stunned silence was replaced by concern. "Why? What's wrong?"

Closing her eyes, she allowed herself to return to Debbie's living room, to the conversation that had started on a serious note yet edged into the territory of fun. "I guess I just needed to bounce my worries about this whole brownie situation off everyone. You know, see if anyone had any ideas that could set me in the right direction."

"Set you in the right direction?"

"In finding the killer." The second the words were out, she realized what she'd said. And, despite the mile or so distance between them, she could imagine the expression on her fiancé's face. Denying her true intentions, though, would be futile.

"Have you ever thought about changing professions?"

"What do you mean?" she asked.

"Seems to me you might be better suited to police work."

She sat up straight. "Give up the library? Are you serious? Never."

His answering laugh dissipated the tension his words had caused. "I'm kidding. Truly."

Slowly, she lowered herself back down to her pillow, her imagination conjuring up images of traffic enforcement and investigations juxtaposed against those of books and schoolchildren. To her, there was no competition. "You know that library is my world."

"I do. But you have to admit you've been donning the investigator hat quite a bit these past two years."

It was true. But still. There'd been reasons . . .

"I only wear it when my friends are threatened. Like now."

"Any leads?"

Her gaze shifted to the sheet of paper she'd left on the nightstand, each of the four names she'd written now followed by thoughts, observations, and even a few unanswered questions. "Leads? No. Paths to explore, yes."

"Anything I can do to help?"

She pondered his question. "I'm not exactly sure yet. So, can I take a rain check on my response?"

"Absolutely." Milo's voice grew husky, a sure sign the topic of their conversation was about to change. "But, just so we're clear, little miss, there's no rain check on our powwow tomorrow."

She swallowed. "Powwow?"

Milo released a sigh. "Yeah, with my mom. To talk about the wedding. Only you didn't remember, did you?"

She considered protesting, yet knew he'd see right through it. Staring up at the ceiling, she mentally chastised herself for the truth that found its way past her lips. "I'm sorry, Milo. I guess I got wrapped up in the whole movie set business and worrying about Leona's part in Anita's death."

The ensuing silence only served to further her guilt. She rushed to make things right. "But don't worry. I can shelve all of that in favor of spending time with you and your mom."

"You sure? Because we could wait."

"I don't want to wait any longer than necessary for our forever," she whispered, pulling the phone closer to her cheek. "Besides, Chief Dallas tends to spend most Saturdays fishing, right? That alone will buy Leona, Margaret Louise, and me a little extra time."

Chapter 17

For the first time in two weeks, Tori didn't wake to the bright sun on her face as it peeked its way through the partially open slats of her mini blinds. No, this time Mother Nature decided to wake her in a very different way—thunder.

It took a moment or two to identify the low rolling booms, but after ruling out a defective car and her own stomach as culprits, Tori swung her feet onto the floor and stretched. Somehow, someway, despite everything that had been plaguing her thoughts when she'd climbed into bed, she'd found a way to sleep, exhaustion pulling a surprising victory from its battle with worry. And she was grateful. Worry tended to multiply in the face of sleep deprivation and she had more than enough without adding fuel to the fire.

Slipping her toes into waiting pink slippers, Tori padded into the kitchen, the promise of a hot chocolate helping to wipe away any residual sleepiness. A smile tugged at the corner of her mouth as she moved about the room in a familiar dance—heat water, prepare mug, pour water, stir contents, top with whipped cream.

Slowly but surely, she'd become somewhat of a routine person since moving to Sweet Briar. On work days, the morning ritual was followed by a second hot chocolate from Debbie's, one she sipped while completing her walk to work. On weekends, the morning ritual tended to include a second cup from Debbie's as well, only *that* one tended to be hand delivered to her doorstep by an impossibly attractive man carrying a bag of still-warm croissants and hand-dipped chocolate donuts. . . .

Her stomach gurgled.

A clap of thunder answered.

Wrapping her left hand around her favorite mug, Tori leaned over the sink and peered out the rain-spattered window into her backyard. As much as she'd been looking forward to a sun-filled day off, the mums Rose had talked her into planting needed a little help in the water department. She took a sip of her hot chocolate and contemplated the mental to-do list she'd compiled in the wake of her last day off.

1. Clean.
2. Help Rose rake.
3. Lunch with Milo and Rita to talk about a wedding date and location.

It had been a good list. But, like all to-do lists made a week in advance, outside factors had come into play and wreaked havoc, making the first two items far less important than they'd once been, and virtually wiping the third item from her radar until Milo had forced it back into play. Now, she just had to pray she could keep the notion of murder suspects and deadly brownies from her thoughts long enough to picture the day she'd officially become Mrs. Milo Wentworth.

While no formal plans had been set in place yet, she'd certainly done her fair share of dreaming. Sometimes she imagined an outdoor ceremony, in the middle of the town square. Sometimes she imagined an evening reception on the library grounds, tiny white holiday lights making the moss trees sparkle and shimmer. But no matter how many locations she fantasized about, two facets of her wedding day remained the same— the cake and the wedding party.

The cake had been a no-brainer, especially when Debbie had offered to make the tiered showcase the moment she learned Tori had accepted Milo's proposal. The only thing left to do in that regard would be to select the cake's filling.

Deciding on the female members of the wedding party had been fairly easy, too, though finding dresses that worked on twenty- and thirty-somethings like Beatrice, Melissa, and Debbie *and* sixty-, seventy-, and eighty-somethings like Margaret Louise, Leona, Rose, Georgina, and Dixie was sure to be a challenge.

A staccato knock at the back door made her jump. Glancing at the clock above the stove, Tori couldn't help but smile, her heart rate settling into its familiar Milo-induced pitter-patter.

Time for croissants . . .

She crossed to the other side of the kitchen and yanked the door open, the smile slipping from her mouth at the sight of the burly man standing on her back stoop.

Police Chief Robert Dallas clasped the lip of his hat between his thumb and index finger and tipped his head forward. "Miss Sinclair."

Unsure of what to say, she stood there blankly for a moment as rainwater dripped from his uniform.

"Mind if I come in for a moment? I'd like to ask you a few questions."

She nodded and stepped backward. "Uh, sure. I guess."

"I suppose if I had to cancel my fishing trip on account of work, this kind of rain ain't such a bad thing." Chief Dallas stopped just inside the doorway and wiped his feet on the mat. "Makes me feel less cheated, I guess."

Tori reached around the chief and shut the door, every mental radar device she possessed pinging a warning signal inside her brain. "What can I do for you, Chief?"

The chief's eyes hesitated on the mug of hot chocolate in her hand. "Am I interrupting your breakfast?"

She doubled her hands on her heart-shaped mug and shrugged. "Not exactly." She knew she should offer him a cup of hot chocolate as well, but she couldn't. She'd been on the receiving end of Chief Dallas's surprise visits more times than she cared to count. "So what can I do for you?" she repeated.

"Seems there's been another murder in town." The chief reached up, pulled his hat from his head, and tucked it under his arm.

"Oh?"

Narrowing his eyes, he studied her closely. "Seems as if Anita Belise was murdered."

She swallowed, then repeated her one-word inquiry, her voice a bit more squeak-like the second go-round. "Oh?"

"Seems someone gave her food with nuts in it despite the fact that she was deathly allergic to them."

"That's awful," she managed to eke out.

Chief Dallas pointed at her hands. "Is something wrong, Miss Sinclair?"

She glanced down, saw the liquid moving inside

207

207

her mug, and quickly set it on the nearest counter. "No. Nothing is wrong. I guess I'm just a bit chilled from the door being open just now."

"It's seventy degrees out."

Busted.

"I—I guess I'm not sure why you're here. Shouldn't you be questioning people on the set?"

"I spent all of yesterday doing just that," the chief explained, his eyes never leaving her face.

"And . . ." she whispered.

"And, just like always, my car essentially steered itself here. To *your* house, Miss Sinclair."

"I didn't know Ms. Belise." It was a lame response but it was all she could think to say. And besides, it was the truth.

"But you knew about her allergy, yes?"

"I—I guess so, yes. It was mentioned a time or two this past week."

"Did you share that information with anyone?" he asked.

All she could do was nod. And swallow.

"Who might that have been?"

She glanced at the hint of whipped cream still evident in her mug and sighed. If she answered the man's question, she'd essentially be throwing Leona under the bus. To not answer him might make matters worse.

Chief Dallas simply waited as she weighed her options, the steely glint in his eyes making her more than a little wary. She shot her hands behind her back as they began to tremble once again. "I mentioned it, offhand, to Leona Elkin."

"You mean, Pooky?"

Crap. He'd done his homework.

She forced a smile to her lips. "She was looking for a way to have some alone-time with Warren Shoemaker."

"And you felt that Ms. Belise's allergy provided a way to achieve that alone-time?"

"If nuts were in the room, Anita would be forced to stay away," she explained with a voice she hoped sounded as carefree and light as she intended.

The chief nodded ever so slightly. "These brownies . . . Where did they come from?"

Carefree and light became a bit shaky. "She made them."

The man's left eyebrow rose half an inch. "*Leona Elkin* made them? You mean the same Leona Elkin who calls the station every so often because she misses a digit when she's calling for takeout?"

She silently cursed Sweet Briar's size.

"She—she solicited some help." It was all she could think to say as her mind raced ahead for contingency plans.

"From whom?"

"From whom?" she echoed.

"That's what I asked." Folding his arms across his chest, Chief Dallas waited for Tori's response, the steely glint now reminding her of a wild animal stalking his prey.

She considered a variety of responses, but, in the end, she went with the truth. He'd find it out eventually, anyway. "Margaret Louise made them for Leona."

"Did she know about Ms. Belise's allergy?"

That was a good question. One she couldn't answer with absolute certainty and she told him so.

Chief Dallas reached into his jacket pocket and extracted a small notepad and pen. Flipping it open, he jotted something down then looked up at Tori once again. "Do you know how one of the brownies ended up in Ms. Belise's hands?"

This she could answer without hesitation or worry about repercussions. "No! And neither does Leona."

He pinned her with a stare. "So the two of you have already discussed all of this?"

She nodded. "I wanted to get to the bottom of things."

Leaning forward, Chief Dallas paused his face mere inches from Tori's. "That's *my* job, Miss Sinclair, remember?"

Tori took in a deep breath only to release it through pursed lips, images of Chief Dallas and his job capabilities playing through her mind and bringing her to the only response that fit.

"I remember, Chief Dallas. Do *you?*"

・ ・ ・

There were many times in life she wished she had a remote control, with Rewind and Skip being her preferred features. But if given a remote control at that very moment, she'd choose a split screen feature with the ability to pause one side.

If she had that, she could pause the part of her brain that was neurotically picking apart every word Chief Dallas had uttered while standing in her kitchen and focus, instead, on the part with Milo and his mom smiling at her from a corner table inside the Red Mill Inn.

"Tori, you're here." Milo rose from his chair and met her as she approached, his gentle kiss on her forehead making her feel more than a little guilty. "I was getting worried something had happened."

Torn between the desire to fib and to pour the contents of her unexpected morning all over him, she merely shrugged before turning her focus on the attractive gray-haired woman beaming at her like a lighthouse amid a storm. "Rita, it's so good to see you." She leaned over and planted a quick cheek kiss on Milo's mom. "I'm sorry if you've been waiting for too long."

Rita waved off Tori's concern with a flick of her hand. "We're just glad you're here now. Sit. Sit."

Milo pulled out the empty chair between them. "Yes, please. I ordered you a glass of water to start and the waitress will be back shortly to see what else you'd like to drink."

She found a smile and flashed it in Milo's direction. "Thank you." Inhaling deeply, she willed herself to leave the last hour or so of her life behind temporarily and focus, instead, on planning for the future. "I've given some thought to the location for the ceremony but I'm at a loss for where to hold the reception. I want it to be nice, of course, but I also want to keep the cost down as much as possible."

Rita nodded. "An autumn wedding in South Carolina certainly makes an outdoor event possible if that's what you'd like. Though it might be wise to have a contingency plan in the event of a storm."

She felt Milo's eyes watching her and she rushed to erase any concern she sensed there. "I think an outdoor wedding would be perfect."

And she did. She just hoped she didn't miss the big day because she was sitting in some South Carolina jail, labeled a murder accomplice.

Milo pulled his attention from Tori just long enough to address his mother. "Tori and I have batted around the notion of getting married on the Green. Perhaps at the gazebo?"

"That would be lovely." Rita reached out, patted both of their hands with her own. "Would you want to have the reception there as well?"

She shook her head along with Milo. "No. But maybe the library grounds would work."

"Either of our backyards could certainly be an

option as well, depending on how many folks we invite." Milo gestured toward a sheet of loose-leaf paper resting on the table in front of Rita. "Is that a list of people we need to invite?"

"It's a list of possibilities, son. Who is actually invited is up to you and Victoria." Rita scooted the list in Tori's direction. "This wedding needs to be the way you want it to be. I had my special day a long time ago."

Oh how she wished she'd met Milo's father. She'd heard so many lovely things about the man who'd raised her fiancé. . . .

"We know who's going to make the cake," Milo offered. "That's going to come from Debbie's Bakery here in town."

"And I know that I'd like my sewing circle sisters to play a part in the ceremony." Tori took a sip of water then placed her glass back on the table, shaking her head at the sound of Chief Dallas's voice in her head. "Um . . . finding a dress that works on all of them may be a bit difficult, though."

"You could always match by color rather than actual style," Rita suggested.

She considered the idea. "That could work." Closing her eyes momentarily, she tried to imagine her friends all dressed in a royal blue, each outfit chosen based on personality rather than a particular style. "Ooh, I like that idea very—"

A burst of laughter from a nearby table cut her off mid-sentence. Stealing a glance to the side, she froze.

There, less than ten feet to her left, sat three familiar faces. All happy. All laughing. All seemingly oblivious to the tragedy that happened right under their noses.

She felt her mouth gape, her body instinctively lean in their direction.

"Tori? Are you okay?"

Oh, what she wouldn't give to be sitting just a little closer . . .

"Tori?"

If she were, maybe she'd overhear something that might point Chief Dallas in the right direction. . . .

"If you'll excuse me a moment, I think I'll take this opportunity to use the ladies' room, give you two kids a little time alone." Rita's voice, coupled with the feel of Milo's hand on her arm, snapped her back to her own table and the fact she'd just checked out on her fiancé and his mom.

Her face grew warm as she met Milo's questioning eyes. "I'm so sorry. I guess I got a little distracted just now."

"You guess?" he asked.

"It happens sometimes, son." Rita pushed her chair back and stood. "I'll be right back."

Tori watched her future mother-in-law walk away, the guilt over being late suddenly overrun by a more all-encompassing guilt. Nervously, she unfolded the napkin at her spot and dropped it into her lap before meeting Milo's troubled gaze. "I'm sorry, Milo, I really am."

"You still want this, right?"

She drew back. "You mean the wedding?"

"To me," he added.

She reached across the table, sandwiched his hand between hers. "There's nothing I want more."

His shoulders dipped in relief. "Phew."

"How could you even think I wouldn't want to marry you?" she whispered through a voice suddenly ripe with emotion.

He shrugged. "Let's be honest. It took you a while to even accept and—"

"I explained all of that."

"You did. But then, when it comes time to make some plans, you forget. And when you're finally here, you check out in the middle of a conversation."

It was hard to argue with the truth. However, the reason for her missteps had nothing whatsoever to do with marrying him and absolutely everything to do with the glare from yet another murder in good old Sweet Briar, South Carolina.

She glanced from Milo to the nearby table and back again, her vow to keep Chief Dallas's visit to herself for the day falling by the wayside. "I wasn't late today because I forgot. I was late because I was being given the third degree in my kitchen."

"Third degree?" Milo parroted.

"By Chief Dallas."

Understanding dawned on Milo's face. "Man, I'm sorry, Tori. You should have called, I'd have come right over."

"And done what?"

"I don't know. Ask him a few questions back . . . demand he leave you alone . . . be there to support you."

Tori dropped her voice to a near whisper. "This will go away."

"And if it doesn't?"

She inhaled slowly. "It has to. Because I don't believe Leona had anything to do with Anita's death. She doesn't have it in her."

Silence settled around them momentarily as Milo seemed to ponder Tori's words. "*Someone* does."

"Someone does, indeed," she whispered as her focus shifted, once again, to the threesome sitting less than ten feet away. Hatred and revenge were powerful motives for murder. Therefore, Margot, Glenda, and Todd had more than earned their spot on her list of viable suspects in Anita Belise's death. Whether it was an all-inclusive list, though, remained to be seen. But if it wasn't one of them, Tori suspected the killer wasn't far.

"We can put the wedding on hold if that will help."

She looked back at Milo. "Why would we do that?"

A knowing smile spread across his face, stopping just short of his eyes. "Because you have a murder to investigate."

Her heart fluttered. "I do. But, I'm a rather accomplished multitasker when I put my mind to it. Just ask Nina. Or Dixie."

Flipping his hand inside hers, they entwined fingers. "You sure?"

"I've never been more sure of anything," she whispered. "Except saying yes to you."

Chapter 18

She suspected she looked like a drowned rat, sitting there, on a park bench, waiting for Todd to emerge. But the last time she checked, desperate times called for desperate measures.

The hardest part so far, though, had been convincing Rita she didn't need a ride home from the restaurant despite the sideways rain that pelted their faces the second they stepped outside. In fact, it was only after Tori assured her future mother-in-law that she needed to stay behind in order to help a friend that the woman had reluctantly climbed into Milo's car and waved good-bye.

Yet now that she thought about it, perhaps she should have waited. Surely there would be another opportunity to question Todd out of earshot from his coworkers, right?

Before she could give the notion of hailing a cab from five towns over much consideration, Todd stepped from the restaurant and popped his umbrella into the air.

Hmmm. An umbrella. Genius . . .

Squaring her shoulders, she stood. "Got room under there for one very wet librarian?"

Todd's eyes widened. "Tori?"

"That's me." She swiped the back of her hand across her wet face and released a well-timed shiver. "A very wet, very pathetic me."

His long arm moved to cover her with the umbrella. "Didn't I see you inside having lunch with friends?"

She sidled up close beneath the canopy and nodded. "That was my fiancé and his mom, actually."

"And they left you behind in the rain?"

Uh-oh . . .

She racked her brain for a story that would sound even halfway feasible. "Um, well, I"—she glanced up, took in the various storefronts surrounding the town square—"had a few errands I wanted to run."

"Those were some fast errands. They couldn't wait for you?"

"I—I got a call. From the library. Dixie needs me to come in." Oh, how she hated to lie . . .

"Oh. Okay, then." Extending his index finger outward, Todd began walking, his ultralong legs necessitating a virtual trot from Tori. "The library is over there, right?"

She followed the path made by his finger and nodded. "Have you been inside?"

"I haven't had time. Though, with the way things are now, I could probably use a book or three to keep me busy while the studio execs decide when or if we resume filming."

There was so much she wanted to ask, questions she wanted to hurl in his direction, one after the other. But it was better to take things slow. To build a sense of camaraderie with occasional questions scattered in along the way. If all went well, she'd still get the same information, maybe even more.

"What kind of books do you like?" They crossed the street and followed the sidewalk that bordered the west side of the square, the trailers and tents associated with the movie set at their backs. "Fiction? Nonfiction?"

"I prefer nonfiction, mostly. Though there's a fiction title I've been meaning to read."

"Oh?" She broke into a near run to keep pace with Todd as they reached the spot in the sidewalk

219

where they could either turn right and follow the square or head across the road to the library. "What's that?"

He cleared his throat. "*Memories of Autumn.*"

She stopped in the middle of the road, rain smacking her face as Todd and his umbrella continued on. "*Memories of Autumn*? Are you serious?"

Todd spun around when his foot hit the next sidewalk, alone. "You're getting wet just standing there."

"Yeah, but you just said you haven't read the book your movie is based on."

He shrugged and held out the umbrella. "Trust me, I'm willing to bet I'm not the only one."

"Wow." She joined him once again. "Well, I'll see what I can do about finding it, but no promises."

His legs slowed to a more normal pace as they approached the building, his head peeking out from their covering. "This is one very cool building. How old is it?"

"Over a hundred years old," she said as she motioned toward the stone stairs that would take them to the front door. "It's been renovated a time or two in the years since, but the structure, of course, remains the same."

He followed her up the stairs, holding the umbrella over her head instead of his own. "People still come here much?"

She stopped at the door. "Of course. It's a library."

"Yeah and most people are doing things online these days—research, newspapers, e-books, you name it. Seems the notion of a library is becoming rather obsolete."

"Bite your tongue." She tugged the door open and waited as he closed the umbrella and stowed it beneath an overhang. "A library is like any other business. We need to adapt to people's needs, find new ways to be appealing, that's all."

"Such as?"

She led the way inside, hushing her voice as she did. "Well, that's a work in progress. But, so far, we've added a children's room that provides our youngest patrons with a place to act out their favorite stories, we've started a teen book club that's made the notion of reading more hip for the high school set, and we have a program set up with some of the assisted living facilities in the area to bring their book requests *to* them."

Dixie looked up as they approached, irritation chasing the smile from her pencil-thin lips.

Tori met the former librarian's narrowed gaze. "I'm sorry it took so long to get here. I guess the rain slowed us down a bit."

"Us?"

"Yes, yes, this is Todd . . ." She stared up at the man standing beside her, the volume of infor-mation she didn't know about this particular murder suspect staggering. "I'm sorry Todd, I don't know your last name."

"McNamara." With a quick duck of his head in Dixie's direction, the man, who was no more than a year or so younger than Tori, rocked back on his heels and scanned the room. "I think this is the first library I've been in since I was like five or something."

And just like that, Dixie forgot all about Tori showing up on her day off and focused, instead, on the potential patron in her midst. "Then you've been missing out, young man. Come . . ."

For a moment Todd looked as if he was about to protest, but, in the end, followed along behind Dixie's stout frame like a soldier falling into step behind his commander. Tori watched them head down the hallway toward the children's room, a familiar excitement bubbling up inside her chest. It had been nearly two years since she'd transformed the library's storage room into a space for young readers, but she still found it just as exciting as ever when she knew someone was about to see it for the very first time. Especially someone with a creative bent, someone who would enjoy all of the details that took the room from nice to memorable.

Details . . .

Shaking her head, Tori forced her thoughts back where they needed to be—on Todd as a potential suspect.

She stepped behind the information desk and grabbed a pencil and a slip of paper. Slipping onto the stool, Tori began listing the things she knew about Todd. . . .

1. His last name was McNamara.
2. He . . .

She paused. He, what? He was tall? He wore a lanyard name tag around his neck at work? He plucked extras from a line?

Groaning, she crumpled the slip of paper in her hand and threw it into a nearby wastebasket. She knew nothing. Nothing of any consequence, anyway.

But that was about to change. Come hell or high—

"Wow, that room is really cool."

She straightened up, mingling glances with Todd as she did. "What was your favorite part?"

"The murals. Those kids did a great job."

"They did, didn't they?" She swiveled on her stool and settled her hands on the keyboard of the main computer. "Shall I check on that book for you?"

He nodded.

"What book is that?" Dixie asked, her feet moving toward the bookshelves before Tori had time to digest her question let alone formulate an answer. "Perhaps I know if we have it."

She put words to the letters she typed on the screen. *"Memories of Autumn."*

Dixie stopped in her tracks, pinned Todd with wide eyes. "You can't be serious."

Todd laughed. "Oh, I'm serious."

The former librarian tsked beneath her breath. "How long has this movie been in the works?"

"The book was optioned two years ago. The screenplay was completed about six months ago. Roles were cast shortly thereafter. I got the call about a month ago."

"A month is more than enough time to read a 350-page novel, young man."

Tori peeked around the computer monitor, mouthed an apology in Todd's direction. If he was bothered by the grilling he was getting, though, he didn't let it show. In fact, if the slight rise to his eyebrows was any indication, he seemed to be enjoying Dixie's persistence.

"True." He widened his stance. "But during that time, I had to pack up enough belongings to be gone for however long we're on location, put a hold on my mail, find a sitter for my dog, attend planning meetings ad nauseam, and oversee all the phone calls that had to happen to make a location shoot possible. By the time I finished each day, I was too tired to think, let alone read."

"Do you enjoy it?" She hadn't planned to ask the question, yet somehow, it was there, on the tip of her tongue at the exact moment Dixie spun around on her penny loafers and disappeared into the aisle formed by the third and fourth shelves.

"Most of the time, sure." Todd made his way around the outer edge of the information desk's circular countertop and propped himself against the opening. "There's something exciting about taking something that's purely on paper—in script form—and turning it into something much bigger."

Abandoning the keyboard altogether, she turned on her stool to afford a better view of Todd. "That's how I felt about the children's room. It started as this idea I'd carried around in my thoughts for years. But when it finally became a reality it was . . . it was *magical*."

A knowing smile crept across Todd's face. "Then you understand."

Indeed she did.

Dixie reappeared in the mouth of her chosen aisle and held a book in the air. "If Mrs. Deland hadn't been called out of town at the last minute *and* Mrs. McClacken wasn't the speed reader she happens to be, I would not be giving you this book right now, young man." With determined strides, Dixie closed the gap between herself and Todd. "Think you can read this in four days?"

"I—uh—"

"Just say yes, Todd. It's easier that way." Tori stepped down off her stool and rested a hand on

Dixie's shoulder. "I'm shocked we have a copy on the shelf."

"Mrs. McClacken returned it just this morning. Only reason it's on the shelf at all is because Mrs. Deland released her hold until after she returns from her trip."

"In four days?" Todd interjected.

"In four days," Dixie confirmed.

Todd took the book from Dixie's outstretched hand and studied the cover, the fingers of his free hand moving to trace the whimsically written title. "I'll have it read by then."

"That's good. Courtney Deland isn't the sort of woman you want to tangle with, is she Victoria?" Dixie looked left, then right before lowering her voice despite the empty library. "She doesn't take too kindly to not getting her way."

Todd's finger paused just above the final letter. "You get those here, too?"

"Those?" Tori asked.

"Yeah, you know, the-world-revolves-around-me-at-all-times type."

Dixie snorted. "Of course we do, young man. And so does Leeson's Market . . . and Debbie's Bakery . . . and every other place you can think of from here to Kingdom Come. It's life. There's not much we can do about them except grit our teeth."

For a moment, Todd said nothing, his finger resuming the *n*'s path until it cleared the cover. When it did, he looked up, his focus moving from

226

Dixie to Tori and back again before reaching into his back pocket and securing a business card from its depths. He held it out to Tori. "My cell phone is on here. Will that do in place of a library card?"

She took in the rectangular slip of cardstock, her gaze coming to rest on the tiny director's chair graphic in the lower right corner. "I like the picture."

A flash of crimson caught her by surprise. "At the moment, it's a stretch. But not for long. Not if I have my way."

Dixie plucked the card from Tori's hand and studied it closely. "You want to be a director?"

Todd gave a single nod. "More than anything."

"Then make it happen," Dixie said as she handed the card back to Tori.

"I intend to." Tucking the book under his arm, Todd pushed off the counter and made his way over to the front door, stopping briefly when he reached his destination. "Thanks for the book. You'll have it back on your counter by tomorrow night."

"You can have four days," Tori reminded.

"I only need one." He pushed the door open then pulled the book from beneath his arm and pointed it toward them. "Hey, for what it's worth, sometimes you don't have to grit your teeth. Sometimes, if you're really lucky, a brownie will do the trick."

Chapter 19

Tori loved each of her new friends for a reason specific to them, a quality or trait that set each of them apart from the other.

Nina, her assistant, was both calming and grounding, like the library they shared in common. Rose, although prickly at times, was the quiet hand Tori needed when life got a little uncertain. Dixie was a constant reminder that people and attitudes could change. Beatrice's quiet innocence was a breath of fresh air if she simply took the time to notice. Debbie was a living, breathing example of the importance of hard work. And Melissa's devotion to her husband and children made it impossible to ever forget what mattered most in life.

But it was Margaret Louise who'd impacted Tori's life most significantly, teaching her about steadfast loyalty and the healing power of friendship in a way no one ever had before. So while she hated to see any of them in distress, knowing Margaret Louise was hurting was downright painful.

With the sides of the fabric square back-to-back, Tori began pinning the batting into place, her focus torn between the rag quilt starting to take shape on her lap and the need to ease Margaret Louise's worry. "Please know I'm trying to figure out what happened to Anita Belise. And I will, I promise you that."

Margaret Louise looked up from the batting she was cutting and forced a smile to her lips. "I ain't worried, Victoria. The truth has a way of landin' right where it needs to be, even it if seems to take its sweet time gettin' there."

She thought back to her impromptu meeting with Todd and her stomach tightened. If she'd replayed his parting comment once, she'd replayed it a million times, her mental jury just as torn on his meaning as it had been at the beginning. Yet she couldn't run his statement past Margaret Louise, couldn't seek the opinion and insight she'd come to value like no other.

No, she needed to put all of that aside and be for Margaret Louise what Margaret Louise was for her.

Realizing she'd made an error with the pinning, Tori painstakingly removed each one she'd placed, the unfamiliar lines around her friend's mouth making it hard to concentrate on much of anything. "Is your mamma all right?" she finally asked.

Margaret Louise bowed her head over the yards of batting, carefully measuring and then cutting each six-by-six-inch square, the faintest hint of a shrug lifting her shoulders a smidge. "I s'pose."

"You suppose?"

This time her friend's shoulders rose and fell more noticeably. "She's got a safe place to lay her head each night so I s'pose she's all right."

Tori's stomach churned at the sadness in Margaret Louise's voice, the woman's normally happy tone missing in action along with her smile and her optimistic disposition. "It's hard for you to have her there, isn't it?"

"I hate myself for it."

She dropped her strawberry-shaped pincushion and stared at her friend. "Margaret Louise, please. You did nothing wrong putting her in Three Winds. You have such a full life with Melissa and Jake's family . . . and your cooking and your sewing, too. You simply don't have the time to attend to Annabelle's every need."

"That's not an excuse. Jake Junior and the others are just fine without Mee-Maw hoverin' 'round all the time. They've got a fine mamma and daddy of their own. And if my mamma was with me, I could still cook. And even sew most days."

Squeezing her eyes closed, she tried to think of something to counter what she was hearing, something that would help loosen the guilt that had Margaret Louise in its unrelenting grasp. "And you're right," she finally said, opening her eyes to meet her friend's. "You could back off from Jake Junior and Julia and Tommy, and Kate, and Lulu and Sally, and even little Molly Sue.

But then seven of the sweetest children I've ever known would be missing something very important in their lives, something they've known since the first day each one of them came into this world."

A single tear slipped from the corner of Margaret Louise's left eye, a pudgy hand reaching upward to swipe it away. "They have each other . . . and the new baby that'll be here just as spring is dawnin'. But Mamma, she's got nobody 'cept me. And she's feelin' mighty lonely at Three Winds. I see it every mornin' when I stop by with her favorite breakfast pastries, and I see it every afternoon when I go back to read with her."

Pushing the top row of fabric squares from her lap, she scooted over to the section of sofa that put her in closer proximity to her friend. "She's got Leona, too. Let her take on some of this burden."

"Mamma is not a burden," Margaret Louise whispered. "Some people are good mammas in spite of the mamma they had . . . because they want to make things better for the next generation than they had themselves. Me? I'm the mamma I am *because* of Mamma."

Tori nodded. "Anyone who sees the two of you together knows, beyond a shadow of a doubt, that you love Annabelle. Annabelle knows it, too."

"Does she?"

She reached out, rested her hand atop Margaret

Louise's. "I wish you could see the way she looks at you sometimes. The love, the admiration, the pride . . . it's all right there on her face when Annabelle looks at you."

The woman worked to control her emotions. "All I see when I look at her is loneliness."

"Then you're not seeing what's there." Tori held Margaret Louise's hand a few seconds longer then released it with a quick squeeze. "But let's say you're right to an extent. Let's say she is a little lonely where she is. After all, she lived with her sister until just recently, right?"

Margaret Louise nodded.

"She's had a lot of changes lately. Her sister, whom she's lived with for years, passes away. She leaves behind her home to move here to Sweet Briar to be closer to you and Leona. She is surrounded by new faces every day. Perhaps what you're seeing in her eyes, Margaret Louise, is anxiety . . . or stress. Leaving behind all that is familiar can be rough on anyone, let alone a ninety-two-year-old woman."

"Mr. McAllister said something similar to me this mornin'. In fact, he seems to think Mamma's increased confusion is because of all the changes in her life lately."

"Makes sense to me," Tori said. "In fact, I'd bet good money that's what all of this is about. Give her a little time, and you might be surprised how things turn around."

Margaret Louise picked up her scissors only to set them down again a few seconds later. "It's still hard to see her like this, though."

"Of course it is. She's your mamma. But you can't take all of this on yourself. This kind of stress isn't good for you, either."

Margaret Louise's cutting hand stilled. "My blood pressure was sky-high yesterday mornin' at the doctor's. I had to beg and plead for him to let me go."

Worry knotted in her chest. "Your blood pressure was high?"

"I guess I've been more worried 'bout Mamma than I realized."

She watched her friend for a few moments, a question forming on her tongue. "Is Annabelle the only thing you're worried about?"

Silence hovered around them as Margaret Louise cut yet another square of batting.

"Margaret Louise?" she prompted again.

"I s'pose I'm a bit worried 'bout that actress's death and whether or not helpin' Leona is gonna land me in jail. 'Cause if that happens, Mamma won't have nobody lookin' after her." Margaret Louise pulled the scissors from the batting and plucked a few stray pieces of fuzz from the blades. "Now don't get me wrong, Melissa would try her best to care for Mamma, she'd probably even bring the whole brood over to see her on a near-daily basis, but that sweet thing has enough on her plate without havin' to worry none about my mamma."

She pushed off the couch and walked to the center of the room. "You're not going to jail, Margaret Louise, you're just not."

"Do you have another suspect?"

Spinning around, she met her friend's questioning eyes. "No. Not yet. But—"

"*I* made those brownies, Victoria. Leona might have asked me to, but *I* made them. That's gonna land me in a whole tub of trouble."

"I'm gonna figure out who killed Anita." She retraced her steps back to the couch and dropped onto the very corner of the last cushion, her knees touching Margaret Louise's chair as she did. "We could figure it out together, you know. We've done a pretty good job with that in the past."

For just a moment, a glimmer of excitement flashed in Margaret Louise's warm brown eyes, only to disappear just as quickly. "I have to focus on Mamma right now. She needs me."

"She needs both of her daughters, Margaret Louise." There, she'd said it. "Leona needs to do her part, too. For Annabelle, *and* for you and your blood pressure."

Margaret Louise continued cutting, her hands guiding the scissors through the yards of batting. "Leona was always closer to Daddy. It's not that she didn't love Mamma, 'cause I know she did, but she just couldn't handle Mamma's . . . little quirks. They embarrassed her."

She felt a swell of irritation and released it through her words. "Leona isn't a little girl any longer, Margaret Louise. She doesn't have to worry about what her friends will say when Annabelle . . ." Her words trailed off as she searched for the most delicate way to complete her sentence.

"Steals things?"

Her face grew warm. "When she helps herself to things."

"It's okay, Victoria. I'm used to her stealing things by now. But Leona still struggles with it and I can't fault her for that."

"She doesn't have to be okay with what Annabelle does, but she can still help with Annabelle."

A slow smile inched its way across Margaret Louise's face, the welcome sight hitching Tori's breath. "Everyone is different, Victoria. And everyone handles hurt differently. No one way is wrong and no one way is better. It's just simply the way God made us. All we can do is learn to accept one another and lend a guidin' hand when we're able."

She peered at her friend through lashes that were suddenly tear dappled. "Margaret Louise, I've never known anyone quite like you before. How did you get to be so wise?"

"Don't know that I am wise, Victoria. I certainly make my share of mistakes. But as long as I let my heart guide my actions and my decisions, any mistakes I do make are made with the best of intentions. I can live with those."

She felt a lump of emotion form in her throat, knew it wouldn't be long before the tears that clung to her lashes began to escape down her cheeks. "There are so many things about the people I've met in this town that I like, qualities that I'm trying to inherit. But of everyone I've met since moving here, you are the one who's taught me the most. I only hope the things I'm learning from you can make me half the person you are, Margaret Louise."

Margaret Louise swapped the batting for fabric and noted the larger, seven-by-seven-inch squares she needed to cut. "Funny, but I said almost the same thing to Mamma just this mornin' . . . only I said it 'bout you, Victoria."

"Me?" she whispered.

"Yes, you. And there's not a person in this town who wouldn't agree."

She had to laugh, her rebuttal example coming fast and furiously. "I suspect Chief Dallas would argue that point, Margaret Louise."

"He pay you a visit this mornin', too?"

"Too?"

Margaret Louise sat up tall in her chair. "He was waitin' on the porch when I got back from pastries with Mamma. He tried to act all cute and coy, but I knew why he was there. That man couldn't sneak his way out of an empty forest."

Anger rose inside her at the notion of Margaret Louise being peppered with questions that didn't fit. Sure, she baked the brownies. Sure, she put nuts in them. But she did it because Leona asked her to bake them.

Leona.

Reaching up, Tori raked her hands through her hair, the spasm of anger shifting its focus from one bumbling person to another.

Police Chief Robert Dallas was still clueless. And, chances are, that would never change. But Leona Elkin knew better. She'd been taught better.

"I'm going to make this right, Margaret Louise. You just wait and see."

Chapter 20

Tori pulled up in front of Elkin Antiques and Collectibles at half past eleven and shifted the car into park. As tempting as it was to honk, she knew Leona would never let her live it down. So, instead, she waited.

And waited.

And waited.

And waited.

Lifting her left wrist into view, she took in the time: 11:45.

"So much for getting an early start," she mumbled as she pushed open the driver's side door and stepped into the street.

"I'm here. I'm here." She looked across the roof of her car in time to see Leona emerge from the shop, handbag and keys in one hand, Paris in the other.

"You're bringing Paris?"

Waving away her inquiry as if it were ludicrous, Leona continued. "I'm sorry we're a bit late but once we finally made it into the shop, we had to make sure Beatrice was squared away on the cash register before we could leave. That one can be a little dense at times."

Tori made a mental note to pick something up for Beatrice—a book, a necklace, a box of English teas. Something, anything to thank the young nanny for giving up her lone day off so Tori could get through to Leona.

After Margaret Louise had headed home the night before, Tori had wracked her brain for a way to make things right. She'd considered a simple heart-to-heart with Leona but had discarded it fairly quickly. Leona didn't like to be told anything. Except, of course, that she looked beautiful. Or that some man half her age was drooling over her from across a crowded room.

She'd even given some thought to letting Leona play shotgun on a stakeout of sorts. But unless the subject of their attention was six foot three and sporting muscles, Leona would grow bored. Asking her to sit in a car and note Margaret Louise's tired eyes through a pair of binoculars wouldn't do anyone any good.

In fact, it wasn't until she was just about to give up that she'd come to the one and only viable possibility.

Leona loved to shop.

Leona loved to chitchat while she shopped.

And sometimes, when she was shopping, Leona even seemed to listen.

It was worth a shot, anyway.

She slipped back into the car, Leona sliding in beside her from the passenger side door. "I think that girl spends too much time with that little boy."

Pausing her hand on the ignition, she glanced at the woman to her right. "Beatrice is a nanny, Leona, it's her job to spend time with Luke."

"But must she hum children's songs all day long?"

She closed her eyes and counted to ten. "Do you realize today is Beatrice's only day off all week?"

"Oh?"

Opening her eyes, she pinned Leona with a stare. "And she's spending that day covering for you . . . so you and I can go shopping."

Leona set her purse on the seat next to her and pulled the seat belt across her shoulder in such a way as to cover Paris, too. "Hmmm. That's rather silly of her, isn't it?"

"You mean, *kind? Nice? Sweet? Special?*"

Leona tipped her head forward, took in Tori atop her stylish glasses. "Is there something I should know, dear? You seem to be wound a bit tight this morning."

She opened her mouth to answer, yet closed it just as quickly. There would be a time and place to speak her mind. Now was not that time. Instead, she merely shrugged and pulled away from the curb.

"I heard from Warren this morning," Leona shared as they left the streets of Sweet Briar and headed west.

"And?"

"He seemed rather distracted."

"That makes sense. He certainly has a lot on his plate right now." Trees whizzed past the car as they traveled the two-lane country road that would eventually bring them to the outlet mall that had just opened three towns over.

Leona sniffed. "A plate he should clear when he calls me."

She cast a sidelong glance in her friend's direction. "Maybe he's hoping you'll be someone he can share his frustration with, someone outside the movie business he can vent to."

"I've offered to step into that horrible woman's role. What more does he want?"

"Y-you offered to star in his movie?" she sputtered in disbelief.

Leona's eyebrow arched. "Of course I did. It's the least I could do under the circumstances." Stroking her hand across Paris's back, Leona turned her attention out the window. "I make these kinds of gestures all the time yet no one ever seems to notice."

What to say . . . what to say . . .

"That must be hard." She drew back as the words left her mouth.

"It's been like this my whole life." Leona sighed and laid her head against the seat back, her perfectly coiffed hair barely moving. "I was always seen as the pretty one . . . the one with the angelic face and model-like bone structure. Margaret Louise was always the kindhearted one. It was like that all the way through college. Still is, even now. Only now it's not just Mamma and Daddy making that distinction but everyone else, too."

"Do you think it's a fair distinction?" She knew the answer, yet asked the question anyway, hoping the distorted reply she was sure to get would be the springboard she was seeking.

"I most certainly do not. Neither does Paris." Ever so gently Leona raised the bunny off her lap long enough to shower it with air-kisses.

"She knows her mamma is special, don't you, sweetie?"

Funny thing was, if Paris could talk, she would say Leona was sweet. And the animal wouldn't be wrong. In fact, Leona's nurturing of the garden variety bunny had surprised many in the sewing circle. Including Tori.

"I know I can be a little impatient at times. But I just don't have much tolerance for people who are slow and stupid. Never have."

"You mean like Beatrice?"

Leona gasped. "Victoria! I've never said Beatrice was stupid. Slow, yes, but not stupid. Any young thing who would travel so far from home for a job is courageous in my book."

Surprised by the answer, Tori opted to see how far the revelations might take them. She pressed on. "Oh, so you mean like Rose . . ."

Leona bristled in the passenger seat. "Rose may be slow, physically, but it's only because she's getting up in years. But even with that she's still on her hands and knees planting those flower gardens she loves so much. I admire that."

She held fast to the steering wheel, righting the car as it swerved onto the shoulder. "Y-you do?"

"Not the flower part, of course, but the staying active part, yes." Leona swiveled her legs to the left. "Me? I would use that energy for being squired around town by a handsome man, but I understand Rose doesn't have the same appeal that I do."

"You think she's stupid, though, right?"

Leona's grip tightened around Paris. "Rose? Are you kidding me? That old bat is sharp as a tack. Gaining the circle's sympathy every time we spar isn't by accident, Victoria. That woman sets me up every single time."

She opened her mouth to argue but let it die on her tongue instead. Rose was, indeed, sharp. Razor-sharp. And while she was hesitant to admit it out loud, Tori suspected Leona was right on some level. Then again, Leona's sullen expressions and holier-than-thou attitude made it easy to showcase her as the villain.

Casting a sidelong glance in Leona's direction, she decided it was time to say her piece. "You could prove them wrong, you know."

"Prove them wrong about what, dear?"

"Show them that you're kind and loving, show them that you don't dislike small children, show them—"

"I *do* dislike small children."

She ignored Leona's comment and kept going. "Show them that big heart I know you have." Turning onto the highway, Tori substituted open windows for air-conditioning. "You're safe with them, Leona. You can show them the real you."

"You mean like I did when I gave you that antique sewing box that reminded you of your grandmother? You mean like I did when I gave one of Paris's babies to Rose so she'd be less lonely?"

She zipped around the cars in the slow lane, the shopping mall they sought no longer quite so necessary. Everything she'd been saving to say for their outing was unfolding right there in the car. "Leona, that box meant the world to me—still does. And I know that Rose treasures Patches in much the same way you do Paris. But sometimes what people need isn't just a material thing. Sometimes they just need to know you're there, that you have their back . . . that you understand."

"We're talking about Margaret Louise now, aren't we?" Leona pointed at an approaching sign, the name of the mall and the upcoming exit clearly marked. Nodding, Tori decreased her speed and moved into the right lane.

"Yes, we are."

"My sister has everything under control. Always has."

She glanced across the seat at Leona. "Oh?"

"When Rose was having treatment for her rheumatoid arthritis a few months ago, who did she choose to bring along?"

Tori turned off the highway and pulled to a stop at the bottom of the exit ramp, the red light giving her a moment to respond to a conversational turn she hadn't seen coming. "She asked me to go with her."

"And?"

"Margaret Louise."

Leona barreled on. "And when Colby Calhoun went missing, who did you ask for help?"

A car honked behind them, prompting her to focus on the road and the now-green light in front of them. "Uhhh . . ."

"Margaret Louise," Leona supplied.

"You were there, too! You stood right next to me on that porch while Margaret Louise found the moonshine—"

"I stood there beside you because I invited myself along. Same as I have many times."

Suddenly the points she'd been hoping to make came back to choke her with a hefty slice of that humble pie Margaret Louise was always touting. And it didn't taste all that good.

Groaning inwardly, she pulled into the outlet mall's lot and found a quiet spot in the back to park. She turned off the engine, hiked her right knee onto the driver's seat, and turned to face her companion. "Leona, please know that I didn't purposely leave you out all those times, I just asked Margaret Louise because—"

"She's the dependable one," Leona finished.

She opened her mouth to protest yet couldn't find the words she needed. Leona was right and she knew it.

"From the time we were little girls, Daddy counted on my sister to make things right whenever Mamma's hands got sticky. He'd usher me to the side and send Margaret Louise in to clean up the mess."

She studied her friend closely. "Did those roles bother you?"

Leona's delicate shoulders rose and fell. "Maybe a little, in the beginning. I loved my mamma just as much as my sister did. But over time, while Margaret Louise picked up after her, I began to see all the pitying looks they got—from classmates, classmates' mothers, neighbors, and relatives—and, well, I started to realize the role I'd been given wasn't so bad, after all."

The role she'd been given . . .

Sitting there, listening to her friend, Tori couldn't help but notice the role perspective played in life. By Leona's perspective, the role of nurturer had been handed to her sister. And now, countless decades later, everyone who knew Leona saw the role she played as being a deliberate choice—one made out of selfishness rather than learned habit.

"I didn't know." It was a simple statement but the most accurate Tori could make at the moment.

"Most people don't." Leona leaned over, set Paris on the floor beside her feet, a smile lifting the corners of her mouth ever so slightly. "That's why I love Paris so much. She has no preconceived notions about me."

She turned her head to the left, took in the

246

limited number of cars parked in this portion of the shopping mall's lot. As much as she'd been mentally preparing for a chat of this nature with Leona, the unexpected twist left her scrambling for something to say. Something that could accomplish what she needed to accomplish yet be respectful of a situation she simply hadn't understood until that moment.

Leona beat her to the punch. "I see the worry in my sister's eyes. I really do. And I don't like it one bit. But I don't know how to fix it."

"You could ask about Annabelle. Maybe visit her sometimes, too."

Shifting in her seat, Leona wiggled a finger in Paris's direction, a pained smile negating her obvious attempts to remain unfazed by their discussion.

"I'm not trying to be pushy, or overstep my—"

"We do," Leona whispered, cutting Tori off mid-sentence. "Every day."

She stared at her friend. "Who does what every day?"

Leona stretched out her arms and plucked Paris off the ground, bringing the animal onto her lap once again. "Paris and me. We visit Mamma every day."

"You visit Annabelle every . . . wait. When?"

"Every morning, we sit in the parking lot of Three Winds and wait until Margaret Louise leaves to meet those grandbabies of hers for breakfast. When we see her drive off, we go inside."

She had nothing to say, so, instead, she simply listened as Leona continued, her friend's voice strained and hushed. "The first day or so, we simply watched her from a corner of the community room. I guess I didn't know what to say and I was terrified she'd steal something from one of her neighbors and I'd have to find a way to explain it away like my sister always does."

"Did she see you?"

Leona shook her head, sadly. "She's always in her own little world. Has been since Daddy passed on ten years ago."

Suddenly, the comings and goings outside her window faded away and she prompted Leona to continue. "And after that . . ."

"On the second day . . . the day after Anita was apparently found murdered, Paris got unusually wiggly. Before I could get a firmer grip on her, she wiggled from my arms and landed on the floor. My gasp must have snapped Mamma into some sort of semifocused state because she looked up and saw me." A faraway expression claimed Leona's eyes as she seemed to travel backward in time. "Mamma smiled the most beautiful smile at me. And then she saw Paris . . . and she got all excited."

"What happened?" she asked, anxious to hear the rest of the story.

"We stayed for about an hour. We went back the next day, too."

"Does Margaret Louise know?"

Leona shook her head. "No. And I don't *want* her to know. Not yet, anyway."

"Why not?" She heard the shrillness of her question, saw the answering rise of Leona's left eyebrow, but it was too late. The question had been posed.

"Perhaps I don't want our time together picked apart and analyzed. When someone has assumed the caretaker role for as long as my sister has, they tend to think they know everything."

It made sense. It really did. But still, she was floored. She'd had no idea, no idea at all.

"I'm trying to get to know Mamma again but it's hard. It's hard to ignore all those looks I saw growing up, looks I still see now every time her hands start swiping again . . ." Suddenly distracted by something outside the window, Leona's words trailed off only to resurface in a completely different spot. "Now there's one who would step on the face of his dying mother if it would get him to the next level."

Tori followed Leona's visual path to find a vaguely familiar face stepping from a nearby car. "Wait. I've seen him before . . ." She cast about for a name to go with the twenty-something but came up blank. "He's from the set, right?"

"His name is Rick. Rick Manning. He's related to Warren in some distant cousin way, I believe."

Rick . . .

Rick . . .

"Rick's been after Todd's job since the day Fifth-Cousin-Once-Removed Warren got him this gig in the first place."

Tori sat up tall. "That's right. Margot doesn't like him."

Leona continued to track the young man across the parking lot with her eyes. "I don't think many people do, except maybe Warren. Though why he would is a mystery to me."

Pulling her focus from the subject at hand, she fixed it, instead, on her friend. "So why don't *you* like him, Leona?"

"He's conniving."

Tori laughed. "Conniving, huh?"

Leona met her amused gaze and raised it with a hint of irritation. "That's what I said, isn't it, dear?"

The smile slipped from her lips. "What makes you say that?"

"He threatened me."

She stared at her friend. "What do you mean he *threatened* you?"

"Apparently, Warren is distracted by me." Leona lifted her left hand from Paris's back and bobbed it beneath the tips of her hair. "I tend to have that effect on men as you well know, dear."

It took everything in her power to offer the obligatory head nod rather than beg and plead for an answer to her question, but she did. It was the surest way to get back on track.

"Anyway, the night I brought over the brownies, he was there. In Warren's trailer."

"Rick?"

Leona rolled her eyes. "That is who we're talking about, isn't it, dear?"

Again, she nodded. And waited.

"When I arrived, Warren cut short their meeting and asked Rick to leave." A self-satisfied smile spread across Leona's mouth at the memory. "Warren wanted to bask in my presence. Alone."

"Do you know what they'd been talking about?" she asked, her curiosity at an all-time high.

"He was trying to secure a higher spot on the totem pole."

She stared at her friend. "A higher spot?"

"Todd's spot, to be exact," Leona mused. "Though why Warren would even consider swapping the two was beyond me. Todd is sharp and hardworking. Rick is unpleasant and lazy."

Taking in the information, she asked the first question that sprang to mind. "So, was he?"

"Was he what, dear?"

She clenched her teeth and counted to ten. Snapping at Leona to get to the point would only slow the process more. Instead, she willed her voice to sound calm. "Was Warren considering swapping their jobs?"

"I believe he was. Until I showed up and put an

end to Rick's pandering." Lifting Paris in line with her face, Leona looked into the rabbit's wide eyes. "Mommy has that effect on men, doesn't she, sweetheart?"

Slowly, Leona lowered the rabbit back to her lap and continued. "He wasn't happy when Warren asked him to leave. In fact, if looks could kill at that moment, I'd be six feet under with one of Rose's precious flowers planted on top."

"He was that angry?"

Leona nodded. "After he left, that awful woman showed up, determined to horn in on my time with Warren. But, thanks to those wonderful brownies my sister baked, she, too, left."

At the mention of Anita Belise, Tori's mind threatened to wander off, but she refused to be sidetracked. Not yet, anyway. "So when did he threaten you?"

"When I left that evening."

"Tell me," she urged.

Releasing a quiet sigh, Leona stepped her feet firmly into the limelight. "Rick must have been hovering around Warren's trailer, waiting for me to leave. In fact, when Warren opened the door and kissed me good-bye, Rick was waiting on the steps. He asked if he and Warren could finish their meeting. Of course, I knew how it was going to go, as I'd already taken an opportunity to voice my opinion to Warren, but I left the two of them to their meeting, nonetheless.

"The next thing I know, that Kelly fellow at the gate is thanking me for the brownies I handed out to everyone, when Rick runs up behind me and grabs hold of my arm." Leona paused long enough to lift the sleeve of her silk shirt and point to two bruises near her elbow. "He was angry. He told me to stay out of his business or else."

"Or else what?" Tori pleaded.

"Your guess is as good as mine, dear." Wrapping her fingers around the door handle, Leona pulled, her feet meeting the pavement before Tori could even blink. "Now, can we please quit all this yakking and go shopping?"

Chapter 21

By the time she'd dropped Leona and Paris off at the antique shop to relieve Beatrice, Tori's head was ready to explode. It had taken every ounce of willpower she possessed to follow Leona in and out of virtually every shop they passed. And when they'd spent nearly an hour agonizing over a beaded tote bag Tori knew Leona would never be caught dead carrying, she'd actually considered screaming.

But the shopping trip had been her idea, her avenue for trying to convince Leona to spend a little time with Annabelle. It wouldn't have been right to scratch the whole outing the moment she'd heard about Rick and his threat.

Rick and his threat . . .

She glanced at the clock on the dashboard and compared it to her plans for the rest of the evening—plans that included some much needed time alone with Milo.

Thirty-five minutes.

That was surely enough time to make a pit stop at the set, right?

Her mind made up, Tori turned left onto Main Street and parked the car in the lot usually inhabited by the classic car enthusiasts during any and all of Sweet Briar's festivals. Reaching behind her seat, she pulled her purse onto her lap and rummaged around inside until she found her notebook and pen.

Leona's account of the hours leading up to Anita's murder had intrigued her, setting off a list of questions she'd been forced to command to memory until Leona had made all of her purchases and been delivered safely back to her shop. The key, now, was trying to remember them all as she positioned the pen between her fingers and began writing . . .

- What is Rick's background? Where did he work before being hired by Cousin Warren?
- What position is he ultimately after?

- How did he get along with the rest of the crew?
- What was his relationship with Warren really like?
- Did he have anger issues across the board?

She stared down at the questions, her mind registering their importance even as a new one— the biggest of all—formed on their heels . . .

- How would killing Anita benefit Rick?

Feeling a familiar sense of excitement bubbling up inside, Tori closed the notebook and shoved it back inside her purse. She needed to get to the bottom of her first five questions before she could truly speculate an answer to the sixth. To do so any sooner would be premature.

Still, she wondered. . . .

Was Rick threatened by Anita's role in Warren's life the way he seemed to be about Leona? Was he trying to get rid of Warren's distractions so he could have the attention of his big shot director cousin all to himself? In which case, were the bruises on Leona's arm a mere sampling of things to come?

The notion sent a chill down her spine.

"One step at a time, Tori, one step at a time," she whispered. With a deep, measured inhale, Tori stepped from the car, her feet guiding her toward

Stan Kelly's post while her mind searched for a reason for her visit. She'd used the missing-notebook excuse once already.

"You're back." Stan sat forward, the back of his chair parting company with the fence post. "Still looking for that notebook?"

She considered the notion of extending the fib, but chose, instead, to go another route. An honest one.

"No. I found it, thanks." Pointing at an empty folding chair on the other end of the table, she met Stan's tired eyes. "Mind if I sit for a minute? I'd like to ask you a few questions if I could."

The security guard's broad shoulders rose and fell in rapid sequence. "Sure, go ahead. Not much else going on at the moment."

She sat, her thoughts zeroing in on the list of questions tucked away safely in her purse.

"How far do you think a person would go if they thought their job was in jeopardy?" she asked, the unplanned inquiry bringing her up short.

For a moment, Stan said nothing, his gaze locked on hers. "Why do you ask?"

It was her turn to shrug. "I'm not sure, exactly. Except that I'm worried about a friend of mine."

Pursing his lips, Stan merely nodded, his chair tilting backward once again. "Well, in that case, I suppose it would depend on how much she needed the job."

She opened her mouth to correct the man on his

choice of pronouns, but changed her mind at the last minute. Really, what harm could it do if he thought the person she was inquiring about was a female friend? If a time came to tweak that assumption, she'd worry about it then.

"I don't know if she needs it so much as she wants it. And by wants it, I mean *wants* it. I guess it's a once-in-a-lifetime kind of job."

He seemed to take that in, mull it around. "I guess she'd do whatever she had to do . . . kiss a few butts, sleep with the right folks, maybe spread lies about her competition."

"Kill off anyone who stands in her way?" She sat up tall, mortified the question had passed her mental filter and made its way out of her mouth.

He pinned her with a squirm-inducing stare. "Excuse me?"

Desperate, she searched for a way to salvage any shot she had of getting her real questions answered. She opted for the dumb female routine complete with a giggle. "You can tell I fell asleep last night watching a crime show, huh?"

Stan said nothing as his death stare continued.

She leapt to her feet, her hands retreating into her purse and withdrawing the first thing she could find . . .

A picture of Milo.

Ggrreeaatt . . .

And then it hit her. A way to get the answers she needed without looking like an idiot any longer.

"My fiancé is a third grade teacher at Sweet Briar Elementary. Every year, he brings in people representing different careers to talk to the students. So they can learn about all sorts of jobs for the future."

The man's stance softened ever so slightly. "And you want me to come and talk about being a security guard?"

Bypassing the truth in favor of pulling her foot from her mouth, Tori nodded. "I—uh, think the little boys would love to hear about what you do."

"When?"

She blurted out the first answer that came to mind. "Tomorrow? Say around two o'clock?"

"I suppose I might be able to accommodate that. If I can find someone to cover me, of course."

"Of course." Squaring her shoulders against the lie that would have her in debt to Milo for the next umpteen years, she posed another one. "Do you think we could get someone connected to the movie, too?"

The legs of Stan's chair hit the pavement. "Mr. Shoemaker is much too busy."

She rushed to explain. "Oh, I get that, I really do. Besides, I'm not sure if a bunch of third graders would really grasp the role of a director. But someone who deals with extras or sets or something like that might be interesting. Maybe someone like Rick?"

Stan laughed. "You mean the kid who takes a

break every chance he gets? The one who pawns his work off on Margot, Glenda, and just about anyone else he can find? The one who tries to get Todd fired every chance he gets?"

She opened her mouth to speak but let it shut as the security guard continued. "You think Mr. Hotshot-in-Training would be interested in talking to a bunch of kids?"

"If there was a human interest reporter there, perhaps . . ."

A second, louder laugh followed the first. "Will it be picked up by the wire services?"

Her shoulders sank. She could only pull so many strings. "I doubt it."

"Then he ain't coming. Unless . . ." Stan tapped a finger to his chin. "Unless I concoct some reason he *has* to do it. Then he'd actually have to work for twenty minutes or however long it takes without expecting everyone around him to pick up his slack and make him look like he's a superstar in Mr. Shoemaker's eyes."

"I—"

A mischievous grin crossed Stan's lips as he took his plan one step further. "Any chance this fiancé of yours has some real stinkers in his class? Kids who could send Rick screaming for the hills?"

Although she was a pretty levelheaded person, Tori had certainly made her fair share of bad choices. Some had hurt her terribly—like falling for her ex-fiancé, Jeff. And some had kept her from the truth. But inviting Stan Kelly and Rick Manning to a career day in Milo's classroom that Milo, himself, didn't know about? *That* took the cake.

Yet even as she stepped onto her front porch and saw him sitting there, waiting, she knew he'd agree to play along with her crazy idea. Chances are, he wouldn't even pepper her with questions.

"I'm sorry I'm late. I stopped by the set to have a quick word with Stan Kelly."

Milo rose from the wicker rocker and met her midway, his arms pulling her close. "No worries. I haven't been waiting more than five minutes."

"Five minutes?" she teased, reveling in the warmth of his touch.

"Okay, maybe ten." He whispered a kiss across the top of her head then dropped it to her lips for a kind of hello that made her knees week. Pulling back, he flashed a smile. "Fifteen, at the most."

"Sorry—"

He hushed away all further apologies with the tip of his finger before pointing to the wicker swing that hung from heavy chains affixed to the porch ceiling. Following his lead, she set her purse on the ground and sat down beside him, resting her head on his shoulder.

"So who is Stan Kelly?" he asked.

"The security guard for the movie set. He's the

one who caught Annabelle swiping items during her tour just before all hell broke loose."

"Ahhh." With a quick tap of his foot, they began to swing, the gentle motion calming. "Is there something wrong?"

"I wanted to ask him about one of the people working on the crew."

"Oh?"

She nodded against his shoulder. "From what I've been able to gather so far, this guy, Rick Manning, has a really poor work ethic yet expects his fellow crew members to cover for him."

"I hope they don't."

"He's Warren Shoemaker's cousin."

Milo's snicker echoed in her ear. "So he's got the nepotism thing going on, huh?"

She nodded again. "So when Leona made Warren think twice about a title switch Rick wanted, he wasn't exactly happy. In fact, he threatened her."

Bracing his foot against the floor, he stopped the swing. "This kid threatened Leona?"

"Leona is fine. I was shopping with her today, remember?" Without waiting for a response, she continued, the slow rhythmic sway of the swing resuming once again. "Anyway, that threat got me thinking . . ."

She felt him smile against the top of her head. "Is that what they call investigating these days?"

Popping her head out from underneath his chin,

she stared up at him. "Think about it, Milo. Maybe Anita did something to threaten his stance in his cousin's eyes. Or maybe she was *planning* to. Maybe he killed her to keep her quiet. Or maybe he killed her to frame Leona."

He reached out, traced the side of her face with his finger. "That's a lot of maybes, Tori."

She gave him that. "But that's why I want to ask him some questions. Good ones." Leaning forward, she plucked her purse off the ground and extricated her notebook from its depths. She flipped it open to the page of questions she'd compiled prior to talking with Stan Kelly. "See?"

His eyes skimmed her list then came to rest on her once again. "Yeah, but other than the first three, those aren't exactly the kind of questions you can come right out and ask him. Not if you want the truth, anyway."

Milo was right. But still, his answers to the first three would certainly give her a better feeling about the next three. . . .

"Chief Dallas is already circling. He's talked to Margaret Louise and me. Leona, too. But the more I think about it, the more I'm starting to think Leona is being used as a scapegoat. She brought the means with which to kill Anita and provided a perfect person to pin it on. And, unfortunately, if Leona goes down for the murder, Margaret Louise stands to go down with her as an accomplice."

He nodded. "I saw Margaret Louise today. She

was so distracted she walked right past me on the way out of church. Passed by Lulu, too."

Tori stopped the swing. "Oh, Milo, seeing her like this is killing me. For Margaret Louise to walk by one of her grandbabies and not notice them?"

"What struck me most when I saw her was how sad she looked. I've honestly never seen that woman without a smile from ear to ear."

"Between doing what's right by Annabelle, and the guilt I know she's feeling over having baked a treat that ultimately killed someone, Margaret Louise is carrying the weight of the world on her shoulders." Pushing off the swing, she stood up, wandered around the porch, Milo's eyes tracking her every step of the way. "Margaret Louise has stood by me since the moment I moved here. It's my turn to do the same for her."

"How can I help?"

She stopped mid-step and turned to face the man she loved more and more each passing day. "You can forgive me for volunteering your class for something tomorrow afternoon."

His left eyebrow shot upward. "My class?"

She took a deep breath, found her best sales voice. "For a very special Career Day that features people who work behind the scenes of a movie."

A sparkle lit Milo's eyes a full five seconds before being joined by a smile. "What a wonderful idea, Miss Sinclair. Perhaps you could be on hand with some homemade cookies . . . and maybe a few questions to get the kids started."

She crossed back to the swing and into Milo's waiting arms. "Why, Mr. Wentworth, I'd be happy to help."

Chapter 22

Talking to twenty wiggly third graders was no small task, but somehow, Stan Kelly made it look easy. Bypassing the chair Milo had set out for him, the security guard sat on the floor among the kids, regaling them with the kind of stories that kept eight- and nine-year-old boys wide-eyed.

There'd been a stint in a movie theater that had him dealing with teenagers who snuck from one movie to the other, paying for just one.

There'd been a few months in a local mall that had him spying on petty shoplifters as they stuffed their pockets with compact discs and makeup.

There'd been a one-month-long job at a bus station that had landed him on the front page of a newspaper for thwarting an attempted kidnapping.

Job by job, Stan took them through the past two years of his life until he got to his work on the movie set. Suddenly, the little girls in the class, who'd remained relatively quiet during his talk thus far, came to life, peppering the guard with question after question.

What movie stars had he met?

Did he get to go to the Nickelodeon Kids' Choice Awards?

How many autographs did he have hanging on his wall?

And without so much as a flinch or an eye roll, Stan answered each and every one as if they were the cleverest questions he'd ever heard.

Tori smiled at Milo as he, too, raised his hand with a question.

Stan nodded in his direction.

"How did you get involved in the movie set to begin with?" Milo asked. "And where are you from?"

"I grew up in Havlock, which is about thirty minutes west of here. Worked as a guard in a prison there for nearly twenty-five years."

"You mean a jail?" a little boy with white-blond hair asked.

"Yes, I do," Stan replied. "Best job I ever had."

"Why did you stop?" a petite brunette asked from the other side of the circle.

"The jail was closing. So I needed to find a job that would enable me to support myself and my boy." Stan released a long, tired sigh. "Had to leave him behind with his mamma while I found work where I could."

The brunette cocked her head and stared up at the man. "I bet you missed him bunches."

Stan said nothing for several long moments and then finally, "I missed his growing up on account of all that job chasing. But no more. And I'm gonna make it up to him by staying close to home and being a part of my grandchildren's lives."

A hand shot up next to the brunette, this one belonging to a stocky little redhead named Seth. "My Daddy says there ain't gonna be no movie here anymore 'cause some lady ate a brownie that killed her."

Stan shrugged. "We'll have to wait and see about that. But the company I'm with will just find me something else to do in the area if that happens."

"Whoa!" Seth suddenly rocked forward and pointed at Stan's waistband. "Are those real-life handcuffs?"

"You bet they are." Stan pulled the silver rings from their clip and held them out for the kids to see. "You only have to worry about these if you do something wrong."

"I won't do nothin' wrong," Seth said.

"Me neither," chorused the rest of the children.

"I'm sure Mr. Kelly is as happy to hear that as I am," Milo said. "Now let's thank Mr. Kelly for taking time out of his busy day to come and see us."

"It was my pleasure," Stan said, as he rose to his

feet and came to stand beside Tori with his left foot braced against the wall.

All eyes turned toward the door as Rick Manning jogged in, his hair and his clothes a dead giveaway to a late night spent doing any number of things except sleeping. Tori sent a worried glance in Milo's direction.

"Class, we have one more person from the movie set today. His name is Rick Manning and he . . ." Milo met Rick's eyes. "I'm sorry, Rick, I'm not sure exactly what you do on set."

"Everything."

Stan snorted. "If everything means hiding behind Mr. Shoemaker's trailer while everyone else works, I have to say he's exceptional at what he does," the guard mumbled.

"Why does Warren keep him if he's really that bad?" she whispered back as the children welcomed Rick to their classroom.

"Obligation, I guess." Stan paused long enough to send a contemptuous glance in his coworker's direction. "One of the rest of us makes a mistake and our head's on the chopping block. But Rick? He makes one, he spins it off on someone else."

"Mr. Rick, do you sit in one of those chairs? The one with your name on the back?" Seth asked.

A little girl with reddish brown braids shifted onto her knees. "And talk through one of those big things with a hole in it?"

"Not yet. But soon. Very, very soon."

"If anyone else with his level of incompetency made that claim, I'd say there wasn't a chance in hell . . . but . . . knowing him, he'll pull it off."

Intrigued by the guest's comment, she raised her own hand into the air.

Milo nodded at her. "Miss Sinclair? Do you have a question for our guest?"

"I do. I was wondering how one becomes a director."

Rick strode over to Milo's desk, pushed a stack of papers into the corner, and sat down in the center. "You do whatever it takes."

She tried again. "I mean, do you have to go to school to be a director?"

"Some do, I guess."

"Did you?"

Reaching into his pocket, Rick extracted a pack of gum, unwrapped a piece, and popped it into his mouth. "Didn't have to. I had another way in."

"Is it something you always wanted to do?" she asked.

"Not really. But once I heard the kinds of perks that came with the job and realized I had a ready-made foot in the door, it sounded pretty good."

Stan raked his hand through his thinning hair and scowled. "This kid makes me sick."

The girl with the braids raised her hand again.

Milo acknowledged the child with a smile and a head nod. "Yes, Ava?"

"My daddy said a lady from your movie died. Was she your friend?"

Tori looked from Ava to Milo to Rick as Stan's foot hit the ground beside her.

"Uhhh . . . no," Rick retorted. "A thorn in my side was more like it."

"What's *a thorn* mean?" Seth asked.

"You ever get your pants caught by a bush when you're playing?" Rick asked.

Seth nodded, wide-eyed. "All the time."

"It's a pain, isn't it?"

Again, Seth nodded, along with several of his classmates. "They hurt sometimes."

Shrugging, Rick pushed himself off Milo's desk. "Not if you cut them off they don't."

She stared at Warren's cousin as her thoughts raced in a hundred different directions. Was he saying what she thought he was saying? She glanced at Milo, saw the look of shock on his face, and knew it was mirrored on her own.

"This has been real, kids, but I've got places to go and things to do so I'm outta here." Rick strode toward the door and disappeared into the hallway, leaving the adults in the room to stare at one another with a mixture of surprise and disgust.

"He didn't share his gum," Ava announced to no one in particular.

A chorus of agreement rang up around the room only to subside as Stan approached Milo and whispered something in his ear. At Milo's nod, the guard addressed the students.

"Do you remember that bus station I worked at in Wisconsin? The one where I saved that little girl from being kidnapped?"

The children nodded.

"There was a candy store about two blocks from the station that had the best cherry sucking candy I've ever had. The place went out of business right before I had to move on, but every now and again the former owner sends me a bag or two of that very same candy. This time he sent two so I have plenty to share." Stan pulled his coat off the back of Milo's chair and reached into the pocket, extracting a small gold foil bag from inside. Slowly, he untied the white and gold ribbon at the top and held it open for the children to see.

"Can I have one?" Seth asked.

"Mr. Wentworth said you can *all* have one," Stan said. "So sit tight and I'll pass them out."

Taking advantage of the sweet distraction, Tori sidled up beside Milo, her hand covering her mouth so as to minimize any chance she'd be overheard by tiny ears. "Milo, I can't help but feel like Rick is the one. I mean, did you hear what he *said?*"

"I did." Milo crossed his arms in front of his chest and leaned against the edge of his desk. "But you're going to need a lot more than what he said here. Most of that could be nothing more than a personality conflict between two people with huge egos."

"It could . . ."

"The key is finding the motive."

"He despised her."

"But that's something that happens over time," Milo pointed out. "Think about it. He threatened Leona, right?"

She nodded.

"Why?"

"You mean why did he threaten her?" she asked.

"Exactly."

She thought back to everything Leona had told her in the parking lot the previous day, the details of their conversation shifting to the forefront of her mind. "Because something that Leona said to Warren put the kibosh on a job switch Rick was after."

"Meaning, the threat was triggered."

She pondered Milo's words. "Okay . . ."

"You find a trigger that put Anita in Rick's crosshairs and everything you heard here today takes on a whole new meaning."

Chapter 23

Balancing her sewing bag on one arm and a plate of homemade oatmeal cookies on the other, Tori sent up a silent prayer as she took the wide concrete stairs one at a time. She'd had the best of intentions when she'd first suggested adding Three Winds to the rotation of Sweet Briar Ladies Society Sewing Circle meetings, yet now that it was actually happening, she couldn't help but have a few reservations.

It's not that she was afraid one of the regular members would complain about the institutional feel or the limited privacy it would provide, because she wasn't. Not really, anyway. After all, each and every member of the circle was a class act in their own way, and everyone had been more than welcoming to Annabelle during the first meeting she attended.

But if for some reason it didn't go well—if Annabelle had a bad night or one of her fellow residents did something wrong—Margaret Louise would no doubt blame herself. And the last thing Tori's friend needed was more to carry on her already overly weighted shoulders.

"Victoria, wait up!"

She turned to see Melissa taking the steps two at a time in an attempt to catch up.

"Whoa! Whoa! Slow it down. You're pregnant, remember?"

Melissa pulled her sewing tote higher on her shoulder and continued to double-step her way up to Tori. "Yes, I'm pregnant. But I'm also a mom of seven, one of whom is under two. Trust me, two steps at a time *is* taking it slow."

"I don't know how you do it." And it was true. She didn't.

"I don't think, I just do." When she reached Tori's step, Margaret Louise's daughter-in-law greeted Tori with a kiss on the cheek and a peek at the plate of cookies. "What? No chocolate?"

"I thought I'd shake things up a little." Though, in all fairness, she would have brought something with chocolate if a library patron hadn't brought her a batch of oatmeal cookies ten minutes before closing. At first, she'd felt guilty re-plating, but, in light of everything on her mind at the moment, it was the best she could offer. It was that or not come at all.

"I hope tonight goes okay."

She saw the worry in Melissa's eyes. "I know. Me, too. Your mother-in-law could use a break right now."

"Jake is worried about her, I'm worried about her, the kids are all worried about her." Melissa slowed her pace to one stair at a time as they

273

resumed their climb toward the Three Winds' entrance together. "It's like she blames herself for not being able to cure Grandma of her problems."

"Toss in this whole brownie making fiasco and I'm afraid she's going to get herself sick."

Melissa stopped just shy of the main door. *Brownie making* fiasco? What brownie making fiasco?"

Uh-oh.

She tried to backpedal, but it was no use. Melissa was like a dog with a bone when it came to members of her family.

"Victoria? What's going on?"

Before she could formulate an answer, the front door opened to reveal a very distressed Margaret Louise. "I don't know what I'm goin' to do. Mamma isn't havin' a good day. She's been starin' at the floor for the past hour or so and won't respond to anything I say."

Transferring the cookie plate to the same arm that held her sewing bag, Tori gave her favorite friend a hug. "Maybe, once we start sewing, things will change."

Margaret Louise lifted her shoulders only to let them slump back down once again. "I s'pose."

"Is everyone else here?"

"Everyone that's comin', anyway." Margaret Louise reached out, took the plate of cookies from its precarious perch on Tori's forearm, and motioned for them to follow. "Beatrice isn't feelin' well. Seems she got a bit of a cold from Luke."

"Sally has one, too," Melissa said as she trailed her mother-in-law down the hallway.

"Oh?" Margaret Louise asked. "When did that happen?"

"She's had it for about three days."

Tori stopped mid-step. Sally had been sick for three days and Margaret Louise didn't know? That was unheard-of in Tori's book.

"She sure would love to see her mee-maw if you get a chance." Melissa reached out, gave her mother-in-law's arm a gentle squeeze, and then disappeared into the activity room around the corner, Georgina's and Rose's voices no doubt guiding her steps.

Swallowing back the lump that formed in her throat, Tori stepped in front of Margaret Louise and stopped once again. "I've got a lead on Anita's murder. And I think it's going to pan out. I just need a little time. So don't worry, okay?"

Margaret Louise peered down at the cookie plate, her lips tugging downward in uncharacteristic fashion. "Even if you find the person who killed her, I baked the weapon. How am I s'posed to live with that?"

She inhaled sharply. "Just because you baked them, Margaret Louise, doesn't mean her death is your fault!"

"I knew she was allergic to them," Margaret

Louise whispered so quietly that Tori had to lean forward to hear every word. "I knew Leona wanted to use them as a way to keep that woman away. I baked them knowing all of that."

"Using them to buy someone a wide berth is a far cry from using them to murder someone. The person who did *that* is the only one guilty of anything."

Silence blanketed the hallway as Margaret Louise continued to stare down at the cookies—her unseeing eyes and crestfallen posture nothing short of heartbreaking.

When Tori couldn't take it any longer, she reached out, wrapped her hand around her friend's arm, and fairly pulled her into the room where their lifeline of friends waited. "How is everyone, tonight?" she asked in her best cheerleader voice. "Ready to work on our rag quilts?"

Heads bobbed around the room as Tori took in each member present.

Rose sat to the left of Debbie, the fifty-plus years that separated the pair nowhere to be found as they took turns cutting strips of royal blue fabric over tales of their days. On the other side of the room sat Georgina, the mayor's ramrod posture and tall form dwarfing that of her sofa-mate, Dixie. Tori glanced right, her focus coming to rest on Leona. Despite the travel magazine in her hands, it was obvious to Tori that the woman's focus was elsewhere.

Following the path of Leona's gaze, Tori spotted the newest member of the circle and crossed the room to say hello. "Annabelle, hi! Thank you so much for hosting our circle meeting this week. The lighting in here is perfect for sewing."

Slowly, Annabelle looked up, a flash of something resembling understanding lighting her eyes momentarily. "I'd like to help make the rag quilts."

She heard Margaret Louise's gasp somewhere off to her side, felt Leona's eyes boring into the back of her head, but still, she kept her focus squarely on Annabelle Elkin. "Of course we want you to help. You've probably been sewing longer than any of us in this room."

Rose patted the vacant spot beside her and Debbie on the long couch. "Annabelle, come sit over here with us. We have a big stack of fabric and batting squares already cut and ready to go."

Understanding disappeared in favor of confusion as Tori took hold of Annabelle's arm and led her toward the couch. "I want to sit with you," Annabelle said.

She stopped, looked at the elderly woman closely. "You want to sit next to me?"

Annabelle tightened her grip on the tattered tote bag in her hand and nodded.

"I'd like that, too, Annabelle." She glanced at Rose once again, mouthed her appreciation for the woman's sweet overture, then sought out the one remaining empty couch in the room—a slightly oversized love seat tucked beneath a wall of windows. "Would you like us to sit here?"

Annabelle nodded, backing into the edge of the couch and dropping onto the cushion as she did. Then, pulling her tote bag onto her lap, she looked from Tori to the couch and back again.

Tori sat down and did the same with her own bag. Reaching inside, she pulled out her antique wooden sewing box and set it in the empty space between them. "If you need scissors or some extra needles, I have plenty to spare." She placed those items beside the box, adding her camera and an envelope of photographs she wanted to share with the group before setting the empty bag at her feet.

"Oh, Victoria, Colby told me you called this afternoon." Debbie handed her scissors to Rose. "He said you were wondering whether he had any connections on the movie set?"

She paused, her hand on the top of her sewing box, and addressed the bakery owner. "I did. I was just curious whether he had access to anyone who might be able to provide a record of everyone on the crew. Names, basic background, that sort of thing." With a flip of her hand, she opened the box and removed the top tray of needles and pins to reveal an assortment of colored thread underneath. "I've been wanting to send some thank-you notes out to all the people who were so nice during my brief stint as an extra but I didn't have everyone's name."

Oh how she hated to lie to her friends, but considering who was in the room, it seemed the best decision at the moment. The last time the possibility of Margaret Louise being implicated in Anita's murder had come up in a meeting, Annabelle had retreated into a world that had only caused her daughter more stress.

Debbie stood and walked over to Tori, a piece of lined paper in her hands. "Well, he tracked down a friend of a friend and he was able to get ahold of a pretty thorough list."

Tori's mouth gaped open.

"Anyway, Colby says he hopes it helps. If it doesn't let him know and he'll see what else he can do."

She took the paper from Debbie's outstretched hand and stared down at the names on the list. One by one, each line contained a name, hometown, job title, and length of time associated with the production studio.

There was Margot Anderson, the second, second assistant director. A native Californian, Margot had been employed by the studio for two years.

She read the next few names, her mind conjuring up faces for two or three of them before coming to one on her list of suspects.

Glenda Goodnight was one step higher on the

totem pole than Margot, her title necessitating just one second, rather than two. Also a native Californian, Glenda had started work just two months before Margot, making her I've-been-here-longer-than-you attitude more than a little ridiculous.

Todd McNamara broke the California pattern hailing from Tucson, Arizona. According to Colby's notes, Todd had started with the studio four years earlier, working his way from mail room to first assistant director.

A dozen or so names brought her to the other side of the paper, where she recognized the security guard's name. Unlike everyone else on the page, Stan was employed by a local security firm specializing in concerts and other events in the area. He'd been hired by the security firm roughly four weeks earlier.

Rick Manning's name was listed near the bottom. While his home state of Montana was listed, his job title and time with the studio was left blank. A margin note from Colby simply reaffirmed what she already knew. Rick Manning was employed because of family connections and his job title was left open.

While she was thrilled for the information, she couldn't help but feel a little defeated. Somehow, someway, she'd hoped the murderer's name would leap off the page.

"Thanks, Debbie. I really appreciate Colby's

help." She smiled up at her friend then folded the sheet of paper in fourths and set it in her box alongside the brightly colored spools of thread. "Looks like I can get to those thank-you notes, after all."

"I'm glad." Spinning on her feet, Debbie made her way back to Rose and their strips. "Now let's get these quilts made."

Soon enough, all thoughts of pretend thank-you notes and unhelpful lists disappeared from her thoughts as she lost herself in making a rag quilt. The cutting, the sewing, the gossiping, the eating slowly did what they always did— provided a stress-free environment that was sorely needed. Sure, she—and probably every-one else in the room—was aware of a nearly silent Margaret Louise, but, for the most part, things went on as they always did on Monday nights.

Until a rapid series of movements out of the corner of her eye brought her up short, anyway.

She glanced over at Annabelle just in time to see the elderly woman's wrinkled hand disappear inside her tote bag. Looking left, then right, she tried to see if anyone else had noticed, but even Margaret Louise was engrossed in her rag quilt.

For a moment, she contemplated saying something but discarded the notion as quickly as it came. Besides, a quick inventory of her surroundings revealed only a smattering of missing items—her scissors, her strawberry-shaped pincushion, and a tin of buttons she'd set to the side while looking for a particular thread color. Nothing she couldn't live without for a few days . . .

Especially if living without them brought Margaret Louise a little less stress.

Smiling at Annabelle, she returned to her quilt, her thoughts drifting back to her conversation with Milo. He was right. The key was in finding the trigger.

She stilled her needle just above the fabric and peeked at Annabelle's other daughter. While Tori could find a way to pump Margot, Glenda, and Todd, Leona was the best candidate when it came to gleaning information from and about Warren Shoemaker. Besides, she owed Leona the opportunity to play co-detective. Her failure to do so to that point had obviously hurt feelings in a way she hadn't realized until their shopping trip.

It was time to make amends.

And it was time to catch a killer.

Chapter 24

She was about halfway through the list of upcoming titles she needed to order into the library when Leona called, the momentary distraction both welcome and annoying all at the same time. If she'd started on the entries when she'd first intended, they'd be done by now. But, thanks to a little matter of murder and its threatened impact on two of her closest friends, she was in desperate need of some quiet.

Leaning back, she spun her desk chair so she could look out at the trees that dotted the grounds. "Now where are you again?" she asked, holding the phone tight to her ear as her eyes followed the comings and goings of a dog tied to the base of a moss tree not more than twenty feet from her window.

Sniff the grass.

Sniff the tree.

Sniff the grass.

Sniff the tree.

Quick tail wag.

Repeat.

"I'm outside Debbie's Bakery with Paris."

She waited for more but heard only silence. "Okay . . ."

"They're all inside. Just sitting around a table drinking coffee and talking."

"Is this some sort of telephone version of charades that I don't know?" She knew she was being a smart aleck, but she couldn't help it. There were times that Leona's bent toward the cryptic bordered on exhausting.

Leona sighed in her ear. "Victoria, dear, are you or are you not trying to figure out who killed that awful woman?"

She bolted upright. "Yes, of course I am."

"Didn't you have Margot and Todd and Glenda on that list we put together at last week's meeting?"

"Yeah . . ."

"Well, they're all inside. Maybe you can stop by for a coffee and do a little snooping at the same time."

Spinning around, she closed out the ordering screen on her computer and reached for her purse. "I'll tell Dixie I need to run a quick errand and I'll meet you and Paris there in five."

"We won't be here, dear," Leona fairly purred. "I'm dropping Paris off with Rose. That way my precious little angel can have a little time with Patches, and I can work on Warren the way you suggested last night."

She felt the excitement building inside her chest.

Between the two of them, they were bound to connect the dots to reveal Anita's killer sooner rather than later.

"Thanks, Leona. I really appreciate this." She strode toward her office door and flipped off her overhead light. "Good luck with Warren."

"One doesn't need luck when they've got charm and beauty, dear."

She all but ran from the library to Debbie's, her two-inch heels clicking against the sidewalk in a rhythmic pattern. Talking to potential suspects one-on-one certainly had its merit, but taking advantage of a relaxed group setting held potential as well. Just how much, though, was anyone's guess.

Yanking open the door of the bakery, she waved at Emma then scouted the tables for Margot and the gang. Sure enough, they were still there, to-go cups and baked goods adorning their table. She bypassed the counter and headed straight for them, her most disarming smile primed and ready.

Margot looked up as she approached. "Hey, Tori, how are you?"

She stopped behind the vacant chair separating Todd and Glenda. "I'm good. Busy, but good."

Todd waved his hand in Tori's direction, his words addressing his table companions. "You should see the children's room she did over at the library. It's dynamite."

She felt her face warm at the praise. "Thanks, Todd."

He continued on, his face sporting an animation she didn't normally see in him. "She picked all these scenes from books and had kids draw pictures that depicted those scenes. Then she painted them up on the walls of this room. It's really pretty spectacular."

Margot patted the empty seat. "Sit. We could use a fresh face around here."

Todd slid off his chair and gestured toward the counter. "What are you drinking, Tori?"

She waved him off. "No, let me get it. I'll be right back."

Five minutes later, she was sitting between Todd and Glenda, shooting the breeze as Margot called it—their conversation flitting over such topics as the latest reality show, favorite childhood books, and the best place to find a coffee in California. She played along, contributing on topics she could, listening when unfamiliar subjects took center stage. Minutes turned to an hour as they joked and laughed, their conversation tackling just about every subject under the sun except the one Tori wanted to engage in more than any other.

Eventually, she decided to go for broke and steered them right where she wanted to go. "So I had the opportunity to get to know Rick Manning yesterday."

Margot's snicker was drowned out by Glenda's snort.

Todd wrapped his hand around his paper cup and lifted it to his lips, tapping the bottom of the cup with his free hand in an effort to get every last drop of his double latte. When he was successful, he set it beside his empty plate and nodded at Tori. "My condolences."

"It has to be awfully hard working with someone like that," she said, casting out the best line she could throw and hoping against hope for a nibble.

Glenda bit first. "We didn't really have any problems among the crew until he showed up, but once he did, life around set pretty much became a living hell. Suddenly we had a pipeline back to Shoemaker watching our every move."

"Reporting back moves that never even happened," Margot added. "There was this time I was getting ready to fill out a required form for the town and he strolls in and tells me he's got it covered. I tell him I've got it, that I've done hundreds of these things prior to location shoots. He insists. So I hand him the form. Twenty-four hours later, I'm summoned by my boss. Seems the form was never filled out and turned in. They docked me a day's pay."

Tori gasped. "Did you ask Rick about it?"

Margot shoved her cup forward and drummed her fingers on the table. "Of course I did. And you

287

know what he did? He denied ever taking the form from me."

"Wow." It was all she could think to say.

"Rick did that kind of stuff all the time. But his favorite and most consistent target to screw over was Todd," Glenda said, reaching across Tori and smacking Todd in the arm. "Isn't that right, chief?"

"Chief?" she echoed.

Todd rolled his eyes. "Glenda and Margot are the only ones who ever call me that. It's a joke, really."

Margot shook her head. "Okay, so you don't have a huge, huge title . . . yet. But you at least have a first in front of yours. And it won't be long before all number references give way to the main title. You know everything that's going on all the time. You keep everyone on their toes. You have since the day I started working here."

"Which is why he's had a target on his back where Shoemaker's precious baby cousin is concerned." Glenda pulled her arm back across the table and dropped her chin into her hand. "God, between Rick and Anita, life these past few weeks was pretty close to unbearable."

Sitting up straight, Glenda fussed with her hair in theatrical fashion. "I will not waste my time dealing with—with buffoons. If I wanted to waste my time with buffoons, I'd be working in a grocery store somewhere building pyramids with tomato soup cans."

288

Margot jumped in, her voice mimicking the same nasally sound Glenda had just employed. "For the next five months, I expect to feel as if I'm staying at a five-star resort with room service, attentive help, and absolute discretion when Warren and I want to be alone."

It was Todd's turn to snicker. "I thought she was going to have a coronary when Pooky showed up. She was on the warpath trying to track down the weak link that let that catastrophe happen."

She nibbled her lower lip inward, debating whether to come clean with the truth or let the three of them continue operating under a blatant misrepresentation of facts. Hoping the sense of camaraderie would take her far, she decided to let them in on Leona's little secret.

"That wasn't Pooky," she said.

Glenda and Margot turned and stared at Tori.

"That was Leona Elkin, the owner of Elkin Antiques and Collectibles right here in Sweet Briar." She looked down at her now-empty cup of hot chocolate and cracked a smile at the lunacy of it all. "Leona is one of those people who sees something she wants and does whatever it takes to make it happen. And, when it comes to men, it always has a way of working."

Utter silence was followed by a burst of laughter from Todd. "She wasn't Pooky and Warren let her stay, anyway?"

She grinned. "You met her, didn't you?"

"Indeed I did. And she is certainly one to remember . . . much to Anita's chagrin."

Margot concurred. "Do you remember the moment she first realized Pooky . . . or, rather, fake Pooky showed up? I thought Anita's brains were going to explode right out of the top of her head, she was so angry."

"She became double focused from that moment on," Glenda mused while chasing the last few crumbs of coffee cake around the plate with her finger. "Find and fire the person who let her nemesis in despite strict orders to the contrary, and find a way to make Pooky disappear from Warren's thoughts once and for all."

"Instead, Anita took a bite of the poisonous apple and took us all out of our misery." Margot blew a burst of air through pursed lips, watched stray strands of her red hair drift back onto her forehead, undaunted. "Oh, and put us all out of a job in the process."

"Temporarily," Todd cautioned.

"Can you imagine the stink Anita the Great would have caused if *I'd* have been the one to overlook her EpiPen?" Glenda made a slashing motion near her throat. "She'd have had my head."

"EpiPen?" Tori echoed.

Glenda shrugged. "Yeah, it's this thing she was supposed to use if she accidentally ingested something with nuts. It could have saved her life if she'd just opened the damn drawer she made sure everyone on set knew about."

"Anita even had a spare cell phone in that same drawer for the sole purpose of calling an ambulance if something went wrong." Margot slumped in her chair, closing her eyes as her head drifted backward. "It was Glenda's job to make sure it had a full charge before she left every evening."

"And what does she do after all of that?" Glenda's voice jumped an octave as she hit the top of the table with her hand. "She takes a bite of a brownie filled with nuts and never even tries to save herself. It figures, doesn't it?"

Todd grabbed his empty cup and slid off his stool. "Just be glad it happened before she was able to fire the two of you."

Chapter 25

She was just steps away from returning to the library when she stopped short, snippets of the past ninety minutes looping through her thoughts. Glenda was right. Why wouldn't Anita have grabbed her medicine when she realized there were nuts in the brownie? Why wouldn't she have attempted to use her phone?

It made no sense.

Reaching into her purse, she pulled out her cell phone and dialed a familiar number, her feet retracing their way back to the sidewalk before Dixie even answered the phone.

"Sweet Briar Public Library. This is Dixie, how may I help you?"

She turned right and headed toward the town square and the municipal building that bordered its southern side. "Dixie, it's me. Look, I know I said I'd be back shortly and that it's been much longer than that, but something has come up. Can you handle things there for just a little while longer?"

"I've been handling things at this library since before you were born, Victoria," Dixie reminded in true Dixie Dunn style.

Rolling her eyes skyward, she couldn't help but smile. She'd walked right into that one. . . .

"I figured you could but thought I should check in and ask, anyway." She glanced over her shoulder to gage the traffic, crossing the street at an unnecessarily fast clip. "Dixie? Can I ask you one more question?"

"Of course."

"If you were in a life-or-death situation that wasn't of your own doing, can you think of any reason you wouldn't try to save yourself?"

"No."

The answer, though short, verified what she herself had been thinking. Something about

Anita's actions—or lack thereof—the night she was murdered simply didn't add up.

"Thanks, Dixie. I'll see you soon."

A pause was followed by a semimuted Dixie Dunn. "Does this have something to do with that actress?"

"Yes, it does."

"Then don't worry about getting back here. Take care of whatever you need to do to put that smile back on Margaret Louise's face. Seeing her so stressed just isn't right."

"I know, Dixie. I don't like it, either." She turned with the sidewalk then crossed the road once again, Sweet Briar Town Hall looming larger than life in front of her eyes. "But I'll figure this out. Somehow, someway."

Snapping the phone closed, she tossed it in her purse and took a slow, deep breath. She'd had more than her share of unexpected visits from Police Chief Robert Dallas—the kind of visits that had been met with clammy hands and a churning stomach. In those instances, the only thing that had kept her sane was knowing that he'd leave, eventually.

Yet there she was at that exact moment, about to walk into his official lair and willingly subject herself to whatever questions he might hurl her way just so she could ask one.

She was slowly but surely going nuts. There was no other explanation.

With a second, deeper breath, she made her way into the lobby of the municipal building and turned toward the opening marked Sweet Briar Police Department.

A rather bored-looking woman in her mid- to late fifties looked up from her sentry behind a waist-high wall. "Can I help you?"

"Is Chief Dallas in?"

The woman's eyebrows dipped. "Who's asking?"

"Victoria Sinclair."

Eyes dropped as a calendar was consulted. "He's not expecting you."

Inhaling sharply, she willed her voice to remain steady. "If you just tell him I'm here to speak with him, I'm quite sure he'll see me."

"Does he know you?"

She laughed, the sound echoing around the windowless room. "He's been to my house many, many times."

Eyebrows shot upward as Tori received a second and far more thorough inspection of everything above the wall. "Oh?"

Horrified by the thoughts she realized were running through the woman's head, she rushed to explain. "We've, um, worked together on a few cases."

A beat or two of hesitation was followed by the press of a button. "Chief? There's a woman out here to see you. Says her name is Victoria Sinclair."

"Send her in."

The dispatcher removed her finger from the intercom button and rose from her chair, pointing toward a door to her left. "Right over here, ma'am."

She stepped through the doorway into the station's command center and followed the woman down one hallway and then a second, the sound of her heels muted against the carpet. When they reached their destination, the dispatcher simply spun on her rubber-soled shoes and returned to her post without so much as a word or a nod.

The chief looked up from his desk. "Miss Sinclair. This is certainly a surprise. What can I do for you?"

She entered the man's office and took the chair he indicated, her hands beginning to tremble ever so slightly. Deep down inside, she knew Robert Dallas was a good man. A little narrow-minded and lazy at times, but a good man. Yet something about being in his office made her nervous. She swallowed in an attempt to buy herself a little time.

He tented his fingers beneath his chin and leaned back. Waiting.

"Why didn't Anita Belise use her EpiPen? Why didn't she call for help?"

She hadn't expected to dive in quite so hard, preferring, instead, to ease herself into such conversations, but now that she had, she realized it wasn't such a bad idea. The faster she got to the point, the faster she could get out from under the man's scrutinizing eyes.

"I can't answer that."

She mulled the man's answer even as another question formed in its wake.

"Was the drawer at least *open?*"

The chief sat up straight. "Drawer? What drawer?"

"The one where she kept her EpiPen and her cell phone."

Reaching over, the chief pressed the intercom button at the base of his phone. "Mildy? Is Carl in?"

Tori scooted forward in her chair and listened. Carl Jasper was the department's newest officer, the addition of the academy graduate coming at the hands of a council vote in response to the rash of murders that had plagued the town over the past two years.

The dispatcher's voice filled the office. "He's right here. I'll send him in."

"Thanks, Mildy." The chief released the button and looked toward the door. Sure enough, less than ten seconds later, the well-toned body of the department's youngest officer stepped through the opening.

"Chief? You wanted to see me?"

"You went through all of Ms. Belise's drawers, right?"

Carl shifted from foot to foot. "I think so."

The chief's left eyebrow rose. "You *think* so?"

Crimson rose in the junior officer's face. "I might of gotten distracted with the plate and the brownie. I was trying to make sure I bagged it just the way you said."

A beat of silence was followed by the sound of the chief's chair scraping against the linoleum beneath his desk. "Grab your stuff and let's go. We need to get in the victim's trailer again."

Tori jumped to her feet. "Can I come?"

The chief yanked his desk drawer open and pulled out a camera and a notepad. "I can't allow that, Miss Sinclair. I'm sorry."

At the flick of his wrist, she led the way into the hallway, her feet traveling the same path she'd followed with Mildy. Only this time, instead of mentally reviewing the questions she wanted to ask the chief, she was devising a plan to get the answers she needed.

Step one of the plan had her turning left as the chief and his officer went straight. There was, after all, more than one way to access the Green.

Step two had her banking on the fact that Stan Kelly would be busy with the chief, therefore leaving her an opportunity to track down one of the crew from that morning.

Step three had her waiting for the inevitable scoop as to what was or wasn't found in Anita Belise's trailer.

Her heels resumed their staccato pattern against

the sidewalk as she implemented step one. As she rounded the first, and then the second corner of the square, she felt the smile creeping across her face.

Stan Kelly wasn't at his post.

"Step three, here I come," she whispered, slipping through the unmanned gate and heading straight for the tent where either Margot or Glenda would surely be found.

She was mere steps from her destination when the flaps of the tent parted and Todd emerged, his walkie-talkie clutched tightly in his left hand.

"Oh, hey." She waved and stopped, noting the tense set to Todd's jaw and waging a pretty good mental guess as to why. "Is everything okay?"

Todd released a frustrated sigh. "The cops are back. They're at the trailer with Kelly, going through everything all over again."

"Can I come?" she asked.

Shrugging, he motioned forward with his walkie-talkie. "Yeah, sure, I guess. But stay out of the way, okay? I don't want this to come back and haunt me."

"Of course." She marveled at her good luck as she practically ran to keep pace with Todd's long strides. "Did you know where Anita kept her EpiPen, too?"

"Yeah, I knew. We all knew. But it was Glenda's job to make sure everything Anita needed was there. If Anita did a random check—as she did all the time—and her cell phone didn't have a full charge, Glenda would have been out on her ear. No questions asked, no second chances given."

As the trailer came into view, Todd hurried his pace even more, enabling Tori an opportunity to hover around a grove of trees where Chief Dallas wouldn't see her so easily yet she could make out some of the sounds coming from Anita's open door.

Twenty minutes later, Stan emerged from the victim's trailer along with Carl and the chief. "I want to talk to the girl responsible for maintaining that drawer," Chief Dallas barked. Glancing over his shoulder at Stan, he jerked his head in the direction of the security trailer. "Track her down and bring her to me. I've got some questions that need answering."

Slowly, Kelly raised his own walkie-talkie to his mouth. "Glenda? Can you meet me in the security trailer, please?"

She waited behind the closest tree until Carl and the chief had disappeared inside Stan's trailer. When the coast was finally clear, she stepped in front of a rather flustered Todd. "Can I ask what happened in there?"

Todd raked his free hand through his hair and groaned outwardly. "Glenda's in trouble. Big trouble."

"Why?"

"The drawer was empty."

She stared up at Todd, her mind racing to make sense of what she was hearing. "What do you mean, empty?"

"The EpiPen, the cell phone, all of it. Gone."

"But how?" she stammered.

Dropping his hand from his head to his mouth, he shook his head in disbelief. "I don't know. I guess whoever killed Anita wanted to make damn sure she died."

"They think Glenda is responsible?"

Slowly, his shoulders lifted only to drop back down again. "It was her job to make sure everything was there."

She considered his words, an alternate theory finding its way to her tongue. "But you, yourself, said just about everyone knew where Anita's supplies were kept, right?"

Todd's eyes narrowed in on hers. "What's your point?"

"Just because Glenda was responsible for making sure everything was as it should be, doesn't mean she's the only one who knew where to find Anita's lifelines. You knew, Margot knew, everyone knew."

"Are you trying to insinuate that I had something to do with Anita's death?" Todd whispered. "Do you really think I could do something like that?"

She held up her hands. "That's not what I'm saying."

"Then what, exactly, are you saying?"

Milo's words filled her thoughts, prompting her to ask a question she'd been dying to ask for days. "Did Anita have any sort of run-in with Rick in the days leading up to her death?"

"No, not to my knowledge. Though, that doesn't necessarily mean anything. What I do know is that Rick wasn't a huge fan of Anita, the main reason being the fact that she was around Warren virtually twenty-four/seven." Todd dropped onto a nearby bench. "And as far as Anita was concerned, she, like everyone else around here, was very aware of the familial connection between Warren and Rick. So she tended to be a bit more tolerant of him than the rest of us."

"But it's not out of the question," she insisted. "They *could* have had a fallout, right?"

"I suppose." Todd shrugged. "Why?"

"Did he know where Anita's EpiPen and emergency cell phone were kept?"

"Everyone did."

"Maybe *he* gave her the brownie and then swiped the stuff she would have needed to save her life." She heard the excitement in her voice, knew she'd come up with the perfect suspect.

"Wouldn't that have been great?" Todd rested his elbows on his thighs and hung his head to his chest. "That would have been a two-birds-with-one-stone kind of thing for any one of us who've had our fill of egomaniacs on set. But it couldn't have happened. Not by Rick's hands, anyway."

"Why not?"

Todd pulled his head up and met her questioning eyes. "Because Rick wouldn't have touched a brownie with nuts, either."

"Why not?" she repeated.

"Because Rick Manning is allergic to nuts, too."

Chapter 26

Tori pulled the roast from the oven and set it on the cooling tray, the enticing aroma of seasoned pork doing little to lift her spirits. She'd been so sure that Rick Manning was the key to Anita Belise's death. His attitude, his arrogance, the way he'd threatened Leona . . .

It had all fit.

Yet, with just eight words, Todd had managed to destroy her perfect theory and send her back to square one.

She didn't like square one. She didn't like it at all.

Once the shock of Rick's allergy had worn off, she'd forced herself to consider other possibilities. Margot knew where the EpiPen was kept and she was just as sick of Anita as anyone else. So, too, was Glenda—the one woman who was actually tasked with the job of making sure Anita's emergency supplies were always at the ready.

But nothing she came up with made sense. Not enough, anyway.

She peeked around the corner at Milo, his precise manner of setting the table bringing a much-needed smile to her lips. "I was so hoping I'd figured it out, you know? Then, at least in that regard, Margaret Louise's stress load would be a little lighter."

With a steady hand, Milo poured wine into both of their glasses. When he was done, he set the opened bottle in the middle of the table and crossed the room to take her hands. "You'll get it, Tori. Have faith."

"I'm trying." She relished his quick squeeze then returned to the task of slicing the roast onto a platter as he stirred the homemade mashed potatoes and transferred the rolls into a serving bowl.

"This looks delicious, sweetheart."

"Thanks—"

A knock at the back door made them both turn, Leona's stylish frame visible through the sheer yellow door panel. She dropped the knife onto the cutting board and crossed to the door.

"Leona. How are you?" Backing up, she gestured her friend inside. "Did you find anything out this afternoon?"

She knew the question was futile, especially in light of the theory-buster Todd had dropped, but she was nothing if not optimistic.

"You mean, beyond the fact that Warren is a bit of a bore?" Leona stopped in the middle of the kitchen, her nose twitching in time with Paris's. "Good heavens, dear, what on earth is that delicious smell?"

"A pork roast." Glancing at Milo, she met his quick nod with one of her own. "Would you like to stay and eat with us? We'd love it if you would."

Milo stopped stirring potatoes long enough to plant a kiss on Leona's waiting cheek. "Yes, please stay."

Leona looked down at Paris and then back up at Tori. "Would you have something for Paris to eat? I don't like to eat in front of her."

She nibbled her lower lip inward in an attempt to stifle the laugh she felt building. "Of course, Leona. I have some lettuce and a few carrots if that will work."

Lifting her arms in line with her face, Leona addressed a wide-eyed Paris. "Do carrots and lettuce sound good, my precious angel?"

Paris twitched her ears.

Leona snuggled the rabbit into her arms and smiled. "I believe we'll stay, dear. Thank you."

"My pleasure," she said, turning back to the roast as Milo set another spot at the table. "So what brings you by?"

"Item number four."

She stopped slicing and glanced at Leona. "Item number four?"

Leona nodded. "I saw you with Mamma at the end of the meeting last night. I saw her hand you back the scissors, button tin, and pincushion."

Tori swallowed.

"I thank you for not mentioning it in front of everyone," Leona said. "I'm not sure Margaret Louise could have handled that."

She lifted the platter of meat from the counter and headed toward the dining room. "There really was no need for anyone to know. As soon as I asked Annabelle about the items, she gave them up with no fuss at all. And, to be honest, if I didn't have to make four more rag quilts, I would have let her just keep everything."

"Well, she didn't give you back everything." Leona set Paris on the floor then picked up the rolls and mashed potatoes and followed Tori.

"She gave me back everything I saw her take." She looked around the table then returned to the kitchen long enough to secure salt and pepper shakers and the broccoli and cheese casserole.

"She gave you back three things," Leona said as Tori walked back into the room. "There's always four. Always."

She set the casserole on the table and plopped into her chair. "Why four?"

Leona waved her freshly manicured fingers in the air. "I don't know. There just is. It's been that way since I was a little girl."

Tori took in the information as she passed the

meat and sides to Leona first, and then Milo. "So what did I miss? A package of needles? A spool of thread?"

Leona placed a small spoonful of potatoes onto her plate then reached into the pocket of her silk blazer. "Your list."

Tori stared at the folded piece of paper and piece of white and gold ribbon in Leona's palm. "My list? I didn't have a . . ." Her words trailed off as her memory finally engaged with her mouth. "Oh, wait. I remember now. That's the list that Colby made for me."

Milo looked up from his plate. "What kind of list?"

Tori took the paper and ribbon from Leona's hand and placed them next to her own plate. With quick hands, she unfolded the paper and spun it around for Milo to see. "I asked Colby if he knew anyone connected to the film. I figured a list of the studio employees might reveal some sort of clue. But, of course, there was nothing."

Milo scanned each line, pointing at people he'd either met or heard about via Tori. When he reached the end, he flipped it over, his finger stopping on Stan Kelly. "The kids loved this guy." Flicking his hand at the ribbon beside Tori's plate, he smiled. "And not just for his special candy, either."

Milo's finger followed Stan's information across the page. "I sure hope he's able to stick

306

around this time and keep that promise he made to his son."

"Me, too." Tori cut a piece of pork and brought it to her mouth, her gaze falling on the gold and white ribbon next to her plate. "What's that?"

Leona perked up. "Oh. Sorry. I found that in Mamma's bag when I was going through it this morning. I guess it got caught on your list."

"Why were you going through Annabelle's bag?" she asked.

"Because I gave her that beaded bag I bought at the mall the other day." Leona pushed her meat around the plate, stopping to fork up every piece of broccoli. "I'm hoping a new bag might make for some new habits."

She laid her fork across her plate and studied her friend.

"Yes, dear?" Leona asked.

"You're amazing, you know that?"

Leona folded her hands gently in her lap and batted her eyelashes ever so gently. "Of course I do."

Milo covered his laugh with a well-placed hand, leaving Tori as the sole recipient of Leona's infamous raised eyebrow. "Are you mocking me, dear?"

She rushed to deny the charge. "Of course not. It's just that I said what I said for reasons you've probably not heard before."

"Oh? And what might those be?" Leona drawled.

Lifting the tablecloth to the side, Tori peeked at the bunny sitting peacefully at Leona's feet. "Taking care of Paris the way you do, giving Patches to Rose so she wouldn't feel so lonely all the time, visiting your mamma at Three Winds every morning, buying her a new bag for her things . . . It's special, Leona," she said. "*You're* special."

A hint of crimson rose in Leona's cheeks only to disappear just as quickly. "I have to admit I'm hoping Mamma will use her new bag for her own things instead of everyone else's things." Leona waved her hand toward the list. "It took almost an hour to sort out everything she'd accumulated. But once I started organizing things into Mamma's standard groups of four, it became a little easier."

"I wasn't the only one with stuff in there?" she asked.

It was Leona's turn to laugh, though her laugh was tinged with a bit of sadness, too. "No. Seems she was taken by Debbie's sewing notions, too."

"But how?" Tori protested. "Annabelle wasn't sitting anywhere near Debbie last night."

"We got up for dessert, didn't we?" Leona took a sip of wine and held onto the goblet. "It doesn't take Mamma long. In fact, it's a rare day when she gets caught in the act."

She knew she shouldn't make light of the elderly woman's condition, but it was hard. Annabelle Elkin was a sweet, sweet woman. "So my list was the lone oddball item in the bag, huh?"

"Actually, no. There were three other things in the bag that I imagine belong to one of Mamma's fellow residents."

"But what happened to the fourth?" Milo asked.

"Someone caught her trying to pocket the last one is all. It happens from time to time." Leona took a second, longer sip of wine, setting the glass on the table with a gentle hand when she was done. "I'll try to match the last three items to their correct owner in the morning."

Tori cut through the middle of her roll, spreading a thin layer of butter on each half. "Does Margaret Louise know about any of this?"

"No. I'm capable of cleaning up after Mamma once in a while, too, you know."

She loved spending time with her friends, she really did, but there were times, like that very moment, when she absolutely treasured her time alone with Milo. His gentle ways calmed her, his strong voice encouraged her, and the way he looked at her made her feel as if everything in life would turn out right.

"I'm sorry I've been so distracted the past week or so. I just hate seeing Margaret Louise so upset." Pulling her grandmother's favorite afghan off the back of the couch, she tucked it around her legs and cuddled into the crook of Milo's arm. "It's like someone shook the earth and the dust hasn't quite settled yet."

"I understand, sweetheart. I really do." Milo rested his head against the back of the couch, his hand stroking the side of Tori's face as he did. "I just wish I could do something to help. But since I don't really know any of the players, it's tough to know what to say or do."

"And I *do* know some of the players and I don't know what to say or do, either." She closed her eyes and thought back over the day. "I mean, I guess Glenda could have done it . . . she was certainly on the receiving end of a lot of Anita angst. So much so, she was always afraid for her job."

"Why?"

"From what I've been able to gather, that was Anita's threat of choice to keep her employees in line."

"Did she ever follow through?" Milo asked.

"I don't know. But that's a good question to ask Todd the next time I see him." She snuggled still closer to Milo and deliberately changed the subject, the need to lighten the evening's mood increasing moment by moment. "Pretty wild about Annabelle, huh?"

"I'll say. But Leona seems to be handling it well."

She couldn't help but smile. Leona was a lot of things—ornery, bossy, even a little full of herself at times. But when push came to shove, she was a gem in her own right. "I'm so glad I moved here," she whispered. "To have friends like Margaret Louise and Leona, Rose and Debbie, Melissa and Beatrice, Georgina and Dixie . . ." She peered up at the man sitting next to her. "And to find someone like you . . . I couldn't be more blessed."

Cupping her face in his hands, Milo moved in for a kiss, stopping just short of her lips. "The feeling is quite mutual."

Chapter 27

She was just entering in the last spring title on the ordering page when her cell phone rang. Glancing at the name on the screen, she popped it open and positioned it between her shoulder and her ear so she could finish her task and talk at the same time. "Hi Leona."

"Good morning, Victoria."

"What can I do for you today?"

"I was wondering if you could stop by Three Winds for a few minutes? I've asked all of the residents if they know who the last two items in Mamma's bag belong to but no one seems to know." A loud sigh filled her ear. "So I've come to the conclusion they must belong to someone from the sewing circle. However, I don't want to make things harder on my sister by telling more people than necessary."

She hit End and leaned back in her chair. She hated to leave Dixie on her own yet again, but if she could help spare Margaret Louise any more angst, it would be worth it in the long run. "Are you there now?"

"I am. But if you don't hurry, Margaret Louise will be back and all of this will be futile."

"I'll be there in ten minutes." She snapped the phone closed, grabbed her keys, and made a quick pit stop at the information desk to fill Dixie in on her mission before making the trek out to Three Winds.

Leona was waiting when she walked through the front door.

"You're not very good at watching the clock, are you, dear?" Leona linked her arm through Tori's and led her down a long hallway of closed doors. "You said you'd be here in ten minutes, but it's been much closer to fifteen."

"I was at *work*."

Leona waved away her protests. "Excuses do not become you, dear."

"It's a fact, Leona."

"Semantics, dear." Leona stopped them at a door halfway down the hall and dropped her voice to a near whisper. "Okay, this is Mamma's apartment. She's inside with Paris and she seems to be fairly clearheaded. If we can figure out whom these last few items belong to without involving her, so much the better."

She nodded, then followed Leona into the small yet cozy apartment that was Annabelle Elkin's new home. The narrow entryway boasted a kitchenette on one side, a small sitting room on the other, and what Tori suspected was a bedroom on the end. Although she'd been there less than a full week, it didn't take long to see that her daughters had done their best to make the space cozy and inviting. There were magnetized photographs adorning the refrigerator—one for each of Annabelle's seven great-grandchildren as well as Paris—and photo albums stacked on the bottom shelf of a floor to ceiling unit along the back wall of the sitting room. Scented candles, attractive picture frames, and potted plants were spread out among the rest of the shelves, giving the unit a lived-in feel.

"Hi Annabelle!" She crossed the sitting room to the wooden rocker where Leona's mom sat with a sleeping Paris. "I love your new home. It's very pretty."

Annabelle beamed around the index finger she raised to her lips.

Tori acknowledged Annabelle's request with a smile and a nod and quietly backed out of the room and into the kitchen where Leona was waiting.

"So here's what I've got." Reaching into the familiar tattered tote bag she'd propped on the kitchen table, Leona pulled out a cell phone and handed it to Tori. "Do you have any idea who this belongs to? Beatrice, perhaps?"

Tori shook her head as she examined the powder blue phone. "Can't be. Beatrice wasn't at Monday's meeting."

Leona shrugged. "I suppose these things could have been in Mamma's bag for a while."

"But someone would have spoken up by now if their phone had been missing for more than a week," she pointed out, turning the phone over and over in her hand. "Maybe Melissa's?"

It was Leona's turn to disagree. "No. Melissa called me this morning. From her cell phone."

Turning it right side up once again, she flipped it open and pressed the green button near the top. Instantly the screen came to life with a single digit shown on the screen.

9

"Hmmm. Whoever it belongs to was in the process of dialing someone when they must have gotten distracted and set the phone down."

"A veritable hazard when Mamma is around."

Tori pulled her focus from the phone long enough to fix it on Leona in an attempt to read her mood. If there was any resentment in her friend's words, it was fleeting. She looked back at the phone, pressing the button for stored contacts.

"Okay, that's weird," she mumbled.

Leona's eyebrows rose. "What's weird?"

She turned the phone so Leona could see the screen. "Whoever owns this phone doesn't have a single number in their contacts."

"Did someone mention getting a new phone?" Leona asked.

It was a good question.

Yet Tori didn't have an answer.

She pointed at the bag. "And the next item?"

"You mean the last one," Leona said, reaching for the bag once again.

Tori looked at the phone one last time and then set it on the middle of the table. "Last one? I thought you said there were three things. . . ."

"There were. Yesterday. But now there's only two."

She looked toward the sitting room and the woman rocking to and fro with a very peaceful Paris.

"It couldn't have been Mamma," Leona volunteered. "I had the bag at home with me."

Tori considered her friend's words, an explanation forming in her thoughts almost immediately. "Wait. I have it." Grabbing her own purse from its spot by the table leg, Tori reached inside and pulled out the gold and white ribbon that had been attached to Colby's list just the night before. "Was this one of the items?"

Leona brightened. "Yes, yes, that's it." The

woman plucked the braided ribbon from Tori's hand and dropped it beside the cell phone. "I imagine it's nothing anyone is going to miss but you never know."

She nodded and pointed at Annabelle's old tote bag. "So what's the third item?"

"I have no idea. I've never seen anything like it before." Leona reached inside the bag and pulled out a long cylinderlike object with a series of diagrams depicted on the front.

Tori took it from Leona's outstretched hand and held it under the light, her gaze moving from diagram to diagram. "This is an EpiPen."

Leona leaned forward for a closer look. "What's an EpiPen, dear?"

"It's what people use when they have a serious allergy—like to beestings or certain foods like seafood or peanuts. . . ."

Peanuts . . .

Her mouth went dry as she looked from the object in her hand to the cell phone on the table, her thoughts a jumbled mess.

"How . . . how did Annabelle get these things?" She heard the panic in her voice, saw the accompanying flash of irritation in Leona's eyes.

"Shhh," Leona hissed. "I don't want Mamma to hear what's going on. She'll get all fuzzy-headed again."

"But . . ." The word trailed from her mouth as she realized everything she was looking at could be nothing more than a coincidence. Or it could be the break she'd been praying for every night. She jumped to her feet, glancing back over her shoulder as she ran for the door. "Don't touch a thing. I'll be back in fifteen minutes."

"Fifteen?" Leona challenged.

"Okay, maybe twenty."

By the time she got back to Three Winds with Todd, a good thirty minutes had elapsed. Which meant two things . . .

Leona was more than a little irritated.

And Margaret Louise was now part of the picture.

She mouthed a double apology at Leona as she pulled Todd into Annabelle's apartment and over to the now empty table. "Where is everything?"

Leona squared her shoulders and peered at Tori over the top of her glasses. "I told you I didn't want Mamma involved with this."

Spinning around, she looked toward the rocking chair. No Annabelle. No Paris. She looked back at Leona. "Where is she?"

"She's right here," Margaret Louise said as she walked into the kitchen beside Annabelle, the door at the end of the hall open to the bedroom Tori had suspected it housed. "Isn't this a nice surprise, Victoria." Margaret Louise stopped beside Tori and gave her a peck on the cheek. "Oh, and I remember you. You're the nice man who

317

took Mamma and me on a tour of the set with Victoria that one morning."

Todd dipped his head. "Ma'am."

Leona brought her jeweled hands to her hips and stepped in front of her sister. "What? You save the nice surprise part for him?"

"You bein' here ain't a surprise, Twin."

Leona's eyebrows rose. "It's not?"

"You think *I* put a picture of Paris on the refrigerator?"

"And why wouldn't you?" Leona challenged.

Tori held her hands in the air. "Ladies, ladies, please. While I'm sure this is a worthy discussion, I need to show Todd the . . ." She looked at Margaret Louise, saw the confusion in her eyes.

Damn.

She tried another tactic. "Margaret Louise? When Todd and I walked into the lobby just a few minutes ago, there were lots of residents heading toward the Activity Room. Maybe there's something going on that Annabelle might enjoy?"

Margaret Louise looked from Tori to Leona and back again, all traces of a smile disappearing from her face. "You want us to go, don't you?"

She reached out, took hold of Margaret Louise's hand. "We just need a few moments. That's all."

Nodding, Margaret Louise linked her arm through Annabelle's and led her mother into the hallway, shutting the door in their wake.

318

"You told me fifteen minutes," Leona hissed when they'd gone.

"I had to get to the set, find Todd, and drive all the way back here." She pointed at the table. "So where is everything?"

Leona opened the cabinet above the refrigerator and pulled out Annabelle's tote bag. "Here," she said, thrusting it into Tori's waiting hands.

One by one she pulled out each item. . . .

The gold and white ribbon.

The powder blue cell phone.

And the EpiPen.

She looked up at Todd as she placed the last item on the table, the man's face white as a ghost.

"That's Anita's phone . . . and her medication."

"And the ribbon?" she whispered.

"I have no idea about the ribbon. I've never seen that before."

Leona dropped into one of the kitchen chairs, her voice a raspy whisper. "You mean you think Mamma killed Anita?"

She felt the blood drain from her own face as the reality of what was in front of them was too huge to ignore. "I—I don't think so."

But even as she expressed the answer she knew Leona needed to hear, she couldn't help but play the scenario through in her thoughts. Anita's cell phone and EpiPen had been in Annabelle's purse . . .

Still, it didn't add up. When Annabelle wasn't

in Three Winds, Margaret Louise kept her on a short leash. Sure, she might miss a little swiping like she did at the sewing circle meeting. But a murder? No, the leash was much too short for that.

There had to be something she was missing. Something—

"Wait!" she shouted. "You said the only time your mother takes three items is when she gets caught with the fourth in her hand, right?"

Leona nodded.

"What was she caught stealing in the last two weeks?"

"I have no idea," Leona whispered. "I tend to avoid Mamma when we're out in public."

"But I don't."

The three of them whirled around to find Margaret Louise, wide-eyed, standing in the door. "What did Mamma do this time?"

She scrambled for an answer to ease the worry etched across her friend's forehead but was thwarted by the ring of her cell phone. "Excuse me a moment." Reaching into her purse, she extracted her phone and looked at the caller ID screen.

Milo.

For a moment, she contemplated letting it go to voice mail but, in the end, she picked it up. She could use the infusion of calm his voice tended to bring.

"Milo, hi. Is everything okay?"

"Of course. I just figured I'd take advantage of the kids being in music class and give you a quick call. How're things at the library?"

She wrapped her hands around the back of Annabelle's kitchen chair and closed her eyes. "I'm not at the library. I'm at Three Winds with Leona, Margaret Louise, and Todd."

A beat of silence was quickly followed by a note of surprise. "You mean the guy from the movie set?"

She nodded.

"He can't see you nod, dear," Leona groused.

Her eyes flew open. "Yes, Milo. The guy from the movie set."

"Why is he there?"

She took a deep breath, let it exhale slowly through her mouth. "I needed him to identify a few things."

"Oh?"

"We found Anita's cell phone and EpiPen."

She closed her eyes again as Margaret Louise's gasp echoed in her ears.

"Really? That's great!"

She only wished that were true. "They were in Annabelle's bag."

The silence returned. This time lasting a lot longer than a beat.

"Where did she get them?" he finally asked.

"I guess she got them from Anita's drawer

somehow. Which is why they weren't there when Anita needed them." She opened one eye, saw Margaret Louise slumped in the chair next to her sister.

"Was she in Anita's trailer?"

She posed Milo's question to Margaret Louise, adding a reality that just now dawned in her mind. "When we went on our tour of the set, I left you guys for a little while to take a phone call from Dixie—"

"That doesn't work, Tori," Milo pointed out from his end of the line. "You said the call came in about Anita's death while you were still there, remember?"

Milo was right.

Lowering the phone momentarily, she relayed his comment to the others.

"And Glenda would have had to have made sure the phone was fully charged and in its place before she left the night before."

"The time of death is believed to have been around eleven or so that night . . . which was after Glenda did her check and long before Annabelle had her tour," Tori mused.

"That's assuming, of course, Glenda actually put the phone back into the drawer, yes?"

Tori turned to look at Leona.

"What was that?" Milo asked in her ear.

She repeated Leona's comment into the phone, then used her finger to guide Todd's focus toward the curled ribbon on the center of the table. "Have you ever seen Glenda with ribbon like that?"

Todd shook his head. "Nope."

"What ribbon?" Milo asked.

She switched the phone to her left ear. "You know, that gold and white braided thing that got mixed up with my list last night."

"That's Stan's."

"Stan's?" she echoed.

"Yeah. It's how that candy he shared with the kids yesterday is packaged, remember?"

She racked her brain for a memory to go along with the words in her ear, but she simply couldn't remember. She'd been too preoccupied with Rick Manning to pay much attention to anything that happened after he left the classroom.

"But that doesn't make sense." Lowering the phone, she addressed Todd. "Stan Kelly didn't have any sort of run-in with Anita before she died, did he?"

"If by run-in you mean telling him his job was over for letting"—he motioned toward Leona—"*Pooky* onto the set that first day, yeah, they had a run-in. Fortunately for him, though, she was murdered before she placed the call to his boss."

Slowly, she brought the phone back to her mouth, her heart thudding in her ears. "D-did you hear that?"

"I heard."

"I got my motive."

"You sure did."

She swallowed back the lump that threatened to make it difficult to speak. "I better go. I've got a phone call to make."

Chapter 28

She'd been to a number of parties over the years to celebrate any number of special milestones.

Baptisms.

Birthdays.

Graduations.

Engagements.

Weddings.

And anniversaries.

But a party to celebrate the successful conclusion of a murder investigation? Never.

"I think we should have more of these, don't you?" Rose said, lowering herself onto one of the remaining patio chairs before claiming her plate of food from Milo's helpful hand. "Especially if Margaret Louise is going to make this kind of food."

"Wait until you see the cake," Melissa gushed.

"Debbie outdid herself this time. It's a chocolate lover's dream."

"There's chocolate cake?" Tori looked from Melissa to Rose and back again.

"That's right, Victoria." Georgina pushed Beatrice to the right as she shifted to the left, the break in their bodies affording a bird's-eye view of the four-layer chocolate cake atop the picnic table. "See?"

She gulped. "Um, why?"

"Because we're celebratin', that's why." Margaret Louise hoisted her leg over the picnic bench and patted the vacant spot to her left.

"We've never had cake before. . . ."

Debbie shrugged. "Well, the first three times you solved a murder, we thought it was a fluke."

"Now we just know it's part of knowing you, Victoria." Dixie forked a bite of potato salad from her plate and shoved it in her mouth.

She wasn't sure if she should be flattered or mortified. Either way, she couldn't help but feel as if she'd somehow tarnished Sweet Briar.

"So walk me through your latest case." Debbie scooted back on the cushioned chaise to allow Colby to claim his seat by her feet. "I feel like I was totally out of the loop this time around."

She felt her face warm. "I don't have cases. I'm a librarian, remember?"

"You've certainly solved your share of crimes," Melissa teased as Molly Sue ran onto the patio and wrapped her arms around her mother's legs. "Oh, hey there, sweetie."

"It wasn't really me this time. It was more Milo . . . and Todd," she protested.

"And *you*." Margaret Louise draped an arm around Tori's shoulders and pulled her close. "You took bits and pieces from Milo and Todd and then sewed it up tight before you handed it over to Chief Dallas."

"The rest was easy. Stan Kelly had motive—he was determined to save his job so he could be a part of his grandchildren's lives, he had means—he had keys to all the trailers, and he was caught red-handed with the proof by Annabelle."

"So what was the fourth item?" Leona finally asked, her gaze straying to a clearheaded Annabelle who was gently pushing a delighted Sally on the swing set. "The one she got caught swiping?"

"A pack of gum," Margaret Louise volunteered. "She'd grabbed it right off the middle of the table."

"But where were all the other items?" Colby asked. "The ones she managed to hang on to until you found them in her bag?"

"The pocket of the coat he'd draped over the back of Mamma's chair durin' his interrogation." Margaret Louise, too, looked out at Annabelle, her focus one of curiosity rather than worry. "Mamma's fast."

"She sure is." Leona met her sister's smile and

raised it with one of her own. "She sees what she wants and goes after it."

Tori laughed out loud. "I guess you come by it honestly then, huh, Leona?"

"Huh?" Leona echoed. "*Huh? Didn't I teach you to always use proper grammar? You are in the south now, dear."*

She felt Milo's eyes studying her from across the patio, the look they bestowed nothing short of pride.

For her.

She pushed off the picnic bench and stood, her destination clear. It was time to get serious about planning their wedding. She crossed the patio and sat down beside Milo. "Can I ask them?" she whispered.

"Yeah, you can ask them."

Squeezing his hand in hers, she looked around at her friends, the people who had stood by her in a way no one ever had until she moved to Sweet Briar. Collectively, they'd stood by her through some of life's darker moments, their loyalty, their love, unwavering and true.

They were the perfect choice to stand beside her while she pledged her eternal love to the greatest man she'd ever known.

She blinked back the tears that threatened to give her away and dug deep inside to find some semblance of a steady voice. "Ladies?"

Seven sets of eyes turned in her direction.

She glanced back at Milo, caught the way his smile spread to his eyes in its trademark knee-weakening way.

"What is it, Victoria?" Beatrice asked.

She winked at Milo then turned back to her friends. "I was wondering if I might be able to borrow you for a particular day."

"You have us every Monday night," groused Dixie.

"Hush!" Margaret Louise demanded. "Let Victoria finish."

"I was wondering if the seven of you, plus Nina, would do me the honor of being my bridesmaids when I marry Milo."

Squeals erupted around the patio as six bodies rose from their respective seats and circled around Tori.

"Leona?" she asked as she took in the one member of the circle who was still seated. "Is there something wrong?"

"Do you have a flower girl picked out?"

She nodded, then sought eye contact with Melissa. "I know she'll be approaching twelve by the time we have our wedding, but would it be okay if I asked Lulu to be my flower girl?"

"She would love that," whispered Melissa.

"Well, what about a ring bearer?"

She looked at Milo, saw his shrug. "We don't have a ring bearer yet, Leona. Lyndon will barely be walking when we have our wedding."

Reaching beneath her seat, Leona plucked Paris off the ground and held her up for Tori to see. "Since Nina's son won't be available, perhaps you should consider some other options."

"Such as?"

"Well, being open-minded is most important, of course," Leona drawled.

"Okay . . ."

"For example, no one ever said the ring bearer has to be a boy, right?"

She nodded, her gaze ricocheting between her friends and Leona, the intrigue on their faces surely matching her own. "That's true."

"And no one ever said the ring bearer had to walk, either."

She scrunched up her brow. "Wait. You mean I should send Lyndon up in a stroller with the rings on his lap or something?"

"No, they'd be much too small for a baby his age," Debbie cautioned as Melissa nodded in agreement. "He could swallow them."

Leona waved the notion aside. "Don't be ridiculous. A one-year-old baby has no place in a wedding party."

"Then what are you driving at, Leona?"

"Well, I was thinking more along the lines of a ring bearer who hops."

"Hops?" she echoed in disbelief.

"Paris would do a fine job in that capacity. We'd just need to find her a velvet ribbon to match the color of our dresses and she'd be absolutely precious. The rings themselves would be tied into the bow for safekeeping."

"Good grief, woman, I think you've finally lost your marbles."

Leona glared at Rose from atop her glasses. "I most certainly have not. It's actually a wonderful idea. Victoria was present at the birth of Paris's children. It only makes sense that Victoria would then share her wedding with Paris in return."

Rose waggled her fingers at Margaret Louise. "I think you might have the wrong family member living at Three Winds."

"Come Saturday, I won't have any family members livin' at Three Winds," Margaret Louise declared.

Tori took Margaret Louise's hands in hers. "You're bringing Annabelle home to live with you?" The second the words were out, she met Melissa's eyes, prayed the question didn't sound judgmental.

Margaret Louise shook her head. "Nope. Not with *me*."

"Then where—" She stopped, the meaning behind Margaret Louise's words making her turn and face Leona. "Annabelle is going to live with *you*?"

Leona nodded. "And Paris, too."

"But why?" she whispered. "She was doing okay at Three Winds, wasn't she? I mean, she seemed happy there."

"She was."

"Then why move her again?"

"Because Mamma and I have a lot of years to make up in a short amount of time."

She swiped away a tear as it rolled down her cheek.

"You truly are amazing, Leona Elkin. Simply amazing."

"You're preaching to the choir, dear. Truly." Lifting Paris into the air, Leona turned the bunny toward the bride-to-be. "Now, about that velvet ribbon . . ."

Sewing Tips

(Contributed by readers via Elizabeth Lynn Casey's Facebook author page)

- Measure twice, cut once.

- Keep a lint roller and clothespins handy in your sewing room. The lint roller tidies up stray threads on an ironing board or sewing mat, and clothespins act as a third hand.

- Don't have a ruler or tape measure handy? Use a $1 bill—it is six inches long.

- Use a magnet to pick up stray pins—no more sticking yourself!

- Cut your seams with pinking shears so they don't fray.

- Keep several hand-sewing needles threaded and ready to go, stuck in your pincushion.

- Run the end of your thread across a candle or bar of soap to get the end a bit stiff. This will make it easier to thread a needle.

- Sew in stages to minimize mistakes and maximize your interest.

- Before hemming a dress, a skirt, or pants, let the item hang for a day on a hanger to allow the fabric to settle.

- Thread looks darker on the spool than it will on fabric. Choose thread a shade darker than the material you'll be using it on.

Please visit www.elizabethlynncasey.com to share your sewing tips!

Sewing Pattern

Rag Quilt

Fabric suggestions: Homespun, flannel,
   brushed cotton (size is 42″ x 48″)
Two-color quilt: Two yards of each color
⅝ yard of 90″ batting

Cut:

   56 squares of each color (7″ x 7″ square)
   56 squares of batting (6″ x 6″ square)

Directions:

With wrong sides together, pin one front to one
back and sandwich batting.
   Pin together. Stitch diagonally across square in
one direction then in the other direction.
   Do this to all 56 squares.
   Lay out your squares so there are seven blocks
across and eight blocks down.
   With back sides together, stitch seven squares

together at sides with ½-inch seams. Do not trim.

Do this for the next eight rows. Then, start with one row, adding each row as you go. Do not trim.

When all is together, stitch ½ inch around outside edge.

Note: Make sure all seams are ½ inch.

Clip all seams every ¼ inch, being careful not to cut stitching.

Shake throw to remove any loose threads.

Machine wash to fray seams. Remove from washer and shake again before drying.

Machine dry quilt with fabric softener sheet. Shake quilt again when dry.

Note: When drying, clean lint filter frequently.

Center Point Large Print
600 Brooks Road / PO Box 1
Thorndike ME 04986-0001 USA

(207) 568-3717

US & Canada:
1 800 929-9108
www.centerpointlargeprint.com